Florid

Books by
Tim Dorsey

CADILLAC BEACH
THE STINGRAY SHUFFLE
TRIGGERFISH TWIST
ORANGE CRUSH
HAMMERHEAD RANCH MOTEL
FLORIDA ROADKILL

Coming Soon in Hardcover

TORPEDO JUICE

Florida ROAD-Kill

Tim Dorsey

HarperTorch
An Imprint of HarperCollinsPublishers

This is a work of fiction. Names, characters, places, and incidents are products of the author's imagination or are used fictitiously and are not to be construed as real. Any resemblance to actual events, locales, organizations, or persons, living or dead, is entirely coincidental.

❤

HARPERTORCH
An Imprint of HarperCollins*Publishers*
10 East 53rd Street
New York, New York 10022-5299

Copyright © 1999 by Tim Dorsey
Excerpt from *Hammerhead Ranch Motel* copyright © 2000 by Tim Dorsey
Back cover author photo by Janine Dorsey
ISBN: 0-380-73233-5

First HarperTorch paperback printing: June 2000
First William Morrow hardcover printing: August 1999

HarperCollins®, HarperTorch™, and ❤™ are trademarks of HarperCollins Publishers Inc.

Printed in the United States of America

Visit HarperTorch on the World Wide Web at
www.harpercollins.com

20 19 18 17 16

For Janine, Erin and Kelly

Acknowledgments

A respectful nod to my agent, Nat Sobel, and my editor, Paul Bresnick, two of the most dangerous men in the New York literary establishment.

The Sun will not rise, or set,
without my notice and thanks.

—WINSLOW HOMER

Prologue

Florida even looks good collapsing.

From Loggerhead Key to Amelia Island to the Flora-Bama Lounge, the Land of Flowers has natives caught in seductive headlights.

Millions of residents stayed up past midnight one evening in October of 1997 to watch the south Florida baseball team win the seventh game of the World Series in extra innings.

The next day:

A full-figured maid from Rio ran in a circle in the parking lot, crying and screaming in Portuguese. The motel manager leaned against the office doorway, weary, a thin, bald Honduran, four foot eleven, sixty years. Brown slacks and ocher guayabera with a pink button on the pocket: "Play the Florida Lottery." He had coppery, folded skin, and he rolled his eyes at the paroxysmal woman in the white cleaning uniform who he decided was being overcome either by religion or insects.

The 1960s-era Orbit Motel was a two-story box around a swimming pool. Its east side faced Cocoa Beach and the Atlantic Ocean, and its sign on Highway A1A was an illuminated globe circled by a mechanical space capsule. The Launch Pad Lounge next to the motel office was retrofitted into the Launch Pad Food Mart, which the manager tended without humor.

The maid's hysterics were unbroachable for fifteen minutes, so the manager ate boiled peanuts. Through sobs, the maid eventually communicated her alarm.

Two police officers in a single squad car arrived four minutes after the manager's phone call. Cocoa Beach has a genie and a bottle on the doors of its police cars. The manager led the officers around the ocean side of the motel and up the unpainted concrete stairs to the balcony. The day was hot and sticky, but the second floor brought wind and snatches of conversation from a tiki bar at the end of the Cocoa Beach Pier. As the manager sorted keys, the officers looked through mirror sunglasses at the lone surfer in a black wet suit. A cruise ship sailed for Nassau and Freeport in the Bahamas. Both cops thinking: We shouldn't have gone out drinking after the World Series last night.

The manager turned the knob of room 214 and pushed the door open. He made a gesture into the room that said, "And you've won a brand-new car!"

Inside was an evidence theme park. A six-foot Rorschach pattern of blood and bone across the wall near the bathroom. Bound securely with braided rope and sitting upright in an uncomfortable motel chair was the late, luckless John Doe, his mouth covered with duct tape and eyes wide. The end of a shotgun was tied to his throat and the exit wound in the back of his neck could hold a croquet ball. His chin rested on the shotgun barrel, the only thing keeping his head propped up, and he wore a baseball cap with the *Apollo 13* emblem.

The other end of the twelve-gauge Benelli automatic shotgun was wrapped to a sawhorse with more tape. A string attached the trigger to the shaft of an electric motor. From the side of the deceased's chair hung a bare copper wire with a small model space shuttle dangling on the end. Circling the wire was a metal collar cut from a beer can. A wire ran from the collar to a car battery. Another wire ran from the shuttle to a solenoid switch and the motor.

The television was on the NASA channel. Live video of two astronauts spacewalking during their third day in orbit. The cops looked over the room, gave each other a high five, and burst out laughing. One radioed for the detectives and lab guys. The other grabbed the remote control, looking for something good on TV.

Clinton Ellrod painted white block letters in an arc across the front window of the Rapid Response convenience store. Back behind the cash register, he admired his handiwork through the glass, reading in reverse: "Congratulations, Marlins!"

With the efficiency of a casino worker, Ellrod pulled down two packs of Doral menthols, tore loose five scratch-off lottery tickets (the sand dollars game), rang up a twelve-pack of ice-brewed beer and set pump seven for eighteen dollars. A crew outside was taking down the Rapid Response sign and replacing it with one that read "Addiction World"; they left early for lunch.

During lulls, Ellrod studied notes from classes at Florida International University. When fried from an all-nighter, he daydreamed out the tinted windows and watched traffic on US 1 run through the asphalt badlands between Coconut Grove and Coral Gables. Fast food, anemic strip malls, check-cashing parlors with steel-reinforced pylons out front. There was a desperateness to the commerce, like a Mexican border town or a remote gold-mining settlement in Brazil. Except for weeds in the cracks, the pavement sealed everything up like an icecap. But Ellrod loved sunsets, even here. Soft, warm light glinting off the cars, and the concrete orange at the end. The day people, rushing through checklists of responsibility, giving way to this other group, hustling around after dark to accomplish everything they shouldn't be doing at all.

Rapid Response stood a few blocks in from Biscayne Bay. Through the front door came construction workers filling forty-four-ounce Thirst Mutilators, schoolkids in baggy clothes shoplifting, registered nurses grabbing Evian from the glassed-in cooler, businessmen on cell phones unfolding maps they'd never buy. Nicaraguans, Germans, Tamil rebels, Sikh separatists, scag mules, prom-queens-turned-drug-trollops, armored car guards, escaped convicts, get-away drivers, siding salesmen, rabbis and assorted nonbathers. Ten times a day he gave directions to Monkey Jungle.

Ellrod, like all Florida convenience store clerks, had the Serengeti alertness of the tastiest gazelle in the herd. He studied customers for danger. He ruled out the pair at the chips rack, the tall, athletic guy and the shorter, bookish man exchanging playful punches, debating Chee-tos, puffy or crunchy.

Ellrod made change for a bookie on Rollerblades. A black Mercedes S420 limousine pulled up. Three Latin men slammed three doors. They wore identical white linen suits, shirts open at the collar, no chest hair or gold chains. Thick, trimmed mustaches. They entered the store in descending order of height and in the same order filled three Styrofoam cups at the soda spigot.

The athletic guy used a twenty to pay for two bags of Chee-tos and a tank of regular unleaded; they drove to the edge of the convenience store lot in a white Chrysler and waited for the stoplight at the corner to hold up traffic, then rejoined US 1 south-bound.

The tallest Latin asked Ellrod for the *servicio*, and Ellrod pointed to the rear of the store. All three went inside the one-toilet restroom and closed the door.

Ellrod turned to the beeping gas control panel. He pressed a button and leaned toward a grape-size microphone on a gooseneck. "Pump number four is on."

"About fucking time," said the speaker on the control panel. The pickup truck at pump four sat on tractor tires. It was red, spangled metallic, with a bank of eight amber fog lights over the cab. The sticker on the left side of the bumper read, "English only in the U.S.A.!" The one on the right had a drawing of the Stars and Stripes. It said, "Will the last American out of Miami please bring the flag?"

The driver walked into the store, and Ellrod saw he came to five-nine on the robber height guide running up the doorjamb. He had a crew cut midway between Sid Vicious and H. R. Haldeman, a Vandyke beard and a sunburnt face rounded out into a moon by the people at Pabst Blue Ribbon. He wore the official NFL jersey of the Dallas Cowboys.

"What took you so long, stupid!" said the driver.

"That'll be nineteen dollars," Ellrod said without interest. The man pulled bills from his wallet; his face had a dense patina of perspiration. Ellrod smelled whiskey, onions and BO.

"I asked you a question!" said the driver. He looked up from his wallet and saw Ellrod's T-shirt. "FIU? What the fuck's that? Some new shitty rap band?"

Ellrod, African American, picked up the drift of the conversation.

"Florida International University," he said evenly.

"Oh, you and the homeboys now stealing college laundry."

"I go to school there."

"Don't bullshit me, boy. You're so smart, how come you workin' *here?*" The man pointed to the employee parking space and Ellrod's two-hundred-thousand-mile Datsun with a trash bag for a back window. "That's your car, isn't it? Shit, don't go telling me you're a college boy. I didn't even graduate high school and look at my truck!"

Ellrod glanced out at pump number four and the rolling monument to pinheads everywhere. The store audio system piped in "Right Place, Wrong Time" and it was to the part about "refried confusion."

"Now give me my fucking change, you stupid fucking . . ."

And he said it. The word. It hung in the air between them, an electrical cumulonimbus over the cash register.

The driver realized what he'd spoken and paused to flash back. He'd used the word once to criticize a bad parking job at a Wendy's, and this little four-foot guy went Tasmanian devil on him. He'd received bruised ribs, a jaw wired shut and eight fog lights snapped off his truck.

He panicked. He jumped back from the counter and pulled a switchblade on Ellrod. "Don't try anything! You know you guys call each other that all the time! Don't go getting on me about slavery!"

The tallest Latin was next in line, fiddling with a

point-of-purchase display, keychain flashlights in the shape of AK-47 bullets.

"Hey!" the Latin said to the pickup driver. "Apologize!"

The driver turned the blade toward him. "Fuck off, Julio! You don't even have a dog in this fight! Go back to your guacamole farm and those tropical monkeys you call the mothers of your children!"

The driver never saw it. A second Latin came from behind, holding a bottle of honey-mustard barbecue sauce the size of a bowling pin. He had it by the neck and swung it around into the driver's nose, which exploded. Blood squirted everywhere like someone had stomped the heel of a boot down on a packet of ketchup.

Ellrod witnessed an entirely new league of violence. Everything in his experience up to now, even murder, was amateur softball. The driver was swarmed as he fell, and the Latins came up with makeshift convenience store weapons. Dry cell battery, meat tenderizer, Parrot Gardens car deodorizer. In ten seconds, they had pulverized both elbows, both kneecaps and both testicles.

The tallest Latin walked to the rotisserie next to the soda machine. A dozen hot dogs had turned on a circle of spits for six hours, and they were leathery and resistant to conventional forks and knives. He grabbed two of the spits and held one in each fist, pointing down, like daggers. The others saw him and cleared away from the pickup driver, now on his back. The tall one pounced and drove the spits into the driver's chest, a bullfight *banderillero* setting the decorative spears. One spit pierced the right lung, and the other blew a ventricle. The driver torqued and shimmied on the floor and then fell into the death rattle, two shriveled-up hot dogs quivering on rabbit-ear antennas sticking out of his chest.

The tall Latin stepped over the driver and up to the cash register. He pulled a ten from an eelskin wallet and handed it to Ellrod. "Three Cokes and two Jumbo Meaty Dogs."

Ellrod's legs vibrated under the counter, but he managed to make change. After a half minute, he ran to the window and watched the limousine merge into southbound traffic on US 1. The windows were down and he could see three men sucking soda straws.

Sean Breen ran his finger down the triple-A map on his lap, a steady flow of crunchy Chee-tos going to his mouth with the free hand. In the driver's seat, David Klein had a thing going with a bag of the puffies.

Fifteen miles south of Miami. Sean said, "Cutler Ridge." He looked up from the map and out the window. "Can hardly tell Hurricane Andrew came through. You should have been here five years ago. That business tower there. You could see in all the offices. The east face was gone."

Twelve more miles they hit Florida City. The turnpike came in from the northeast and dumped onto US 1. The end of civilization on the mainland. The peninsula had twenty more miles until the bridge to the Florida Keys, but the only thing left was a two-lane road south through the mangroves. The final building before the wilderness, the Last Chance Saloon, had a "Go Marlins!" banner over the door between the wagon wheels.

Sean and David thought professional wrestling in Florida wasn't what it used to be.

"Jack Brisco was my favorite," said Sean. "His trademark was the Figure-Four Leg-Lock."

"Those were the days, when the fundamentals meant something."

"Like the sleeper hold."

"Remember you had to apply an antidote hold after the sleeper knocked the guy unconscious?"

"Yeah, and one time this masked wrestler wouldn't let anyone in the ring to apply the antidote to his opponent, and Gordon Solie was going crazy in the announcer's booth, yelling, 'Brain damage is setting in!' The guy went into a coma and came out of it the following week to win the battle royal."

David's face turned serious. Ahead, a dark lump sat in the lane. David winced as it passed under the car, and relaxed when it cleared the undercarriage.

He looked in the rearview. "Gopher tortoise," he said. "Ain't gonna make it."

David pulled over and walked back toward the tortoise, which had reached the center line. He stood on the shoulder, waiting for opportunity. Heavy traffic blowing by, but a break coming up. One more car to go and he could run out and carry the tortoise to the other side.

* * *

Serge leaned forward in the passenger seat and tuned the radio in the canary-yellow '72 Corvette. His yellow beach shirt matched the car and was covered with palm trees; his two-dollar sunglasses had ruby frames and alligators at the corners. The first four radio stations were Spanish, then blues from Miami, then Serge found the frequency he wanted as they passed the Last Chance Saloon.

"I just want to celebrate . . . another day of living! . . ."

Serge talked over the radio. "And what was the deal with Coral Key State Park? The place was a deathtrap. If it wasn't for Flipper, someone would have died there every week. Can't believe nobody sued."

"Dolphins like to wear hats," said Coleman, a joint dangling from his lips as he drove. On his head was one of those afro wigs painted in a rainbow. He was wearing novelty sunglasses with slinky eyeballs, and they swung and clacked together when he turned to face Serge.

". . . I just want to celebrate . . . yeah! yeah! . . ."

"What's that in the road?" asked Serge.

"Don't know," said Coleman. "Looks like something fell out of a car and that guy's trying to retrieve it. Some kind of case. . . . Well, not today, fella!"

Coleman swerved over the center line, like Jerry Lewis running over Spencer Tracy's hat in *It's a Mad, Mad, Mad, Mad World.*

". . . I just want to celebrate another day of living! . . ."

And Coleman popped the turtle.

The pair turned around and saw a guy jumping up and down in the road, shaking his fists in the air.

"You sick fuck! Why'd you do that?!" Serge shouted. "You killed a living thing!"

"I thought it was a helmet," Coleman said.

"A helmet? We're in the Keys! This ain't fuckin' *Rat Patrol!*"

Serge plucked the joint from Coleman's lips—"Gimme that!"—and flicked it out the window. He ripped the slinky-eyeball glasses off Coleman's face and tossed them in the open gym bag at his feet. The glasses landed on the packs of hundred-dollar bills and next to the Smith & Wesson .38.

"Pull over," said Serge. "I'm driving."

Twenty miles west of Key West, mangrove islets scattered across jade shallows. Toward the Gulf Stream, the green gave way at once to a cold, ultramarine blue that ran to the horizon. It was noon, a soundless, cloudless day, and the sun broiled.

At the far end of the silence began a buzz, like a mosquito. It stayed low for a long time and then suddenly swelled into a high-precision, motorized thunder that prevented any train of thought, and a forty-foot cigarette boat slapped and crashed across the swells far closer to the flats than was smart.

Orange and aqua stripes ran the length of the speedboat, which had the logo of the Miami Dolphins on one side and a big number 13 on the other.

Behind the wheel was twenty-two-year-old Johnny Vegas, bronzed, built and smelling like a whorehouse. Because he was wearing Whorehouse Cologne, one hundred dollars an ounce on South Beach. Long black hair straight back in the wind, herringbone gold chain around his neck. His workout T-shirt had the sleeves cut off and a cartoon on the front that made a joke about his shlong being big. On the back was a drawing of a woman in a bikini with a bull's-eye on her crotch. He wore the curved sunglasses of a downhill skier.

Johnny's mouth alternated between a thousand-candlepower shit-eating grin and running his tongue over his gums with cocaine jitters. He kept the coke in a twenty-four-karat gold shark amulet he'd bought in a head shop on Key West, Southernmost Bong and Hookah. It now hung from the gold chain. He threw two toggles near the ignition and "Smoke on the Water" shook from sixteen waterproof speakers.

Johnny lived off a trust fund generated by a life-insurance-for-the-elderly program targeting anyone who had ever been, known, seen or heard about a military veteran. He exercised daily in his Bal Harbor condo, and it showed—not muscle-bound but defined at six feet, one-ninety. On weekends he cruised for chicks in the boat, and he had the tan of a professional beach volleyball player.

Other people bought jerseys with the numbers of their favorite Miami Dolphins players. Johnny customized the cigarette boat for his favorite, future Hall of Fame quarterback Dan Marino. He soon found that people assumed it actually was Marino's boat, and that Johnny was a tight friend. Johnny often said, yes, it was Marino's boat. Would you like to come aboard, little girl?

In romance, Johnny was a selective man. He wouldn't just go for anyone. He was attracted to a very specific type: horny, young, binge-drinking women in T-backs. Any event with a hint of spring-break attitude, Johnny's boat was there.

He ranged from Fort Lauderdale to Islamorada in the Keys, where fast boats held effective parties on an offshore sandbar. That was as far as Vegas would take the cigarette. The cocaine he bought for the World Series the night before had taken him the rest of the way down the Keys.

No sooner had he arrived, he was on the business side of Key West, heading out to sea. As the propeller cavitated, Johnny unconsciously fingered the coke talisman hanging at his sternum. At sixty miles an hour, he strained to see as the air pressure flattened his eyeballs, but he had to keep up appearances for the woman clinging to her white leather seat. She didn't really mind, with a tight belly full of Captain Morgan.

She was maybe twenty, a student at Key West Community College, majoring in flirting her way onto expensive boats with powder parties. She was thin, with a deep tan, sun-lightened brown hair, and a cute Georgia face. And she'd learned nothing in life is free when she'd gotten thrown overboard by an Argentinean tycoon on whose yacht she had been partying and whose knee she'd been grabbing before she said, "Sorry, I have a boyfriend back at school."

That morning Johnny had been idling the boat past Mallory Square when he spotted her sitting in a bikini with legs hanging over the seawall, having shown up ten hours early for the sunset celebration.

He tapped his left nostril; she nodded eagerly and boarded. They did two lines at the docks and slugged rumrunners as they passed Sand Key lighthouse.

Johnny's plan was to head south from Key West, pick up deeper water, and chart west. The uninhabited Marquesas Atoll sat twenty-five miles farther with a sandy beach, perfect for scoring.

Which would be a first. Because, despite the boat and the exercising and the cocaine and cologne and money, he never got a babe in the sack. Not once. It was always something. Boat fire, waterspout, sand crabs, Coast Guard search, language barrier, drug overdose and, with rampant frequency, the sudden and complete change of heart. There was even the can't-miss time a statuesque brunette model came right up to him on the dock and said, "I fuck guys with fast boats." They were three miles offshore and she's topless, taking off her bottom, when she hears something. A hydroplane pulls up, a man opens the cockpit, and she gets in and leaves.

This time would be different. This time with— what was her name? One of those double, singsong deals. Something Sue. Betty Sue? Peggy Sue? Ah, to hell with it: more cocaine for everyone!

Indications to the contrary, Johnny wasn't obnoxious, just immature, and the older residents of his condominium regarded him as a lovable, goofy pet.

They also had no faith in his seamanship. They worried that someday he'd hit an awash coral head and there would go Johnny, cartwheeling across the Gulf Stream at eighty miles an hour until he was embedded headfirst in the sand like a javelin. So they broke it down for him. Stay in the blue water and out of the green water. Over and over: blue water good, green water bad.

Johnny and 'Sue raced due south of the Marquesas in solid-green water and skirting closer to yellow and white. The water was clear as a swimming pool, and patches of sand and coral ran starboard. Between two islands was a channel that cut across the flats as if someone had poured a river of lime Jell-O. He looked down and saw the shadow of his boat racing next to him on the seafloor, and he pretended he was the Flying Dutchman.

The bottom was soft, and Johnny's boat plowed a hundred-yard trench that bled off the violence of the grounding. The stop catapulted 'Sue onto the deck on her hands and knees.

"Are we stuck?" she asked, the boat's deck as solid and unmoving as Nebraska.

"Oh, no no no!" said Johnny. He tossed a mushroom anchor over the bow with forty feet of line, which was thirty-nine too many, and the excess coils of rope floated by where 'Sue was sitting.

"How 'bout some more cocaine!" said Johnny, creating a diversion. He tapped the amulet on the fiberglass console. 'Sue poured another rumrunner out of Johnny's titanium tactical party Thermos, having spilled the last one down the left side of her bikini top. Johnny took off his shirt.

The stereo blared "Funky Cold Medina." They climbed up on the bow. Dancing sloppy, not holding each other, rubbing chests. Johnny thought of his buzz and 'Sue and the music and how he was gonna finally get laid. He closed his eyes and saw an infomercial for Veterans' Health and Life on the inside of his eyelids, and he smiled.

There was a splash in the water off port, and Johnny and 'Sue tumbled back together on the bow.

"Jesus, Harry and Joseph!" he yelled.

They looked overboard, out in the blue water, where their boat should have been. They expected to see a bale of dope or an airplane wing, but instead saw a large blob covered with seaweed and algae and gunk, a long-dead manatee or Kemp's ridley turtle.

They stared a half minute, and their crunched-up faces released at the same time with recognition. Out in the water was a man, bloated and distended, chain around his neck. 'Sue gave a prolonged, blood-clotting scream, which Johnny took to mean she was no longer in the mood.

It took a few minutes but 'Sue had started to calm down, just sniffling and her chest heaving a little. Johnny thought, Yeah, there's a blown-up old dead guy all putrid and shit a few feet away, but I got the smooth moves! He put his arm around her shoulder, to console her, and began sliding his hand toward her breast.

*   *   *

A procession of sports cars and RVs was making the grunion run down from Florida City to the drawbridge onto Key Largo. Because of speeding, reckless driving and head-on crashes, the Florida Department of Transportation had erected a bunch of warning signs and built special passing lanes.

One of the signs read "Be patient. Passing lane one mile." Next to it, an Isuzu Rodeo towing a Carolina Skiff jackknifed trying to pass a Ranchero. The Rodeo slid upright to a stop on the left shoulder, but the skiff rolled, sending four cases of Bud and Bud Lite clattering across the road. The rigid column of high-speed traffic became disorganized, like a line of ants hit with bug spray. A Mustang swerved left, flipped and landed half submerged in the water next to the causeway; a Mercury spun out to the right and slid down the embankment sideways, taking out thirty feet of endangered plants. Motorists ran to check on the people in the Isuzu but retreated when the Mercury's driver pulled a nickel .45 out of the glove compartment. He opened fire on the Rodeo, across the street, which returned fire with an SKS Chinese military rifle. The Rodeo's bumper sticker said, "Hang up and drive!"

Behind the firefight, people got out of cars and crouched behind bumpers or ran for cover in the mangroves. Some jumped in Barnes and Blackwater Sounds and swam away.

Twenty cars back from the accident, Sean Breen and David Klein opened their doors for shields and prepared to run. Ten cars back, three Latin men sat in a bulletproof Mercedes limousine playing three Nintendo GameBoys.

One car back was a yellow Corvette. Coleman and Serge stared at the boat in the middle of the road and the foam shooting into the air from the Budweisers.

As they approached Key Largo, breaks in the road-side brush had given first glimpses of the Keys. Hundreds of yards of tangled branches blurring by, and then a two-foot opening, a subliminal view across the sounds. Unnamed mangrove islands in that unmistakable profile, long and low. Serge thought it was the same profile that in 1513 prompted Ponce de Leon's sailors to name them Los Martires, the martyrs, because they looked like dead guys lying down. No they don't, thought Serge, but he was naturally high anyway as he sat in the parked Corvette. The sniper fire was making a racket and it snapped Serge out of it.

"Beer me," he said, looking straight ahead.

"Right," said Coleman. He waited a few seconds for a break in the gunfire and ran out in the road in front of the car, grabbing one of the few cans that wasn't blowing suds from the seams. He jumped back in the car and handed it to Serge.

Serge stared at him. "I meant from the cooler."

The Coast Guard petty officer, a serious young man with a galvanized clipboard, recent haircut and pressed uniform, stood on the back deck of Johnny Vegas's boat and said no unnecessary words as he took down Johnny's version.

Johnny eyed the man's wedding ring, which he noted was quite small and without diamonds. The petty officer hadn't mentioned Dan Marino. Johnny had been noticing for some time that people in authority weren't giving him enough respect. It wasn't that they were rude or patronizing. Worse, he was irrelevant. Maybe I need to work on my image, he thought, and planned to buy a fighter pilot's jacket.

Coast Guard and Florida Marine Patrol boats had arrived. A four-man dive team was in the water. The body had been pulled from the Gulf and lay on a stainless-steel table at the stern of the Coast Guard boat. A man with surgical gloves probed the remains; another took photos with a Nikon.

Johnny sat forlorn with elbows on his knees, his chin in his hands and a rotting buzz in his head, thinking about all the drugs he'd dumped in the ocean after radioing the authorities on the VHF. 'Sue hunched over in fetal position on the port side with a towel wrapped around her, shivering, occasionally lunging for the gunwales to toss up more of her breakfast of cold pizza. She turned to Johnny with a sad, pleading look, not feeling so attractive anymore. He shook his head with impatience and opened a watertight compartment. "Here," he said, holding something out to her. "Have a mint."

Johnny put his chin back in his hands and stared at the flotilla of partially digested pizza being ravaged by tropical fish.

Another boat approached from the east, a forty-foot trihull catamaran. A reporter from Florida Cable

News stood on the tip of the middle bow holding a microphone, facing back toward the cabin and his cameraman. Behind him, hidden under his suit, he had a brace and safety harness, like a barnstorming wing-walker. He raced at top speed toward news.

The upstart Florida Cable News network had to compensate for lack of money, experience, and reputation with raw daring. The coin of the realm was the scoop, and they regularly beat all major Florida affiliates by going on the air immediately with a ground-breaking series of premature, unconfirmed, flat-wrong stories.

But the worse FCN's accuracy got, the higher the ratings. A cult developed and tuned in to see how factually mangled the coverage had become. The closest thing FCN had to a recognizable personality was correspondent Blaine Crease, a former stuntman who was becoming recognized for exclusively reporting incorrect stories while suspended in a harness. Bouncing on a boat in a harness. Standing atop a fire engine in a harness. Bungee-jumping into precedent-setting slander.

On the Coast Guard boat the early bets favored a gangland hit, like the mobsters who occasionally popped up in fifty-five-gallon drums in the Miami River and off the Rickenbacker Causeway. Others leaned toward lunacy, remembering the psychopath who'd dumped three women in Tampa Bay in '89.

They wondered about the single cement block attached to the chain around the victim's neck. After the oil drums, you'd think every professional button man would know what it takes to keep a body down when it bloats during decomposition.

A diver broke the surface behind the boat and spit out his regulator. "We got another one!"

Sean and David were stiff, sweaty and tense from sitting in the car so long. When they arrived in Key West, they skipped checking in at a hotel and drove to a bar on Duval Street.

They arrived in the purple interlude between sunset and night and parked on a side street by the Expatriate Café. The bar nurtured a sinister, desperado atmosphere that could be purchased on the way out in a variety of T-shirts and knickknacks. The tables nestled among fishtail palms, and mature traveler's trees fanned out at each end of the patio. The tables had tiny, dim lamps with white shades. Over the bar was a world map from the 1930s, an antique sign for Pan Am, and a row of black-and-white celebrity photographs: Ernest Hemingway in Spain, Gertrude Stein in Paris, Humphrey Bogart in Casablanca, Roman Polanski in Switzerland, Howard Hughes in the Bahamas, Eldridge Cleaver making Tim Leary wash the dishes in Algeria.

Sean and David grabbed stools at the bar and ordered drafts. A hit-and-run afternoon cloudburst left puddles in the street that reflected pink and green neon. The opening guitar chords of "Whole Lotta Love" pounded out the open door of the bar across the street.

The two sat with their beers watching the pedestrians and mopeds and cars cruising Duval. They looked up at the TV, hanging on the wall between Bogart and Polanski.

"Good evening, this is Florida Cable News. Our top story tonight . . ."

Serge pointed up at the TV over the espresso machine.

". . . Our top story tonight is tragedy in the waters off Key West, where two bodies were recovered. . . ."

Serge and Coleman sat in a cramped Cuban lunch counter on two stools next to the window. The restaurant was a block off Duval Street on Fleming. A blue awning hung over the door, flanked by U.S. and Cuban flags.

They ordered cheese toast. Coleman had café con leche and beer; Serge ice water. They watched TV and chewed.

". . . We take you to correspondent Blaine Crease with this exclusive report. Blaine? . . ."

Blaine Crease bobbed against the horizon as his catamaran sailed toward the Marquesas.

"Thank you, Natalie. A grisly discovery about twenty miles from Key West today as divers recovered two unrecognizable bodies involved in some kind of incident with Miami quarterback Dan Marino's speedboat. . . ."

A large photograph of Marino's smiling face filled the screen.

"It is not known whether Marino himself was aboard. But we have been unable to reach him by phone, and his boat captain refused to be interviewed. . . ."

The TV showed a depressed Johnny Vegas staring at tufts of pizza in the water, then looking up at the camera and angrily waving it away.

Blaine Crease's voice narrated over the video: "... *Heaven only knows what that poor young man is thinking. ..."*

Johnny was thinking, If she would only stop up-chucking, I can still score.

"*... Back to you, Natalie. ..."*

"*Thank you, Blaine. And in other tragic news ..."* said the smiling anchorwoman, who swung to another camera and switched to frown. "*We take you to the Space Coast. ..."*

A skinny, baby-faced reporter walked backward on the beach with a microphone. "*As the space shuttle orbits overhead, police face a down-to-earth murder mystery in the space capital of the United States. I'm here in Cocoa Beach, where police have discovered a crime scene almost as puzzling as it is macabre. Officially, authorities are saying nothing except the deceased is male, but sources tell me he was the victim of the world's most dangerous Rube Goldberg device. ..."*

Coleman gave Serge a worried glance but didn't speak. Serge threw three fives on the counter, individually, dealing cards, and they walked into the Key West night.

One

Eleven months before the World Series, in November, the start of the tourist season, the beaches off St. Petersburg were jammed with pasty people.

As always, Sharon Rhodes knew every eye was on her as she walked coyly along the edge of the surf, twirling a bit of hair with a finger. A volleyball game stopped. Footballs and Frisbees fell in the water. Guys lost track of conversations with their wives and got socked.

She was the *Sports Illustrated* swimsuit edition in person. Six feet tall, gently curling blonde hair cascading over her shoulders and onto the top of her black bikini. She had a Carnation Milk face with high cheekbones and a light dusting of freckles. Her lips were full, pouty and cruel in the way that makes men drive into buildings.

She stopped as if to think, stuck an index finger in her lips and sucked. Men became woozy. She turned and splashed out into three feet of water and dunked herself. When she came up, she shook her head side to side, flinging wet blonde hair, and thrust out her nipples.

There was nothing in Sharon a man wanted to love, caress or defend. This was tie-me-up-and-hurt-me stuff, everything about her shouting at a man, "I will destroy all that is dear to you," and the man says, "Yes, please."

Wilbur Putzenfus was losing hair on top and working the comb-over. No tan. No tone. A warrior of the business cubicle, with women he was socially retarded. Spiro Agnew without the power. A hundred and fifty pounds of unrepentant geek-on-wheels.

Sharon threw her David Lee Roth beach towel down next to his, lay on her stomach and untied her top.

Wilbur studied Sharon with a series of stolen glimpses that wouldn't have been so obvious if they hadn't been made through the viewfinder of a camcorder.

When Wilbur ran out of videotape, Sharon raised up on her elbows, tits hanging, and said to him in a low, husky voice, "I like to do it in public."

Wilbur was apoplectic.

Sharon replaced her top and stood up. She reached down, took Wilbur by the hand and tried to get him to his feet, but his legs didn't work right, Bambi's first steps.

She walked him over to the snack bar and showers. Against a thicket of hibiscus was one of those plywood cutouts, the kind with a hole that tourists stick their faces through for snapshots.

This one had a large cartoon shark swallowing a tourist feet first. The tourist wore a straw hat, had a camera hanging from a strap around his neck, and was banging on the shark's snout.

The bushes shielded the backside of the plywood from public view, but the front faced heavy foot traffic on the boardwalk.

Sharon told Wilbur to put his face in the hole, and he complied. She told him not to take his head out of the hole or she would permanently stop what she was doing. She pulled his plaid bathing trunks to his ankles, kneeled down and applied her expertise.

Some of the guys from the volleyball game had been following Sharon like puppy dogs, and they peeked behind the plywood. Then they walked around the front of the cutout and stood on the sidewalk, pointing and laughing at Wilbur. Word spread.

The crowd was over a hundred by the time Wilbur's saliva started to meringue around his mouth. His eyes came unplugged and rolled around in their sockets, and he made sounds like Charlie Callas.

Finally, nearing crescendo, Wilbur stared bug-eyed at the crowd and yelled between shallow breaths, "WILL . . . YOU . . . MAR-RY . . . ME?"

"Yeth," came the answer from behind the plywood, a female voice with a mouth full, and the crowd cheered.

*   *   *

Wilbur Putzenfus, a claims executive with a major Tampa Bay HMO, was not an ideal catch. But he could provide a comfortable life. Wilbur's job was to deny insurance claims filed with the Family First Health Maintenance Organization ("We're here because we care"). As Family First's top claims denial supervisor, Wilbur handled the really difficult patients, the ones who demanded the company fulfill its policies.

Wilbur was promoted to this position after a selfless display of ethical turpitude that had revolutionized the company. On his own he'd launched a secret study that showed wrongful-death suits were cheaper than paying for organ transplants covered by their policies.

"So we should stop covering transplants?" asked a director during the watershed board meeting.

"No," said Wilbur, "we'd lose business and profit. We should just stop paying the claims."

"We can do that?" asked the director.

"Gentlemen," said Wilbur, grabbing the edge of the conference table with both hands. "These people are terribly ill and in serious need of immediate medical treatment. They're in no shape to argue with us."

"Brilliant," went the murmur around the table.

As the senior claims denier, Wilbur handled only the most tenacious and meritorious claims that bubbled up through lower levels of impediment.

While a simple coward in person, Wilbur became a vicious coward behind the relative safety of a long-distance phone call. Wilbur answered each appeal with the predisposition that no claim would get by, regardless of legitimacy, company rules, reason and especially fairness. When cornered by an airtight argument, Wilbur responded with a tireless flurry of Byzantine logic. If all else failed and it looked like a claim had to be approved, there was the secret weapon. It became legend around the industry as the Putzenfus Gambit.

"It's an obvious typographical mistake on the bill. Why can't you fix it?" the policyholder would ask.

"I don't have that authority."

"Who does?"

"I can't tell you."

"Why not?!"

"I'm not allowed to give out that information."

"What's the phone number of your main office?"

"I'm not authorized to disclose that number."

"Fine! I'll get it myself. What city is your main office in?"

Silence.

"Are you still there?"

"I'm not allowed to talk to you anymore."

Click.

Sharon's engagement ring was from denied dialysis. The wedding floral arrangement from rejected prescriptions and the open bar from obstructed physical therapy. The buffet was subsidized by untaken CAT scans that would have found a tiny bone fragment that later paralyzed a fourth grader. The medical evidence in that case was so overwhelming,

Putzenfus considered his denial of the claim a moral victory.

The white stretch limo slung a cloud of dirt for three hundred yards. Doing at least sixty, too fast for the thin causeway inches above water.

The coastal area north of Tampa Bay was too spongy and harsh for condos. The limo was way out in the sticks, and the view over the marsh opened up for miles. The incongruous sight of swamp and speeding limo suggested an overthrown Central American president or bingeing rock star.

"Are you sure this is the right way?" Sharon asked from the back of the limo, her nose smudged against the side glass. She slid the electric window down. Sharon pressed her right hand on the top of her head to secure the wedding veil and stuck her face out into the wind to get a better view ahead.

Wilbur had proposed only two months before, and that night he'd laid out the plans for their dream wedding. Sharon listened and pictured nuptials on a fancy barrier island. She expected to drive over the Intracoastal Waterway on one of those new gleaming arches of a bridge and into a five-star resort.

Not a swamp.

Sharon fell back into her seat in the limo, lit a cigarette and said, "This blows."

She scratched her crotch through the wedding gown as the limo crossed onto Pine Island. When they pulled into McKethan Park, she could hear the music Wilbur had selected, "Endless Love" by Diana

Ross and Lionel Ritchie. Sharon stuck a finger in her mouth, making the international puke sign.

I need some more coke to handle this, she thought, and stuck a doctored spansule up her nose, snorting like a feral hog.

A cool, light breeze whipped small whitecaps near the shore. Wilbur, in a white tux, waited at the southern point of the island. The watery backdrop was ringed with distant saw grass and sabal palms. A laughing gull flew over Wilbur, catching the last light of day. It dove in the water and came up with a needlefish.

A windblown Sharon stepped out of the limo and walked toward Wilbur with the gait of someone making a trip to the mailbox. An enraptured Wilbur gazed upon the love of his life. Sharon, chewing a wad of Bazooka bubble gum, watched the seagull fly off with its fish and said to herself: I thought they just ate Fritos.

Sharon decided the honeymoon at Disney World stunk and told Wilbur every sixty seconds they were there. She snorted cocaine the whole time, in the Country Bear Jamboree and all over Tomorrowland. She smoked a joint in the Haunted Mansion, and fucked another tourist at Twenty Thousand Leagues, out behind the plastic boulders.

Wilbur thought the honeymoon was nothing less than perfect, due, in no small part, to the steady diet of blow jobs Sharon dispensed to keep him tolerable.

Driving back to Tampa on Interstate 4, Sharon said she felt unwell and climbed into the backseat to lie down. Traffic slowed to stop-and-go at the perpetual road construction outside Plant City. Sharon asked him to roll down the windows so she could get more air.

"Ouch!" Wilbur yelled a few minutes later and slapped the left side of his neck. "Damn mosquitoes."

Police suspected they had another sniper on the Interstate 4 corridor between Orlando and Tampa, another maniac randomly plinking at cars from the cover of palmettos. The autopsy on Wilbur Putzenfus said the bullet was extremely small caliber and had missed all arteries and anything else important. Under other circumstances, it would barely be classified above a flesh wound.

Unfortunately for Wilbur, he received his medical care through Family First HMO. Unbeknownst to him, his physician, Dr. Sal "the Butcher" Scalone, fell under a Florida loophole that waived domestic medical certification for doctors trained in certain overseas venues. This included Scalone, who was fully board-certified in the island nation of Costa Gorda.

Wilbur also had the unremitting bad luck of being shot on the thirtieth day of the month. Under Family First's incentive plan, Scalone was still in the running for Buccaneers skybox seats for keeping the month's lab tests and referrals below a safe level.

But it was close. So close that Scalone instructed his secretary to keep a running total. By noon on the thirtieth, Scalone had come within two dollars of blowing the football seats. A whole half day to go.

He did the only thing any self-respecting HMO physician could do when faced with such a medical emergency. He ordered his secretaries to close the office and planned to hide out on the back nine with his pager and cell phone turned off.

As the doors were locked, Scalone was told of the last patient he had forgotten about in admitting room seventeen. Scalone found Wilbur sitting with skinny white legs swinging impatiently off the side of the examining table. He wore a paper smock that tied in the back, and his left hand clasped his neck.

Scalone examined the wound and came to an obvious conclusion. Unless he just slapped on a Band-Aid, this injury would cost more than $1.99.

Wilbur Putzenfus walked in the front door of his Palma Ceia bungalow and fell asleep in the den watching ESPN. On his neck was a smiley-face Band-Aid that said, "We're here because we care."

Over the next fourteen hours, blood poisoning and other bacterial complications had their way with Wilbur. Sharon drove him to the emergency room at Tampa Memorial, where he appeared in mildly bad shape. Still time left.

The agent at Family First who answered the phone told the hospital admitting clerk that he was sorry, Wilbur was not approved for emergency room treatment unless it was okayed by his doctor, who was not answering his pager or cell phone. When the hospital clerk raised her voice that the man urgently needed care, the agent said he would have to transfer her to somebody higher up. The admitting clerk then listened to a recorded personal greeting from Claim Denials Supervisor Wilbur Putzenfus before being dumped in voice mail.

"We can't get authorization from the HMO," the hospital clerk told Sharon Putzenfus. "Do you want to pay for this yourself?"

And that was the end of Wilbur Putzenfus.

Family First's HMO saved $143 on medical tests and another $2,624 on treatment for the bullet wound. Its life insurance division, which also covered Wilbur, paid out $500,000 to a slightly bereaved Mrs. Putzenfus, who, for unexplained reasons, held Mr. Putzenfus's sparsely attended funeral in Tahiti.

Two

The weekend Wilbur Putzenfus died was the last in January, eight months before the World Series, and it was an eventful one for Tampa detectives. The morning after Wilbur's body was pried out of the recliner in his den, the city's 911 center received a call from the exclusive south Tampa suburb of Manatee Isles. The particular address of the emergency caused a series of off-the-record telephone calls to spiderweb out from the 911 center to the most important homes in Tampa. Seven times the usual number of personnel were dispatched to the residence.

Celeste Hamptons lay peacefully on the living room carpet in a mauve bathrobe, looking more asleep than dead. As many people filled the living room as had attended most of Hamptonses' charity fund-raisers for the hospital, museum and political campaigns. Nineteen uniformed cops and eleven detectives; two teams of paramedics had just given up and were in the kitchen, going through the refrigerator.

There was a representative from the mayor's office and another from the county commission, both in charcoal-gray suits, white shirts, maroon ties with diagonal stripes. The deputy secretary of agriculture, in denim, had driven over from the State Fairgrounds east of town. All were being scolded by a man with no official title who didn't introduce himself. He wore bright white shorts and a teal tennis shirt decorated with navel oranges. Hundred-dollar sunglasses hung from his neck by a pink rubber lanyard. A graphite tennis racket was still in his hand and he shook it at the deputy secretary of agriculture. None of the cops or detectives recognized him, but they followed the lead of the guys from city hall, full of "yes, sir" and "no, sir."

"I don't care if it looks like *cyanide* poisoning, stonewall the bastard! Get rid of these cops—kill the criminal investigation!"

The agriculture man assured him there was absolutely no way the malathion pesticide had come from his Huey helicopters or DC-3 airplanes that were spraying the area for medflies. He was personally supervising the makeshift airfield at the fairgrounds himself. Believe it or not, it appeared to have happened exactly as it had been phoned in to police.

The helicopters and planes had been flying for three months after they had found the insects. A handful of Mediterranean fruit flies had turned up in

Tampa backyards, and their tastes leaned toward Florida's citrus crop.

The next thing anyone in Tampa knew, the state capital hit the city over the head with a billion dollars of agricultural clout. Tampa was placed under a citrus version of martial law, and the helicopters were sent in. Saigon. The Hueys skimmed over neighborhoods spraying a mist of what looked and adhered to cars like Smucker's strawberry preserves.

State officials told Tampa they didn't need local approval and to just sit down and shut up. They repeated in lockstep mantra, "Malathion is so safe you can drink it."

Local officials and ad hoc citizens groups turned in water tests that showed a hundred times the federal pesticide limits in rivers and kiddie pools. Residents took on a Bolshevik swagger. Tallahassee decided to change tactics and commissioned a warm-fuzzy advertising campaign to make up with the residents of Tampa Bay. They hired "Malley" the Dancing Malathion Bear.

They were not remotely prepared for what was to come.

A desk phone rang out at the fairgrounds; simultaneously, fifteen miles away, a cell phone made muffled pulses inside a tennis bag at the Palma Ceia Country Club. When the deputy secretary of agriculture heard precisely what had happened at Manatee Isles that morning, he grabbed his heart. The man on the tennis court bounced his graphite racket twenty feet in the air. "Un-fucking-believable!" He slammed the cell phone shut and stomped out of the country club.

In Celeste Hamptons's living room, the tennis player tore into the deputy secretary. "Who the hell's bright idea was it to say it was safe enough to drink?!"

"But we never thought anybody would actually do it!" said the agriculture official. "She wanted to prove it was safe, support her friends in the citrus lobby. She was planning to make a public service commercial. Drank a whole ice tea tumbler of the stuff." He pointed at an empty glass on the counter with a lemon slice on the rim.

"Of all people! She knows we're liars!" said the tennis player.

The monogram on the tennis bag was "CS," for Charles Saffron, president and CEO of New England Life and Casualty, whose power outstripped his notable wealth. He was the whisper-in-the-ear between business and politics, the behind-the-scenes, connect-the-dots guy who knew everyone, left nothing on paper and couldn't be scathed. He was the crack in the system into which fell accountability and from which sprouted plausible deniability.

Saffron looked around. "Where's Sid?"—referring to Sid Hamptons, her husband, former city councilman, accused of bribery, never charged, resigned, then named chairman of the mayor's task force on task forces.

"You didn't hear? Died five months ago. Freak escalator accident at the aquarium. Got his shoelace caught."

"Shoelace in an escalator? I thought that was a load of crap you tell kids to settle 'em down."

"So did everyone. First case on record."

"Damn."

"She remarried a week ago. Young British guy." The agriculture official pointed to a gentleman in a double-brested navy blazer and taupe ascot sitting at the dining room table. "His name is . . . here, I got it written down. . . . Nigel Mount Batten."

Saffron walked to the table and slapped the young man hard on the side of the head.

"Owwwww!" The man grabbed his right ear. The cops turned toward them for a second, then back to the basketball game on TV.

"Listen, you fucking limey poofter!" Saffron growled, then changed tone. "Is that correct? Is that the proper saying?"

Mount Batten nodded yes nervously.

"Good," said Saffron. "I wouldn't want to get my international protocol wrong, trigger some kind of diplomatic incident, you little colonializing son of a bitch!"

He grabbed Mount Batten by the hair and jerked his head back. "Everything is all wrong here," said Saffron. "Celeste was dumber than a dust bunny, but she never struck me as the kind of person to drink a glass of insecticide." He stuck a thumb hard into one of Mount Batten's eyes.

The terrible screaming forced the cops to turn up the TV.

"I know you killed her, you Tory twat!" He bore in on Mount Batten with champagne-brunch breath. "Now listen good! We've got *bugs* in Florida that can kick your royal butt; imagine what my friends will do. I want you the hell out of my state!"

The agriculture official interrupted and grabbed Saffron's arm. "Hey, if it's true he killed her, we're in the clear," he said. "Let homicide take it. Charge this guy. The program will still have a clean record."

Saffron knocked three times on the agriculture official's skull with his knuckles. "Hello? Shit for brains? Anybody home? Which headline do you like better? 'Woman dies in medfly war' or ' "Safe" malathion used as murder weapon'?"

The deputy secretary sighed and put his hands in his jeans pockets. Mount Batten jumped up from his chair and ran yelling across the living room. He broke through the yellow crime scene tape across the front door like a finish line and kept on running.

Sharon Rhodes, formerly Sharon Putzenfus, nibbled on a baklava and pawed without interest at loofahs in a large wooden basket. The next showing of *The History of the Sponge* was about to start, but Sharon walked out of the museum and down an alley in Tarpon Springs. She walked by Zorba's restaurant, with photos of that night's belly dancers in the window, and by Spring Bayou, where the archbishop throws the cross in the water at Epiphany and the Greek boys jump in after it.

A sponge boat rode deep in the water from its load of tourists and motored up Dodecanese Bayou toward the sponge docks. A fiercely handsome young Greek man with sharp, angular features and solid black hair stood on the bow. He wore an antique diving suit and held the large brass diving helmet under his arm. He had demonstrated for visitors from Palatka, Lakeland, Winter Haven and Brooksville how they used to work when Tarpon Springs was the sponge capital of the country. The audience unloaded into the gift shop to buy souvenir sponges that were cut in rectangles and colored blue, pink, green and yellow.

One tourist said the sponges looked exactly like the ones in the supermarket.

"No! Special sponge!" said the shopkeeper. "From the old country."

Sharon crossed Dodecanese Boulevard and entered a pastry shop with a sidewalk café. She checked her watch and ordered a tiny Styrofoam cup of bitter Greek coffee the shade of ink. Rollicking Greek music played over low-fi stereo speakers that subconsciously made everyone want to dance in a line with a hankie. Sharon sipped the coffee and walked to the rest room in the back of the shop.

She pushed open the door to the only stall. A man lunged and pulled her inside. She struggled and clawed at his cheeks. He smacked her across the face and smacked her again with the backhand returning the other way. He threw her against the side of the stall and her head bounced off it.

With brute violence, he ripped both her skirt and panties down to her knees in one motion. She spit in his face. She cursed him. He violated her, thrusting repeatedly until the bolts securing the stall's wall pulled from the concrete. The wall crashed to the tile floor and fell back against the sink, which also tore loose and shattered in a pile of porcelain chips. The stall door fell into the hand-drying machine.

Sharon melted into his arms. "I've missed you so much," she cooed and sloppy-kissed him.

"I've missed you too," said Nigel Mount Batten.

Two waitresses and a cook rushed in to check on the commotion. Mount Batten pointed at the fallen house of cards that used to be the stall. "Shoddy workmanship!" he yelled. "My lawyers will be in touch!" He pushed through the group, and he and Sharon walked out of the bakery arm in arm.

Mount Batten told Sharon about the tennis player. Under the circumstances, he said, it was better not to mess with probate and just settle for the six hundred thousand in life insurance. Together with Wilbur's half-million policy, they had a decent nest egg, all for the low investment of not seeing each other for two months. Oh, and by the way, Sharon said, "You're a shitty shot. The guy almost didn't die. I had to take him to the hospital or it woulda seemed suspicious."

Mount Batten's laugh was hearty and sophisti-cated. They pulled into the parking lot of Ocean Crown Harbor Club Tower Arms, a thirty-story peanut-shaped condominium on Clearwater Beach.

"I love it!" she effused as a private elevator opened into the furnished penthouse. Across the suite, through the balcony's sliding glass doors, the view over the Gulf of Mexico was as if from an airplane. She ran in the bedroom, shrieked with delight and jumped up and down on the giant round bed.

"Only twelve thousand a week," Nigel yelled from the living room. "See that building to the north? That's Jim Bakker and Jessica Hahn's old place."

Sharon rolled onto her back on the round bed and fired a joint with the crystal lighter from the nightstand; Nigel pulled a bottle of Chivas from a mahogany cabinet. So began forty days and forty nights of eye-crossing debauchery. They had steak and wine shipped across the bay from Bern's, cigars from Ybor City, wardrobe from Hyde Park, the best drugs from four counties: brown tar, china white, yellow jackets, black beauties, Panama Red, Acapulco Gold, blue cheer, orange sunshine; they drew low-echelon glitterati from private bottle clubs and teenagers from downtown raves. Four gallons of mimosas chugged through an electric fountain in the foyer. Nigel ordered a biohazardous disposal vat from a hospital because people weren't being considerate with their spent syringes and condoms. A state judge showed up and after two days he loaded his Porsche Cabriolet on the back of a flatbed tow truck and sat up front with the driver for the ride home. They rented a sixty-foot Bertram for an all-night fishing trip. In perfect weather it beached in a desolate part of Hernando County, not a single fish on board. Someone used a cell phone. A limo arrived on an empty county road a hundred yards away. They abandoned the yacht, hiked to the limo and piled in horizontally for the ride back to Clearwater Beach.

Strangers wandered through their lives, and Nigel and Sharon uncovered them all over the penthouse: on the kitchen floor, behind the bidet and in the closet, slumped over a shoe tree, masturbating into a chinchilla coat. Money and valuables disappeared. Credit card companies called to report charges from around the world. Nobody kept the books.

By day thirty-nine, Nigel and Sharon were thirty thousand in the hole on six bank cards. But they had more important things to think about. Nigel with his Chivas and dusted upper lip, and Sharon constantly sucking on a glass crack stem.

Day forty, Nigel lying supine on the giant white sofa, pouring whiskey into his mouth with a gravy boat. Watching *McHale's Navy*. The phone ringing. Nigel slaps at it and knocks it off the cradle. He sees the receiver lying there, a small tin voice coming from it. He looks atop the end table at a line of coke as thick as a garden snake. He squints at the phone, then back at the coke. He has to make a decision. After a short eternity, he picks up the receiver.

"Uh, hullo?"

It was New England Life and Casualty. Just confirming that they'd received and approved his signed application for five hundred thousand in life insurance on himself.

"Okay," he said, and hung up, his mind laboring at brontosaurus pace, a minute later: But I didn't apply for any life insurance.

He noticed he was sliding down the couch into a deeper and deeper slouch. Man, I'm trashed, he thought. He felt something grabbing his ankles. He was dragged off the couch onto the carpet.

Nigel looked down and saw Sharon gripping both legs, his consciousness getting slippery.

"Sharon . . . what? . . ."

He watched the ceiling go by above, the tight nap of the ecru rug rubbing against the back of his head.

Sharon had thought long, but she didn't have Nigel's imagination or technical ability; she'd never come up with malathion poisoning or highway shooting. About the only thing she was an expert in was slutty clothes.

Nigel stared up from the bathroom floor. His butt felt cold, and he realized he didn't have pants on. Sharon wiggled some of her tightest jeans up Nigel's legs.

When they were buttoned, she propped him against the door and hefted him into the gilded bathtub. She sat him up in the shallow end and turned on the water. He no longer had the strength; his face was one big question.

Sharon turned off the water, the tub half full. She left and Nigel could hear the closing theme of *McHale's Navy* in the other room. He faded in and out for two hours, Sharon checking occasionally and draining the water from the tub. The last thing Nigel thought, shortly before midnight: I can't feel my legs.

Nigel would have been proud. Leave it to Sharon; she knew her laundry shrinkage. Toward the end, Nigel recalled he had told Sharon that depressing someone's general circulation was as good as wringing their neck. The paramedics arrived too late the next morning and found a stone-stiff Nigel in the tub, with an expression that couldn't quite believe Sharon was killing him with a pair of Levi's 501s.

Three

One Saturday afternoon in February, shortly after
Wilbur Putzenfus was found dead, orthodontist
George Veale III fell or was pushed out of a vehicle
into traffic on Bayshore Boulevard. It was the second
time in the same hour.

South Tampa is the polyp of land that dangles into
Tampa Bay like a uvula. This is the old money and
a bunch of the new. Restored bungalows and sprawl-
ing Mediterraneans, garden clubs and Junior
Leagues. Bayshore Boulevard curves along the eastern shore, past mansion row. Along the balustrade is
what's billed as the world's longest continuous sidewalk, filled with joggers and skaters in Lycra and
headphones.

One Saturday afternoon in February, shortly after
Wilbur Putzenfus was found dead, orthodontist
George Veale III fell or was pushed out of a vehicle
into traffic on Bayshore Boulevard. It was the second
time in the same hour.

On another day it could have been fatal, but this
afternoon the traffic was going five miles an hour and
the vehicle behind him was a giant sea serpent. A
black scarf wrapped Veale's head, and a plastic parrot was sewn to the shoulder of his shirt. He had

started the day dressed as a pirate, but now his eye patch was over his ear, the fake scar had peeled off his cheek, and the top half of the parrot was gone.

Other pirates yelled for the float to stop. Brake lights lit up on the pickup truck, which had become an eighteenth-century schooner through chicken wire and crepe paper. Two pirates jumped down to the road, picked up Veale and threw him onto the back of the float like a rolled-up carpet, and he remained unconscious until the Gasparilla Parade reached Euclid Avenue.

Gasparilla is Tampa's annual heritage festival, and Tampa's heritage appears to be about alcohol. The festival is pinned on the legend of José Gaspar, a pirate of disputed authenticity, and run by groups of wealthy secret societies with royalty themes.

Veale's society publicly welcomed minorities, and privately laughed and tore up their membership applications. Two hours after sunrise, Veale poured Johnnie Walker for himself and three other members of Too White Krewe.

The krewe drank and commiserated about the increasing pressure to integrate before the next Super Bowl came to Tampa. There was no getting out of it, and they considered their options out loud. An Uncle Tom, an Oreo, someone "not black enough." How about that guy who helped get the senator reelected? Perfect, they thought, and Veale dialed the phone.

In the oak-paneled den of a home on Bayshore, the men applied swashbuckler paint and strapped on plastic cutlasses. And continued drinking. The host's underage daughter walked by and Veale made a pass. Which prompted a bit of wrestling around on the floor of the den, but the others were able to separate them before the wives got wind. They patched things up with another round of drinks.

They finally presented themselves, giddy and disheveled, to the wives, who registered benevolent irritation and fanned their noses at the fumes.

The parade rolled north from Gandy Boulevard under a cold, dank sky that threatened rain but held back. Residents lined the shoulder of Bayshore, screaming for the pirates to throw plastic beads and aluminum doubloons. The pirates fired miniature cannons.

The *Tampa Tribune* float caught fire, ejecting columnists, and was scratched from the parade. New York Yankees pitcher and off-and-on hometown hero Doc Gooden waved from a mobile baseball-motif pavilion.

Before the procession crossed Bay to Bay Boulevard, Veale was a raging lout, cursing and throwing beads as hard as he could at the crowd, drinking from a flask and grabbing himself indecently.

He blended in.

One of the other pirates spilled a drink down the right side of Veale's face, running the paint, and he looked like a Peter Gabriel album cover.

At Howard Avenue, he yelled at a group of teenage girls, "Show me your fucking tits!" When one complied, he wound up and fired a string of plastic opals into her face.

"Ow! Jesus!" She grabbed her left eye and a friend went to get ice.

By Rome Avenue, Veale was into the doubloons. He gripped them around the rim with his forefinger and slung them the way you'd skip shells off the surface of a lake. "Here, you cocksuckers!" he shouted and skimmed a doubloon off the forehead of a six-year-old boy, drawing blood. A mother yelled back at the float and led the child away, but Veale didn't see it. He was lying in the road again.

When Veale fell off the schooner for the third and last time, the float kept moving because of a marching band behind it, and the brass section had to step over Veale. When the band passed, two pirates carried Veale up to one of the Bayshore mansions and rolled him under the bushes.

Cars crammed both sides of the streets feeding Bayshore, and parade-watchers carried the celebration into the evening and back toward town, walking through flower beds and tossing beer cans on the lawns of bank presidents and city councilmen, a little peasant insolence to give the day symmetry. One commoner sidled up to some shrubs and unknowingly relieved on Veale's pantaloons.

Veale awoke at dusk, lying facedown in the dirt under the hedge of a house he didn't recognize, stinking of liquor and urine, and he said to himself, I have a party to get to.

It was Veale's party, and he staggered with plastic sword dragging on the ground the two blocks from the bay to his home.

Most of the guests had arrived by the time Veale bellowed his entrance. George Veale III, orthodontist to the soccer moms, whose motto was In every five thousand dollars of dental work there's ten thousand dollars to be made. He borrowed his second motto from his Realtor: Location, location, location. Forget Medicare; south Tampa was a cash-only galaxy of liposuction, silicone, Phen-Fen fat farms and Valium bars. Into this stew Veale dropped a staff of eleven dentists, all under thirty, who were paid nothing and could turn the perfectly adequate teeth of a first-grader into the smile of Alec Baldwin. It was absurd, and parents couldn't line up and pay Veale fast enough.

Veale churned out just over eight hundred thousand a year, a million counting tax dodges. He insured his hands for five mil.

His home spread out in a U with the open end facing San Clemente Street. Across the end was a stucco wall topped with two rows of burnt sienna barrel tiles. In the middle was a black wrought-iron gate that led to the courtyard. A Canary Island date palm towered behind the wall as the landscaping centerpiece of the property. At the ends of the U, twin second-story balconies with more wrought iron overlooked the street. Each had bougainvillea in forty-gallon terra-cotta planters shaped like panthers.

Veale thought extra volume in his voice was the key to everything. He grew a beard the way an insecure person does when he wants to conceal a pudgy face, but Veale's was professionally manicured. Also, a ponytail beginning to show gray, a diamond stud earring and small potbelly. He wore dark, three-piece pinstripes and carried a platinum cigar cutter in his breast pocket. Every day after work, Veale shed his shoes, socks and jacket, but left his vest on. He poured four ounces of bourbon in a Waterford rocks glass, with exactly five rocks. He'd hold the drink in the same hand as the short, fat butt of an unlit Cohiba. In the other hand was the leash of his pit bull, Van Damme, and he paced with the dog back and forth in front of his house like a football coach on the sidelines, talking to himself and gesturing with the cigar stub. He was forty-eight and he loved the feel of the St. Augustine lawn between his toes.

At least half his party guests were current or potential clients, because Veale thought a party wasn't really a party unless it was lubricating future revenue.

It had started without him. One of the caterers was upstairs boffing Veale's twenty-year-old fourth wife; in another bedroom a future son-in-law was boffing his twenty-two-year-old daughter.

A red-blue-and-orange macaw sat in a gold cage in front of the wet bar. Veale had put stuff in the cage he thought macaws liked in the wild of the rain forest, a trapeze and a little unicycle, but the bird didn't touch them.

Fellow pirates brought over the cannon from their float and set it up on the wet bar. One of the krewe had panties stretched over the top of his pirate hat.

Two women who sent their kids to Veale leaned against the bar, shorting out on martinis, cackling and throwing olive pits into the cannon.

The bar was chrome and glass block and stood in the living room at one end of the pool. The pool began indoors, stretched under a plate-glass wall and ended outdoors in the courtyard. The pool was aglow from underwater lights and contained seven dropped hors d'oeuvres and two clothed lawyers.

Each year at Gasparilla, when he was completely faced, Veale fired a blank charge from the cannon inside his house, filling it with smoke and the smell of gunpowder. He did it again this year, except he also fired twenty olive pits like a shotgun, blowing the macaw through the plate glass and into the pool.

The sight of the inside-out bird in the water emptied the party. Veale swung into action. He drove drunk to an exotic club on Dale Mabry Highway for two hundred dollars of lap dances from a stripper named Sharon.

Four

David Klein met Sean Breen in gym class at Tampa High School during the Bicentennial. After class, Sean's jock strap was stretched out and padlocked across three lockers. Sean still in it. On his toes, balancing, just able to reach the floor. This was top-shelf entertainment among David's friends from the football team. Sean was so good-natured he laughed along with the gag. David stayed behind and cut Sean down with scissors used to snip athletic tape.

Sean said thanks and they got dressed. David asked why a black kid had such an Irish name.

"Because I'm Irish," Sean said seriously.

David imagined a little black leprechaun and bit his lip to keep from laughing.

Sean asked, "How come an athlete has such a Jewish name?"

David didn't say anything right away, and Sean blurted, "Hey, just kidding, just a joke."

"No offense," said David. He liked Sean right away.

Most cool kids at Tampa High existed at a middle plateau of popularity where they had to constantly push down against the lower strata to stay there. David had the currency of popularity that could be spent freely. Quarterback, homecoming king. His were the rugged good looks and advanced physique of someone in college. He never showed anger, but was reserved with his smile. That he was so laconic and circumspect only increased his draw, a distant, self-assured aura everyone wanted to touch.

The awkward, picked-on misfits loved to see David walking down the halls. They'd wave and call out stupid things like "Great game!" or "You the man!" David always waved back, sometimes pointing at them with a hand made like a pistol, and it was the highlight of their day.

When two guys from David's offensive line thought to amuse themselves at Sean's expense with Nair, David put one up against a locker. When a linebacker made a racial crack about Sean, David pushed his face into the floor. It became an unwritten but thoroughly observed rule: Sean was untouchable.

Two phenomena sealed David's legend. First, he dated nearly every cheerleader. Not because he was after them. Because they asked him out. He was sincere, mannered, heart-palpitating company, and he said no every time they asked him out a second time.

The girls and David were discreet about the dates, and rumors metastasized wildly.

The second phenomenon was the essential ingredient for any legend of school coolness. A single, over-the-top act of public violence.

David's parents weren't actively abusive to David and his sister, Sarah. They were indifferent. The siblings compensated for the lack of acknowledgment and were inseparable. Two years younger, Sarah tagged along everywhere after David. David saw an admiring look coming up from Sarah that said he was perfect. Under Dave's umbrella of protection and praise, Sarah became, simply, well-adjusted. In the wake of her brother's reputation at Tampa High, she developed into one of the more popular girls in the sophomore class.

Sarah left early for school one morning, and David missed her at breakfast. David saw her halfway down the school's main hallway and called to her. She scurried for the stairwell with an armload of books. As the first bell rang, David caught up with her on the stairs. She turned her face away, but not before David saw the two faint black eyes under heavy makeup.

He sprinted up the stairs as Sarah yelled behind him.

Seven classrooms of students at Tampa High that morning remember David Klein swinging open the door, looking around and running to the next room. The eighth class remembers David charging across the room to the last row and tackling Frank Sturgeon in his desk, both crashing into the radiator under the windows.

Frank had at least three inches and twenty pounds on David. As nose guard on the football team, Frank was notches below David in school stature. But he also captained the wrestling team, which held its own separate sphere of popularity at Tampa High. David thought Frank was a moron, walking around with big arms held out a deliberate distance from his triangular torso. David had barely remained civil when Frank had picked Sarah up for their first date two weeks before.

David broke Frank's cheekbone and split the skin over his eye, producing an amount of blood more dramatic than the injury. David's savagery, however, couldn't be understated. Frank, dazed, crawled up the aisle; David grabbed him by the feet and dragged him back, pummeling him, reaching for book bags, purses, anything his hands found to hit Frank over the head and back. Two assistant football coaches ran in the room and pulled David off, David still kicking at Frank's ribs.

David was suspended for a week, which the coach got shortened to four days so he wouldn't miss the annual rivalry with Plant High. "You're suspended from school, but not practice!" the coach reminded him.

Two hundred students stayed late that afternoon in the parking lot, watching the locker-room door for David to run out to practice. Everyone, even David, knew six or seven wrestlers would be waiting. There wasn't a question of David not emerging from the door; everyone knew he'd never run. Because of the wrestlers' size, they also knew he'd have no help.

Out he came, number 12, in gold and green, jogging and carrying his helmet by the face mask. Two hundred people and the only sound was David's cleats on the pavement.

The wrestlers blocked his path to the field. David stopped and tightened the grip on his helmet's face mask. He'd take at least one with him. The wrestlers started fanning out around him.

Someone leaned on a car horn and several doors slammed.

The crowd turned and parted. Three huge black men stepped out of an Oldsmobile; they looked to be in their late twenties. They unhurriedly removed suit coats and ties and folded them.

They walked over and stood beside David. The one closest to David said to the wrestlers, "Four against seven. You need to get some more guys?"

The arrogance in the wrestlers' faces dissolved. The man spoke again, barely above a whisper. "David stubs a toe and we're coming to your houses to ask why."

The wrestlers' exit wasn't even an attempt at graceful. They walked briskly to their cars, yelled something unintelligible and patched out.

The man who had done the talking turned to David. He pointed back to the Olds, where Sean was standing. "Sean's the youngest in the family." The man smiled for the first time. "And the smallest. He says you watch out for him." He slapped David on the shoulder. "Take care of yourself."

David stared at Sean. I'll be damned.

The other students didn't quite know what to make of it. Sean joined David and Sarah as an inseparable trio. Sean's influence opened up David's personality, and he became more jocular when they were together.

Mostly, they fished together, usually off the Gandy Bridge that spanned the bay to St. Petersburg. Not catching anything. It became a tradition, and before they knew it they had not been catching fish together for twenty years. They had not been catching fish both times when Sean asked David to be godfather to his children.

Sean consistently touted the joys of fatherhood to David, and he was always trying to get David matched up with some nice woman from the office. The dates never went badly, but they never clicked either.

"At least they're better than some of the women you find on your own," said Sean.

David had to admit Sean had a point. He'd just gotten his car back from the paint shop after it had been egged and keyed by a woman who later left a weepy message on his answering machine demanding to know what was so wrong with her that he wouldn't call anymore.

"It's genuinely scary out there," David told Sean.

* * *

"It's genuinely scary out there," Susan Tchoupitoulas said to herself at that same moment, four hundred miles away. She had just walked into her house and closed the door following a particularly repugnant good-night kiss.

Susan had dreaded the kiss during the entire pathology of the date. This was no way to spend her night off—more stressed than on many of the stakeouts she'd endured on the Key West Police Department.

Susan was on the tallish side at five-eight and had just enough tomboy in her to be cute. Her blonde hair came to just above her shoulders, and she often used a plain rubber band to keep it in a stubby ponytail. While the fashion runways of New York currently favored thin horse faces, Susan was a throwback beauty—the full-faced, healthy good looks of an Ingrid Bergman.

Susan may have been one of the youngest sergeants in the history of the department, but her father still waited up for her. When Samuel Tchoupitoulas rolled into the living room in his wheelchair, Susan gave him a big hug. She had that look on her face.

"Rough night?" he asked.

"What a loser," she said. "He kept asking me if I was scared being a cop and said he would be. How appealing."

"Yeah, I thought he was a clown when he came to the door," her father said. But it was without any "I told you so" edge.

Susan and her father, a former sheriff's deputy,

lived in a conch cottage on Olivia Street in Old Town. Everything was just how they liked it.

Susan had followed in her father's footsteps and become a cop, and she was a great one. Her father had taught her that far worse than a criminal was a bad cop, whether corrupt or incompetent. She was proud of the Key West police force. Most of the officers, she knew, were as good as any in the state. One problem, however, was that for all its international reputation and the millions of tourists who visited, Key West was still a small town on an island only four miles long by one and a half miles wide.

In the police department, this translated to small-town politics that kept certain well-connected officers in uniform who had no business with a badge and a gun. They gave the department a bad name far out of proportion to their numbers on the force. The problem was so well known that the residents had a nickname for them: "The Bubbas."

Some of The Bubbas tried in vain to date Susan, and then, in the alternative, harass her on the job.

"I can't get a break with men," Susan told her dad. "Either they're telling me idiotic sex jokes at work or wasting my private life." She said it with a smile.

"Someday you'll meet the right guy," her father said.

The Gasparilla festival was held in February, and Sean and his family and David were running up a tab at the Columbia Restaurant. Sean's wife, Karen, had the tenderloin, and Sean and David shared paella served in a bowl the size of a satellite dish. Christopher, four, had a hamburger, and in the fifth chair at the table, the Breens' three-month-old daughter, Erin, woke up hungry.

A waiter prepared a bottle of baby formula with the showmanship of a wine presentation, and neighboring tables applauded. The lights dimmed except for a red glow on the stage of the main dining room. Four people lined up in tight, ornate costume, the women in scarlet silk with lace fans, the men in black cotton. For the next twenty minutes, the crowd was still for the flamenco dancing set.

The stage cleared and the sound system played "Oye Como Va" during the costume change. The dancers returned in tropical colors, the women in short skirts and the men in white shirts and floral sashes for belts. Upbeat Cuban music, metal drums, fast dancing. The tempo rose and the dancers clapped in unison. They marched down off the stage, winding between the dinner tables, and a conga line fell in behind.

As the dancers came by their table, Karen pushed her chair out and got Christopher and they joined the line, laughing. Sean shrugged at David. "Can you watch Erin?" David nodded yes and Sean joined the line. They all ended up back onstage, dancing in opposition to the rhythm.

The music continued, the amateur dancers kicking out legs way out of time, and David smiled in a moment of distilled contentment. The paella was a pile of mussel shells, shrimp tails and chicken bones on a bed of leftover yellow rice and peppers. A long, good day was winding down.

Sean and David had spent the morning out in Sean's fourteen-foot skiff, not catching fish. They drifted with the tide across Cockroach Bay, where they had never seen a cockroach. There was something about the mangrove flats that had a pull on both of them. Out in the middle of the Stone Age, stingrays gliding under the shallow water, ibises on the oyster bars, and the roots of red mangrove grabbing out into the water like spider legs. Sean and David couldn't get any of their other friends hooked on the mangroves, so whenever they got together, they made a beeline down US 41, past the Coffee Cup restaurant, to the boat launch south of the Little Manatee River. They hoped it was a spiritual thing and wondered if they were just rednecks.

Sean cut the engine, and David got on the platform with the push pole. Sean was forward, wearing polarized sunglasses, squinting at the mangrove roots looking for snook. They heard a loud crack and water behind them roiled. Dolphins charged a school of mullet, and one slapped the surface of the water with its tail fluke to stun them, the dolphin version of fishing with dynamite. Two dolphin tossed a mullet back and forth with their bottle noses like it was a football.

"There goes every fish till the next tide," said Sean.

The Columbia Restaurant had been built in 1905 in Tampa's Latin quarter, Ybor City. Ybor had been the Cuban-Italian core when Tampa was "Cigar City USA." After the heyday, Ybor was boarded up. This attracted bohemians, who loitered, which attracted businessmen, who opened nine hundred bars and restaurants. David thought the place looked like a gene splice of Greenwich Village and Havana, and run by Planet Hollywood.

After dinner, the group stepped out of the Columbia onto Seventh Avenue. They strolled west into the heart of the district. The oncoming sidewalk traffic was heavy with body piercing, tattoos and beepers. A white Rastafarian operated a marijuana pipe kiosk. He explained to a customer that it was legal because you could somehow use the devices to smoke cigarettes.

A man with a kettle of oil, potatoes and a power drill was making curly fries. A seventeen-year-old girl in a halter top and pigtails chewed on a pacifier because Ecstasy made her grind her teeth.

In the courtyard beside an industrial-dance club, a trailer sprouting a large antenna. A man in a Stetson hat sat behind a table and microphone. It was the famous radio talk show host Mo Grenadine, broadcasting *The Mo Grenadine Show*.

"Isn't that the guy you used to promote?" David asked. "You did his advertising campaign."

"Don't remind me," said Sean.

Mo's success was based on demographic research that showed talk radio audiences were predominantly male, bitter, undereducated, untraveled, did not know how to figure percentages and unfailingly blew all major life decisions. Research also showed Mo's ratings spiked when he called homosexuals "fudgepackers," which he had to do constantly to fill airtime because he did not possess talent or knowledge.

The problem with Mo's audience was that it had an incredibly low per-capita income, which is why *The Mo Grenadine Show* was sponsored by Hot-to-Trot Jerky Sticks, Red-Eye Beer ($1.99 a six-pack) and The Galactic Wrestling Federation.

Grenadine, fifty-one, had started unlikely enough as a private investigator specializing in fabricating evidence to deny insurance claims of legitimate and generally poor accident victims, some of whom were now his listeners. Sitting home one afternoon, he had a bad medical reaction to drinking nine scotches. He saw something on TV about a Tampa city council hearing that evening on a gay rights ordinance. Grenadine went out and bought a gay porno magazine and made a hundred Xeroxes of a man giving another man oral sex. On each he drew a red circle with a slash through it. He stood next to the doorway of the city council chambers and handed a copy to each person who entered.

The following morning he was in the newspaper, the next afternoon a guest on talk radio. The next week he was the host of the radio show. And that November, Mo Grenadine surfed a wave of homophobia into the Florida senate, also picking up the overlapping assault-rifle vote.

To fertilize his power base, Grenadine called press conferences to attack AIDS benefits, gay public speakers at the University of South Florida, lesbians in general and those who wouldn't date him in particular.

Grenadine kept open his private eye practice to launder the bribes of insurance companies with pending legislation.

Then the scandal.

Grenadine and two call girls were in the hot tub at his condo one night and he somehow got his penis caught in the pool pump's intake valve. His subsequent engorgement left him inextricable. The women fled and in the morning the neighbors found him incoherent and pruney-skinned. The sheriff's department dive team used rescue equipment to cut into the pool's wall and remove the entire mechanism in front of TV crews.

"Stick a fork in him, he's done" was the thinking man's bet in the newsrooms. In the face of all contrary facts and accounts, Grenadine called a press conference in his hospital room and claimed he'd been attacked by a platoon of perverts who'd molested him in an unspeakable manner because of his courageous, God-fearing work in the legislature. The attack emphasized the need to vote for him and stop the sodomites who break Jesus' heart. The performance brought convulsive laughter at the television stations.

Grenadine was reelected in a landslide.

On the radio he started calling himself "Holy Moly."

Sean and David listened from the sidewalk in Ybor

City as Grenadine screamed "fudgepacker!" into the microphone.

On the way home, Sean said he'd gotten a phone call that morning inviting him to a Gasparilla party. One of the social clubs was recruiting him to join.

"Too White Krewe? I dunno," said David. "They probably think you're an archconservative because of your work on the senator's campaign. Are *they* in for a surprise!"

"Let's give 'em a chance," said Sean.

They gave 'em a chance and stopped at George Veale's party, leaving quickly when a parrot was blown through a plate-glass window by indoor artillery fire.

Later that night, when Gasparilla fireworks burst over Tampa Bay, Sean and Karen were standing over the crib in their nursery, smiling at a sleeping baby.

David walked alone and admired Tampa's skyline from the Ballast Point Pier.

Coleman stumbled along Seventh Avenue on the downhill side of a twelve-beer buzz and stopped to buy curly fries from a man with power tools. Serge took photographs of a historic marker honoring José Martí.

Sharon Rhodes gyrated in George Veale's lap and thought about absolutely nothing.

Mo Grenadine was passed out in his one-bedroom condo with his pants around his knees, a dominatrix tape on the video, and a plastic novelty device from Hong Kong attached to his penis with rubber bands.

Five

March, seven months before the World Series.

The Florida National Bank branch office sat in an alcove near the rest rooms of the Tampa Bay Mall, and Coleman's note told the teller no funny stuff, just give him the money.

The teller hit the silent alarm as she filled the bag and yelled bloody murder when Coleman fled around the corner. Next to the bank was the Gold Coast Arcade. Dark and loud, lots of distracting flashing lights. Coleman stuffed the money bag down the front of his pants and climbed in the cockpit of Tail Gunner. In eight seconds, he peeled off his mustache and wig and pulled the red shirt up over his head. He dropped it all inside the Tail Gunner cockpit and retrieved a baby carriage hidden under a pinball machine. The pillow under the blanket looked like an infant.

Cops and security guards flew in from all directions, and Coleman walked through the middle, toward the food court.

The cops formed a perimeter around the mall, and Coleman planned to wait inside, have a little lunch, and head out when the authorities packed it in. Coleman sat on a bench, removing pickles from a Chick-fil-A.

A field trip was in progress. Two nuns led second-graders in their little Catholic uniforms through the mall. As they passed Coleman, two of the children became curious about the baby carriage and tried to peek inside. Coleman edged the carriage away from them.

"Now, now, musn't wake him up," said Coleman. One of the nuns leaned over to take the children by the hands.

Suddenly, there was a loud bang in Coleman's crotch. An explosion ripped open the front of his pants, and a shower of warm red liquid splattered in the faces of the nun and the children. Pandemonium ensued. Coleman writhed on the floor of the food court, grabbing his sore nuts and cursing the bitch who had put the dye pack in the money bag. The nun and kids screamed inconsolably. The closest they could make of it was something they'd seen in a science-fiction movie. Coleman had unleashed The Horrible Dick-Worm from Outer Space.

Two skinheads ran to the screams. They didn't know what to make of it either, so they kicked Coleman unconscious.

Coleman arrived at his cell in the Hillsborough
County Jail in a wheelchair. A long, skinny guy lay
on the bottom bunk not looking at him, reading a
paperback, *The Cockroach Bay Story.* The guy slid a
bookmark between the pages, turned over and held
out a hand. "I'm Serge."

Coleman shook the hand. "Hi, I'm Seymour," he
said, "but friends call me Coleman. Enemies too."

Locked in the cell with the lights out, Coleman
needed a beer; Serge needed his psychiatric medicine.
Serge lay on his side in the bunk, propped up on one
elbow, becoming manic. Coleman sat cross-legged on
the floor next to the bed, listening in awe for hours
as Serge recited the unabridged history of Florida.

From the Calusa Indians to the space shuttle, Coleman hung on every word. Serge told him about great
artists and pioneers and carpetbaggers and an entire
world just outside Coleman's awareness.

The exploding dye pack was about to put Coleman
in the headlines for the third time in his sorry, ran-
dom life. The first time was twenty-one years ago,
when he was four. Coleman was born Seymour Bunsen, the puny child of a working mother, and he constantly sought the approval of his unemployed
father.

One Sunday afternoon Mr. Bunsen and the usual
suspects lounged in front of the television in the Bun-
sens' living room, enduring another football ship-
wreck of the Tampa Bay Buccaneers. Full ashtrays
and empty longnecks covered the coffee table. In

front of the table was a sixty-quart cooler holding a bath of ice water and no more beer.

Seymour kept coming up to his dad, pestering him with questions about what was going on in the game, tugging on his shirt and pants legs. The Buccaneers fumbled into their own end zone in the fourth quarter, and young Seymour poked his dad in the shoulder. "What's happening? What's happening?"

"Jesus Christ!" Mr. Bunsen screamed. He grabbed little Seymour, stuffed him in the cooler and sat on the lid. His drunken friends laughed and Mr. Bunsen drained his beer and laughed too, and they watched the rest of the game.

Seymour was blue and near death when he got to the hospital. He spent three months in intensive care, a month more than his dad would spend in jail. Doctors weren't sure whether psychological trauma or brain damage caused him to withdraw and wither. He seemed emotionally adrift; he would never again seek anyone's approval.

The football angle of the child abuse made it a natural for the media. A TV newscaster opened with "The Buccaneers weren't the only ones to take a beating yesterday. . . ." A sports talk show blamed the Bucs' poor play as much as Seymour's dad.

In Tallahassee, one senator held up a newspaper that said in large letters: "Dad benched for unnecessary roughness." He demanded the Florida Department of Health and Rehabilitative Services take action. Another lawmaker used the attack to try to secure public funding for a new football stadium.

The story followed Seymour Bunsen from school to school, as he was moved around often in a series of disciplinary transfers for fighting with taunting classmates.

At every school he was initially nicknamed Bunsen Burner. But as soon as his classmates heard about him being stuffed in the cooler, they responded with the compassion for which schoolchildren are known. The nickname "Igloo" lasted only three weeks. "Coleman" stuck.

The second time Coleman made the headlines, he was twenty-two. A small-time burglar, he decided he needed a wealthier clientele if he was going to better himself. He bought golf magazines to pick tonier neighborhoods to hit. One night while inside a home on the Palma Ceia Country Club, he fell asleep playing video games. He awoke with a joystick on his stomach and laughing police officers in the room. Coleman jumped over the balcony and ran onto the golf course.

As he sprinted, Coleman heard cops behind him, still laughing. While burglarizing the house, Coleman had put on the teenage son's new basketball shoes, the kind with red lights in the heels that flash on each step. The cops followed Coleman's blinking red lights down a par five and two par fours until Coleman ran into the pin on the number eight green and knocked himself cold.

The bank robbery was the third-time charm. But it was Coleman's sentencing, not the heist or dye-pack explosion, that made news.

Florida had become infamous for its abbreviated prison sentences. Through overcrowding, mandatory gain time and other caveats, prisoners were serving fractions of their terms. This drew a backlash of legislative lip service and ineptly written law.

The chairman of the senate's criminal justice committee had been caught up in a sexual harassment case for a year, distracting him from the little work he would have accomplished otherwise. He survived the scandal with a secret hundred-thousand-dollar payment to his accuser diverted from campaign donations. He held a press conference to announce that he had a sex addiction and, therefore, he too was a victim.

During the scandal, the lawmaker found himself in charge of writing the get-tough legislation against early releases from prison. He never wanted to write such legislation. He just wanted to demagogue in front of the television cameras that he "would personally write the legislation myself!"

Now, his aides said, there was no way out. He had publicly promised.

"I don't have time. I've got this sexual harassment case to deal with," the senator responded, pulling up his pants. On the sofa in his office, his newest legislative aide was sliding panty hose back on. "These accusations are so unfair," he continued. "I can't tell you how hard it's been on me."

The aide on the couch, reapplying lipstick in a compact mirror, said, "Let me write it. I'm good with words."

"There!" the senator said to the other aides. "She'll write it. I don't have time."

"But . . ." one aide started to object and was rebuffed with a cocked fist.

When hiring the newest aide, the senator had passed on ten more capable applicants before settling on the one with the big tits.

Coleman's case was the first to fall under the new law. After the numbers were crunched—the advanced good behavior and federal capacity mandates and parole and the complex formulas the aide had written into the law—the state of Florida ended up owing Coleman time. The judge thought it was a mistake and had his clerk add it up again. Then the judge added it up himself. Each time Coleman came out ahead, and the judge had no choice but to order Coleman's release. What couldn't be accomplished in the realm of reality was achieved through legislative fiat. The senator who sponsored the bollixed-up bill went on television to blame liberal, criminal-coddling judges.

In the first week of October 1962, Serge A. Storms was born at West Palm Beach Memorial Hospital, a Kennedy baby. Just after two in the morning, Serge's mother was in her room under anesthesia. His father nodded off in a chair in the lobby. The television showed a four-jet formation in the clouds during the national anthem, closing out a broadcast day in Miami. In the distance, a freight train clacked along the rails next to Old Dixie Highway, carrying military supplies to the Keys for the Cuban Missile Crisis.

They lived in Riviera Beach, in an upstairs apartment near a citrus packing house on Blue Heron Boulevard. The drugstore down the street had a giant bottle of Coppertone on the roof. Serge's mother was a sales clerk at Burdines, and his father was the worst jai alai player ever to have taken the court at the Palm Beach Fronton.

His name was Pablo, but he played under the sobriquet "Testarondo." He made up the name and it meant the same thing in Spanish as it did in Italian, which was nothing. His number was 7.

Pablo played, as it's sometimes said, like a man possessed. He'd climb up the jai alai walls to field a shot. He'd roll on the floor and come up slinging the ball. He skidded into the screen at least once a game. The fronton featured Pablo prominently in its TV ads, programs and promotional literature.

Pablo's returns were arguably the fastest in the Florida league. Accuracy was another matter. When brute force was crucial, Testarondo was a sure bet. But when merely vague precision was required, Pablo was money down the drain.

Pablo's lack of accuracy went beyond not being able to hit the target. Because of the curved basket of a jai alai cesta, even standing behind him was not safe. Pablo's missed shots were distributed in a 360-degree spray of rock-hard pelota. His *dos paredes* were frightening, his *cortadas* a catastrophe, his killshots deadly.

The other players hated him as much as the fronton managers loved him. In the predictable matches with heavy favorites, the level of betting dipped. Pablo's presence in a match threw the odds board into bedlam. Pablo never threatened to beat the favorite; he threatened to maim him. The wagering broke records.

Every Saturday morning, little Serge sat with his mom in the vacant fronton spectator seats and watched his daddy practice. Pablo practiced like he played in real matches, at full speed. The other players went through the motions, but Pablo ran up the walls like an insane man and sent the pelota whistling by their ears. After nearly decapitating another player, Pablo would look for Serge and his mother in the audience and wave. Serge thought his daddy was a huge sports star like Mickey Mantle.

One night in November, during the daily double, Pablo caught the ball five feet from the back wall and reached back with all his might for a full-court *rebote*. The other players hit the floor. Pablo let fly. He released late, from his hip, and the pelota flew out in the opposite direction, behind him. It ricocheted off the back wall and struck Pablo in the right rear quarter-panel of his skull. His casket was carried beneath a canopy of crossed cestas; his widow was given a number 7 jersey folded in a triangle.

For his part, the energetic Serge soon displayed a precocious antisocial streak. At age five, Serge was picked for the studio audience of *Skipper Chuck's Popeye Playhouse*, a morning children's show produced in Miami and hosted by Chuck Zinc, the emcee of the Orange Bowl Parade. Each time something caught Serge's attention, he'd wander away from his seat, only to be returned by stagehands bribing him with candy. During a segment where four sock puppets played "I Wanna Hold Your Hand," Serge ran up to the puppet window and pulled Ringo by his yarn hair. Ringo head-butted Serge in the chest, and Serge bit Ringo's face, which wasn't Ringo's face but the hand of the puppetmaster, who screamed and cursed and chased Serge around the studio until the show went to test pattern.

For the next thirteen years, Serge's well-meaning mom tried to find a suitable role model for the boy and invariably took up with a series of thieves and pawnshop owners. The steadiest was a cat burglar named Henry who tossed pop flies to Serge through two seasons of Little League. The rest of the time Henry ate their food and slept under their roof. When Serge's mom got on Henry's back about not carrying his weight, he'd rip off a house in Lake Park or Palm Beach Gardens.

One night Henry thought he'd finally found his angle. He guessed he could hold his breath a minute, maybe a minute and a half, and he made twenty-six trips into a split-level being tented for termites off Northlake Boulevard. He carted away enough electronics, silverware and jewelry to last them six months. The next morning Serge found Henry mottled on the living room sofa, eyes and mouth agape from a fatal dose of methyl bromide that curled his arms and legs like a dried-up lizard in the garage.

By now, Serge's behavior had its own signature. Everything with him was an on-off switch; there was no volume control. Half his grades were A's, the other half F's. He began to hang at the Palm Beach Mall. As people walked out of a bookstore, he'd punch them in the stomach and step back in detachment to study the effect.

This last quirk resulted in Serge being classified as criminally insane by the Palm Beach County Health Department. Serge's attention-deficit disorder was the first of many hyphens. Obsessive-compulsive, manic-depressive, anal-retentive, paranoid-schizophrenic. He was believed to have been the only self-inflicted case of shaken-baby syndrome.

Some of the same dysfunctions also made Serge animated, charming, entertaining and sporadically brilliant. Serge was the star of his high school drama club, playing Death in a Woody Allen production. He decided to master the free throw through Zen and five hundred practice shots a day. He set a conference record for consecutive shots, lost interest and quit the basketball team midseason. He was a voracious reader and technologically inclined, with a gadget fetish. He became expert in varied subjects by stalking librarians, teachers, toll-free operators and any other resource with an unending line of questions. Until he obsessed on another subject.

He became fascinated with the space program, the minting of U.S. coins, submarine warfare, Chinese table-tennis technique, masonry, cryptography, literature of the counterculture. And Florida. The full range of native interests, flora and fauna, art, history, culture, anything.

After graduating from Suncoast High School in Riviera Beach, he became a world-class drywaller, which paid no more than the ones who smoked joints at lunch. Other than the occasional beer, Serge eschewed drugs and alcohol, not from piety but because they made him berserk. If Serge wanted a recreational drug experience, he would skip taking his Prozac, Zoloft, Elavil and lithium.

This usually resulted in brief incarcerations for petty mayhem, vandalism and unexplained acts of psychosis like putting on a top hat and tails and shooting up a cemetery.

As Serge moved into the adult correctional system, a series of underpaid psychiatrists listened to his emerging Florida aesthetic. He launched torrid bursts about the Everglades photography of Clyde Butcher, the written body of Rawlings, Douglas and MacDonald, and the vernacular architecture of crackers. *Flipper* and *Gentle Ben* were state treasures.

Serge would typically arrive at a friend's house. After five minutes he still hadn't sat down. "Can I get some water? I need to use the phone. Mind if I change the channel?" Pacing hard. "Where's your newspaper? Let's make some coffee. My legs are hot—do you have some shorts I can borrow? I gotta split."

One doctor told Serge that he was longing for his mother and seeking the womblike Florida of his childhood.

Serge mentally aimed a .44 Magnum at the doctor and blew a black-purple hole the diameter of a nickel in his forehead. The doctor asked what Serge was thinking. Serge told him. The doctor spilled hot coffee in his lap. He ran into the hall screaming and grabbing between his legs. Three guards ran into the room and promptly beat Serge with rubber truncheons.

Psychiatrists controlled Serge, early, with Ritalin, then tricyclics, and later said screw this incrementalism and loosed the spectrum of psychotropic drugs.

What couldn't be explained or excused was his unmagnetized moral compass. On broad philosophical issues, Serge was compassionate and stridently moral; on a personal level, he was predatory.

There was never cruelty; Serge's conscience just seemed to go blank from time to time. His motto could have been Think globally, act criminal locally.

Serge functioned more or less normally when he stuck to his medicine, which he refused to do as often as possible. He seemed to know just how far to take the system without triggering a lengthy prison stay. The younger psychiatrists thought Serge was harmless and were uniformly fascinated by his verbal tapestries. The older doctors thought he was sick and would end up killing someone. That's how differently they interpreted the incident on Interstate 75.

Serge hadn't taken his lithium and Prozac for two weeks when he woke atop a green information sign over the northbound lanes of I-75 near the Busch Gardens exit. It was morning rush hour, and cops and

TV trucks clustered on the shoulder of the highway as Serge awoke to the locomotive in his head. He looked down at the semi whizzing under his feet and had no idea how he had gotten there.

The police closed down all lanes. Various emergency lights flickered off the green sign. With TV cameras filming, Serge stood up on the light supports, cleared his throat, and began in an evangelical voice:

"There was no Disney World then, just rows of orange trees. Millions of them. Stretching for miles. And somewhere near the middle was the Citrus Tower, which the tourists climbed to see even more orange trees. Every month an eighty-year-old couple became lost in the groves, driving up and down identical rows for days until they were spotted by helicopter or another tourist on top of the Citrus Tower. They had lived on nothing but oranges and came out of the trees drilled on vitamin C and checked into the honeymoon suite at the nearest bed-and-breakfast."

The crowd grew.

"The Miami Seaquarium put in a monorail and rockets started going off at Cape Canaveral, making us feel like we were on the frontier of the future. Disney bought up everything north of Lake Okeechobee, preparing to shove the future down our throats sideways.

"Things evolved rapidly! Missile silos in Cuba. Bales on the beach. Alligators are almost extinct and then they aren't. Juntas hanging shingles in Boca Raton. Richard Nixon and Bebe Rebozo skinny-dipping off Key Biscayne. We atone for atrocities against the Indians by playing bingo. Shark fetuses in formaldehyde jars, roadside gecko farms, tourists waddling around waffle houses like flocks of flightless birds. And before we know it, we have The New Florida, underplanned, overbuilt and ripe for a killer hurricane that'll knock that giant geodesic dome at Epcot down the turnpike like a golf ball, a solid one-wood by Buckminster Fuller."

Some who had pulled over nodded in assent that Serge had a point. Firemen unfolded a rescue net under the sign.

"I am the native and this is my home. Faded pastels, and Spanish tiles constantly slipping off roofs, shattering on the sidewalk. Dogs with mange and skateboard punks with mange roaming through yards, knocking over garbage cans. Lunatics wandering the streets at night, talking about spaceships. Bail bondsmen wake me up at three A.M. looking for the last tenant. Next door, a mail-order bride is clubbed by a smelly man in a mechanic's shirt. Cats violently mate under my windows and rats breakdance in the drop ceiling. And I'm lying in bed with a broken air conditioner, sweating and sipping lemonade through a straw. And I'm thinking, geez, this used to be a great state."

There was a scattering of whistles and clapping.

"You wanna come to Florida? You get a discount on theme-park tickets and find out you just bought a time share. Or maybe you end up at Cape Canaveral, sitting in a field for a week as a space shuttle

launch is canceled six times. And suddenly vacation
is over, you have to catch a plane, and you see the
shuttle take off on TV at the airport. But you keep
coming back, year after year, and one day you find
you're eighty years old driving through an orange
grove."

Serge's footing slipped and he fell into the firemen's net. He made all the nightly newscasts. That
Friday, one station aired Serge's speech in its entirety
in the weekly editorial slot. They titled it "I, Flori-
dian." The station sent an agent to the jail to offer
Serge a contract for social commentary. They'd even
build him a set. A giant road sign. He'd be "The I-
75 Prophet."

Serge looked at him and asked, "What happened?"

Coleman was released two days after Serge and
immediately took him up on his invitation to visit.
Serge owned an old cigarmaker's shotgun cottage in
Ybor City, vintage 1918. It had been a condemned
crack house; Serge had picked it up for one dollar
and a promise to restore it, which he did with ma-
terials stolen from three Home Depots. He had dry-
walled the interior in one psychotic sixty-hour death
march that landed him in the hospital taking glucose.
At the curb was a rusted-out '65 Barracuda. Serge
loved its wraparound rear window tapering to the
trunk. The car had been green but was now brown.

Coleman walked up the front steps with a suitcase
in one hand and a rainbow afro wig in the other.

Serge met him on the porch and looked at the suitcase. "I said visit, not move in."

Coleman looked sad.

"Okay, but only a few days. You gotta find a place of your own."

Serge flopped on the couch and set his bottle of mineral water on the coffee table, a big wooden spool from telephone cable.

"Make yourself at home," said Serge. So Coleman drank all of Serge's beer and grabbed a frozen pizza from Serge's freezer. He wanted to microwave it for seventy-five seconds but punched seventy-five *minutes* on the keypad.

After finishing the last beer in the house, Coleman lost his balance in the bathroom and snapped a towel rod off the wall.

He dropped Serge's favorite souvenir glass from the Dolphins' 1973 Super Bowl. He found a model Saturn rocket from Serge's childhood and ran through the house making rocket noises, tripped, and fell on it.

"Sit down on the couch!" Serge ordered. "Don't move!"

Coleman sat down, didn't move. He set a glass of grape juice on the cushion next to him and it tipped over on the upholstery.

"What the hell is that smell?" Serge said.

"My pizza's done," said Coleman.

Coleman said he and the rest of the cell pod had watched Serge's highway speech on the news.

"I'm secretly a tourist too," Serge confessed. "The native tourist. I love Florida cheese."

It was late Saturday afternoon. Serge was kneeling over his bed, a naked mattress on the floor. He opened a fishing tackle box and removed the contents piece by piece, arranging them in a precise matrix on the mattress.

"We've got nobody to blame if we prostitute ourselves," said Serge.

Coleman nodded, making a wrong interpretation. He tried to detect a trend among the items Serge carefully positioned. Plier-head utility knife, Dristan, micro-TV, duct tape, Alka-Seltzer, windproof lighter, halogen flashlight, surveying compass, hemostats, vitamins and analgesics, socket wrenches, Chap Stick, signal mirror, shatterproof flask, funnel, mini-binoculars, tape recorder, a can of Fix-a-Flat, bottle opener, taser, whistle, gizmos, gee-gaws and gimcracks. He placed a second box on the mattress, a large wooden cigar box with dovetail joints. It held matchbooks, imprinted napkins, coasters, postcards and swizzle sticks.

"The problem isn't the tourists. It's the criminal element," said Serge. "That, and untended mental health problems. We have all these insane armed hobos coming from the Midwest, usually Ohio."

Serge sat back on his feet and admired the configuration on the mattress. He began replacing the items, this time in different pockets, drawers and compartments of the tackle box. The box had a row of stickers around the outside from St. Augustine,

Thomas Edison's House, Bok Tower, the Suwanee River, Fort DeSoto and Daytona Beach.

"What gripes me the most is all the garbage they give us Cubans. All of that 'Oh my God, we're being overrun by rafters!' Hell, we've worked hard to help build Key West and Tampa and Miami," said Serge. "Forget the Marielitos. What about the *Ohio*-litos?!"

"Sounds like you're prejudiced," said Coleman.

"Fuck Ohio," said Serge.

He flipped down a panel on the outside of the tackle box, revealing a revolver and an automatic pistol held in place with Velcro straps. He removed both, checked the chambers and cleaned them meticulously.

"Next time you drive around this city, take a good look at the people," said Serge. "They have room to bitch about tourists? This is trash state U.S.A. We're in no position to be calling people Philistines."

Coleman nodded again without understanding. He fished in his suitcase and came up with a switchblade comb. He showed it to Serge and offered it toward the tackle box. Serge shook his head no.

"I take it you wanna party tonight," Serge said, wiping down the guns. Coleman gave him two thumbs up and a giant smile.

"Okay," said Serge, washing his hands in the bathroom sink. "I'm gonna give you The Tour."

Serge toweled off his hands and washed them again. Then he closed the drain and filled the sink with ice and water. He got in the shower, opened the cold-water handle and danced and yelled in the frigid stream. After three minutes, he turned the knobs as hot as he could stand it, and then a little more. Steam escaped into the hall.

He jumped out of the shower and slammed his face in the sink of ice water.

Coleman watched from a chair by the kitchen table.

"I like to subject myself to rapid temperature changes," Serge explained. "Makes you feel alive." Serge washed his hands again and dressed quickly in jeans and a Skipper's Smokehouse T-shirt. He grabbed a suit bag from the closet and said the magic words to Coleman: "Let's rock."

Serge was close to no one and in love with Florida. For every corner of the state, Serge had a Julie Andrews list of his favorite things—lists that could only be executed all at once in a hyperactive road rally, pinballing from restaurant to museum to monument. That was Serge, every day of his life.

They got to La Teresita on Columbus Drive. Businessmen sat at the lunch counter trying to keep mounds of saucy food off ties and long-sleeve white dress shirts. There was a constant patter of Spanish. Serge said it was never spoken in his house growing up, but it still sounded like music. He ordered *bistec en cazuela* and Coleman the *arroz con pollo*.

"This is great!" said Coleman with the chicken.

"Heaven," said Serge. "But wrap it up, we gotta go." He knocked back hot Cuban coffee and savored the afterburn like brandy.

They raced over to the Hub, downtown on Zack

Street, which looked like a corner tavern in downtown Chicago in the forties. A horseshoe bar, drinks to drop pachyderms. Eight bohemian college students pushed two tables together; a pair of toothless people necked at the bar.

"Kill that drink," Serge said. "We're on the move."

They drove over to Franklin and Platt streets.

"This was the beginning of Tampa," said Serge. "They built Fort Brooke here in 1823. It protected the pioneers during the Second Seminole War."

Serge started the car again. He crossed the Hillsborough River at the Kennedy Boulevard Bridge and pulled over by the old Tampa Bay Hotel on the University of Tampa campus. The architecture was nineteenth-century Moorish with crescent moons above minarets.

"This is where Teddy Roosevelt and the Rough Riders waited before heading to free Cuba in the Spanish-American War. The ride up San Juan Hill and all that jazz."

Serge opened the trunk and got out a wooden shoeshine box from the thirties. Inside were four clamps, masking tape, a shock of natural sponge, a pencil, camel-hair and synthetic brushes, eleven metal tubes of color and a round tin mixing tray.

Serge clamped a thick piece of textured paper to a square of plywood and wetted down the top half. He spread cerulean blue lightly with the one-inch brush. He was going to put down a heavier layer to outline the clouds, but the initial covering had to dry first.

"Come on, come on, come on!" Serge said rapidly,

tapping hard on the edge of the plywood. He held it up at an angle and saw it was still wet. "Screw it!" he said, and threw the watercolor supplies back in the trunk.

They got in the car and headed west.

"Remember Jules Verne? That book he wrote about going to the moon?" Serge asked. "He had the astronauts take off from Tampa—here's the plaque. But actually, he had them take off from Belle Shoals, a wide spot in the road way out in the eastern part of the county. Early this century, there was a pipe sticking out of the ground out there, irrigation or something. A lot of people thought it was the cannon that fired the astronauts to the moon. True story."

Coleman inhaled a Budweiser. "I'm hungry again. And thirsty."

"We're on our way," said Serge. They raced up Howard Avenue for Cuban sandwiches-to-go at the Fourth of July restaurant and backtracked to the Old Meeting House for creamy shakes from the fifties. They hit the Tiny Tap and the Chatterbox.

Coleman was halfway in the bag, playing darts, when he nearly hit someone coming out of the rest room, and Serge had to smooth it out with money and a promise to leave.

The setting sun glinted first from the tail of the silver 727. The reflection ran the length of the jet to the nose as it landed at Tampa International Airport.

Seven floors up, from the top deck of short-term parking, Serge took photos of the Whisperjet. Coleman popped another sixteen-ounce Bud.

"Here's a tip: If you ever want to gauge the status of a civilization, check out its convenience stores and airports," said Serge. He snapped more pictures. "I saw the SST land here. That's a French plane."

Serge opened the trunk and stowed the camera. He removed his suit bag and slammed the trunk lid. "Saw a night space shuttle launch too. It was going to meet the Mir space station so it took off at a fifty-one-degree inclination thataway"—Serge pointing—"instead of the regular twenty-seven degrees that way. You could actually see it attain orbit and go down over the horizon."

Coleman nodded, thinking of food.

Serge told Coleman to take off his shirt and pants. He threw the suit bag over the roof of the car and unzipped it. Coleman looked around but the only other people were a couple waiting for the elevators.

"*Miami Vice* changed television—and Florida," said Serge. "There's this one episode where a chick comes up to Don Johnson next to a swimming pool. She takes an ice cube out of Johnson's drink and rubs it between her breasts."

Serge handed Coleman dark slacks and dress shoes. Next, a white pinpoint oxford cloth shirt, black tie, and a gold tie tack that looked like an eagle.

"The chick drops the ice cube back in Don Johnson's drink, like he's supposed to get flustered," said Serge. "Johnson just picks it out of his drink, tosses it in his mouth and starts crunching."

"Now that's class," said Coleman.

"It was a golden era," said Serge.

Serge had Coleman slip on a dark suit coat with gold bars on the shoulders and gold rings around the cuffs. He put on a cap with gold braiding on the visor.

Serge grabbed the lapels and tugged, straightening the fit on Coleman. Coleman stood at attention. "How do I look?"

"Like the man who just landed that jet," said Serge.

Serge had picked up the uniform when he'd rolled two pilots in their hotel room the month before. He and Coleman took the elevator down from the parking garage to the concourse, where they grabbed the monorail for Airside D. Airport and airline employees nodded politely and some called Coleman "captain."

Serge and Coleman parked themselves at the airside lounge. Coleman ordered a shot of Jack Daniel's and a beer chaser. The bartender raised his eyebrows at the pilot's uniform. Serge said, "Mineral water."

Serge asked the bartender to change the TV to the Tampa Bay Lightning, who were playing the Florida Panthers. The hockey game joined the sunset and the view of planes landing and taking off to fulfill Serge, and he hammered his mineral water in one pull and slammed the glass on the bar.

"Hit me!" he told the bartender.

"Me too!" said Coleman, slamming down his empty whiskey.

For two hours, Coleman went though bourbon and beer. Travelers double-taked at the pilot on the stool, laughing and pounding his palm on the counter, spilling drinks and scattering bowls of peanuts. An eighty-year-old man wandered the concourse, clutching a Publishers Clearing House sweepstakes letter and looking for Dick Clark.

"Another drinky-winky, mister bartender man. Make it shnappy," Coleman slurred, "I have a plane to catch." He howled and pounded on the bar some more. Travelers pointed in horror.

The bartender cut Coleman off and they left and walked down the concourse. Coleman's shirt was untucked and his pilot's hat on sideways as he weaved down the airside. The crowd at each gate tightened as Coleman approached and sighed as he passed.

Before leaving for the parking garage, Coleman walked up the last gate and addressed everyone: "Has anybody seen my keys? I have to get to Kansas City." As the crowd stared at Coleman and recoiled, Serge worked behind them, silently stealing two briefcases and a laptop.

Residential Ybor City had a crime problem. All of Serge's windows were barred. He kept a Ruger between the cushions of the couch. Once or twice a month he'd hear low voices outside the house, possibly a knock after midnight, car trouble.

At such times, Serge would turn off the TV and rack his Beretta twelve-gauge. The distinct sound made problems vanish.

While Serge took every precaution, Coleman stumbled around town all fucked up, openly making friends and inviting everyone back to the house.

Serge constantly awoke to find strangers searching his cabinets or shouting at invisible demons.

"And what the hell is *this!*" Serge asked Coleman, pointing at the naked wino passed out on the living room floor with bagpipes and a Viking helmet.

Once Serge woke with a gun in his face and two men going through his valuables. Another time the place had already been ransacked by the time he got up.

"This shit's gotta stop!" Serge kept saying.

One night, Serge awoke at three A.M. on the living room sofa and thought he heard talking in another part of the house. And a faint buzzing sound. He checked in the kitchen and the bathroom. The bedroom door was closed and the slit underneath was bright with light.

Serge opened the door. On the bed, on top of the sheets, was a striking blonde. Lightly curling hair on the pillow. She wore red pumps, and that was it. The buzzing sound was a vibrator.

Coleman sat on the side of the room in his rainbow Afro, thumbing a *Mad Magazine*. A row of empty beers on the windowsill. "Oh," he said, noticing Serge, "meet Sharon." He leaned down over the nightstand and vacuumed up a line of cocaine, then returned to his magazine.

"What's wrong with this picture?" Serge said. Nobody answered.

Coleman burned the scrambled eggs on the gas stove and ate them anyway. The sky was getting light, but nobody had slept. Sharon sat at the breakfast table, looking dazed at the ashtray as she tapped a Marlboro. Thinking about her bad luck, the insurance company denying Mount Batten's life insurance and threatening to go to the cops if she didn't sign a waiver.

Serge read three newspapers.

"So I see her by the railroad tracks at Fifteenth Street," Coleman said with a mouth full of yellow. "And I say, 'Hey, hey, why you lookin' so down? This is a party town!' and she says, 'I like coke.' "

Serge interrupted, "So she says she knows where you can get some great stuff but she's all out of money."

Coleman gestured at Serge with toast. "You know her?"

"Metaphysically."

Against Serge's expectations, Sharon didn't split at the first opportunity and tagged along with them to the Lowry Park Zoo.

"I love the zoo," Coleman said at the suggestion. Sharon had Coleman stop and get some more coke and she walked around the zoo doing it every place she could. Her blonde hair was matted, wild-looking and sexy in a trampy sort of way. Her shiny blue bicycle pants showed off even more of a striking figure than Serge thought he'd seen the night before. Her sunglasses were impenetrable, and she snorted brazenly above the rhino pit. Two preppies from the University of South Florida tried to hit on her with cocaine jokes.

Sharon positioned her body between them and her powder and snapped, "Get your own!"

Three days later the trio was still intact. Coleman and Sharon were in the living room, watching TV. Serge in the kitchen, slicing white onions. His mom had never cooked native dishes, and Serge hadn't discovered Cuban food until he'd moved to Tampa, which made him appreciate it as a foreign delicacy. He had yellow rice going on one burner and dropped the onions in the pot of black beans. He stirred shredded flank steak in the frying pan with tomato paste, peppers and more onions. The bread was on the table: The Cuban bakery on Florida Avenue dropped a palm sprig in the bag with each thin three-foot loaf, for religious good luck. Coleman wandered in. "Those bananas are really bruised."

"They're plantains," said Serge and sliced them fat. This was his favorite part. He quick-fried them a little burnt, the way he liked. He could hear Coleman back in the living room with Sharon, watching *Wheel of Fortune*.

"Skirting with disaster?" Sharon guessed at the secret phrase.

"No," said Coleman, "I think it's Shirting with disaster."

Great, thought Serge, The Three Freakin' Musketeers. A ringleader, a mascot and a hood ornament.

Six

The state of Florida was in a heat wave in early spring.

Three stove-bellied men marched abreast down a sidewalk in Sarasota, forcing visitors and retirees into the gutter. Their leather jackets were festooned with nonfunctional chains. The back of each jacket had an unfaded zone in the shape of a large patch, bordered by broken stitching.

"Who ever heard of bikers without bikes!" one said. "Now we just look like goddamn drunks."

"But we *are* drunks," said a second.

"Shut the fuck up!" said the third. "I need to think."

They waited. Nothing.

The first biker sneered at an old lady, who hissed back and raised her walker at him like a lion tamer.

"See what I mean?" he said. "No respect."

The men sat on a street bench next to a pair of

fashionably depressed students from New College, who gave the bikers the creeps.

The trio had been kicked out of every self-respecting criminal biking outfit on both coasts until they were forced to cling to the bottom rung of Florida's biker community: The Riders of Eternal Doom, Sunshine Chapter.

The Riders had wanted a flaming skull and lots of daggers for their emblem, but they could only afford factory seconds from the uniform company. So instead they settled for reembroidered patches originally rejected by a Siesta Key ice cream parlor. The riders' logo became a cobra wrapped around a triple scoop of Rocky Road.

The Riders had kicked out the three bikers that morning, tearing the patches off their jackets and confiscating their motorcycles.

Maybe it was their names, they thought. Stinky, Cheese-Dick and Ringworm. Maybe they should have gone with a more violent tone instead of the antihygiene theme Ringworm had suggested.

Ringworm was the obvious leader of the crew, based purely on his hugeness. Stinky was excitable and easily panicked. Cheese-Dick got beat up a lot.

Ringworm was nothing less than a giant. About six-six and three hundred and fifty pounds, he usually wore an open leather jacket with no shirt. His belly was so swollen it extended up to the nipple line, and it had a large tattoo of the *Hindenburg* going down. Stinky was the middle in size, same proportions as Ringworm, just more in scale with the general population; he got his nickname from his nonstop nervous perspiration. Cheese-Dick was short and wide and had scars everywhere from his cavalcade of ass-kickings.

They walked down to the waterfront and signed on with a band of wildcat shrimpers who beat them up—Cheese-Dick first—and threw them overboard ten minutes later.

They swam ashore on Lido Key and kicked in a sand castle.

Sharon thought Serge and Coleman were insufferable boobs. To think that she allowed Coleman to finance her cocaine habit!

She had intended to flop in the cigarmaker's cottage only until her next grifter or smuggler boyfriend came along. If she hadn't been in a world-record drought, she would never have allowed Serge to force her into stripping at The Red Snapper to help with room and board. Not that she had anything against stripping; she had a thing against ambition.

Sharon's vixen looks instantly made her the most talented lap dancer in The Red Snapper, even though she refused to pay attention and stop chewing gum or smoking during the daily grinds. Her sole motivation was determining whether the next customer might be a Carlos Lehder or Robert Vesco. If one looked promising, she planned to take him to the spare office in back that some of the girls used for the high-rollers. Except that all her customers seemed to be fat guys in bowling shirts.

A strip club is one of the few places where two groups voluntarily come together who have such precipitous contrasts in net worth and familiarity with violence, each group with a head-and-shoulders edge in one category. The basic math of a tropical storm.

Serge told Sharon to stand lookout. A couple of times a week, he'd come by for tips on robbery candidates, looking for married, drunk, wimpy out-of-towners, preferably from overseas.

Serge, getting the report from Sharon one night, stopped and thought he heard something. "Is that a tuba?"

"From the back room," Sharon said. "Don't ask."

Serge and Coleman followed the marks to their hotels, usually out on West Shore Boulevard. As the tourists chuckled and stumbled and began closing the hotel room door, Serge would kick it in and level revolvers in both hands.

"Which one of you dirty fucking cowards beat up the dancer at The Red Snapper? One of the girls pointed out your car!"

Usually they'd freeze or faint. One time four guys actually started pointing at each other. "It was him, I swear!"

By the time it was over, they were thrilled to give Serge all their money and jewelry and anything else he wanted.

"Okay, you guys look honest. I'll just take this stuff as good faith. But if you're lying . . . !"

They never called the cops.

Inside a month, Serge and Coleman had collected two thousand dollars, eleven watches, three cameras, a laptop computer, two camcorders, six cell phones, a derringer, a night vision scope, a leather jacket and another complete airline pilot's uniform. When Sharon received her first one-third cut, she got with the program and more aggressively sought victims.

Between dances, Sharon worked on her two-pack-a-day cigarette hobby and wondered whether to get another tattoo. While straddling a customer, she noticed the two Canadians across the room.

Later, she made small talk with the tourists. She was bored, wanted to get something to drink and unwind after work. Hey—they were cute! Where were they staying? The Porpoise Inn on Waters Boulevard? Sure, she might hook up with them.

At four A.M. a delightfully surprised but groggy Canadian opened the door of room 14 at the single-story Porpoise Inn, circa 1953.

"I'm tipsy," Sharon giggled, and stumbled into the room. The other Canadian turned on the light and squinted. She put her arms around the neck of the first and tongue-kissed him silly. Coleman and Serge ran into the room, and Sharon pulled back and punched the one she was kissing in the balls. She pointed at the tourist still in bed. "Shoot that fucker if he moves!"

Serge ripped apart luggage and dumped drawers, and Sharon and Coleman snorted lines of meth on top of the dresser. Between lines and ransacking, the trio realized the tourists were gone.

They ran to the door and saw a rented Taurus speeding out of the parking lot, west, toward Interstate 275, and they hopped in Sharon's red Camaro. Northbound on the interstate, past the Bearss Avenue exit, there was nothing for twenty miles—no traffic lights, no exits and generally no cops as the road headed into Pasco County.

The Taurus was in the left lane and the Camaro caught it ten miles from the county line, pulling up on the right side. Serge drove with his right hand and shot a .380 automatic at the Taurus's tires with his left. Sharon was in the front passenger seat, trying to hold her left hand still, snorting meth off the back of it.

The right front tire blew out and the Taurus careened into the median. The Camaro pulled over and Coleman and Serge sprinted down the embankment. The tourists were neutralized with a single punch in the head each. Wallets and watches were removed.

Sharon came running down the embankment, sizzling on meth, screaming, "Fuck you! Fuck you! Fuck you!" She pushed her head and arm into the front seat of the Taurus and shot both tourists in the face with the .380 that Serge had left on the Camaro's front seat.

Serge and Coleman leaped back from the car.

"Oooo, that had to hurt," said Coleman.

"That'll teach 'em not to tip," said Serge.

Coleman and Serge never mentioned the killing of the Canadians to Sharon after that night. It had taken them five high-wire minutes to get her to take her cranked-out finger off the trigger and hand them the gun. A half hour later, as they drove over Tampa Bay, they had brought up the topic—maybe she was a smidgen out of line, putting them at risk—and Sharon went apeshit. She bounded up from the backseat and grabbed Serge from behind, around the neck, as he drove. Serge fought with the steering wheel, smacking the guardrail on the Howard Frankland Bridge. He bent her fingers back, turned and scrambled over the top of the driver's seat into the backseat, abandoning the driving duties. Coleman casually reached over with his left hand and grabbed the wheel, driving from the passenger side.

Serge pinned Sharon in the backseat and punched her in the face and stomach, again and again. Coleman straightened the car out and slowly climbed over the center console into the driver's seat. Sharon was cursing, clawing and beating on Serge, who bashed her in the left cheek, trying to shut her up. But Coleman noticed a certain rhythm develop in the Camaro's suspension. He glanced in the rearview mirror and saw the moonlight off Serge's bare rear, popping in and out of view. Sharon spit in Serge's face, grabbed his hair and pulled his face down for a hard kiss that busted both their lips. Coleman thought it was too violent to qualify for rough sex. More like an alley fight with a quickie worked into the choreography.

Sharon's profanity grew louder, meaner and more poetic. They were westbound, Tampa to St. Petersburg, and when they hit the hump on the Howard

Frankland, Sharon went off like an Apache warrior charging over a hill.

"Yi-Yi-Yi-Yi-Yi-Yi-Yi!!!!!!"

It startled Coleman so badly he swerved into the lane on his left, overcorrected, and almost went in the water. He got a handle on the problem and accelerated.

Coleman took the exit at Twenty-second Avenue North and found an Addiction World convenience store on Fourth Street. It was five A.M. For breakfast, Coleman bought three sausage biscuits and a forty-four-ounce Thirst Mutilator, Serge a quart of OJ, Sharon cigarettes. She and Coleman each dropped a Roofie in front of the clerk, to cut into the crank, and washed it down with the soda. Coleman set the Thirst Mutilator down next to the cash register and poured in half a flask of Jim Beam. The clerk watched and yawned.

Serge took over the driving again, motoring aimlessly in the empty, predawn streets of St. Petersburg as Sharon and Coleman passed the spiked soda in the backseat, adding a joint to the mix. Nobody talking, relaxing, the twilight at the top of the ballistic trajectory when the day's drug battle finally turns in favor of the downers. The radio was on medium volume, Led Zeppelin's "Kashmir" as the car rolled under a series of synchronized stoplights. *"I am a traveler of both time and space . . ."* The sky toward Tampa started to glow, and Sharon and Coleman drifted toward crash. Serge drove out on the pier, sending gulls and pelicans into the air, and parked in the valet section. Coleman and Sharon were out. Serge got a stolen Pentax from the trunk and took a dozen shots as the sun rose across the bay.

Sharon and Coleman awoke in a broken-down hotel on Fourth Avenue that had a palm-green canopy out to the sidewalk. It reminded Serge of St. Pete in its prime. He had checked them in, dragged each into the room. Told the clerk they had eaten bad seafood.

When they awoke, Serge was wired from skipping his medication. He said he was going to teach them to appreciate Florida.

"Let's not and say we did," said Sharon, and they slapped each other.

He took them to the Salvador Dalí Museum, but Coleman's and Sharon's brains only registered static.

"This is the epitome of the surrealist movement," Serge tried to explain.

"Why does that guy's head have a crater filled with seashells?" asked Coleman.

"Can't you read?" said Serge. "It's because he's a bureaucrat!"

He drove them over to Treasure Island, where Serge said the motel strip reminded him of early Las Vegas: the Sands, the Thunderbird, the Bilmar, the Surf. He took them by Haslam's bookstore, the art deco in decline on Fourth Street and the International Museum.

Sharon had her standard pissed-off expression, but she surprised herself by starting to enjoy the day. They went to a spring training game at Al Lang Stadium on the waterfront. She bought a baseball jersey that came down so low you couldn't see her hot pants. She stood against the bullpen fence, attracting New York Yankees.

When a pop foul left the stadium, Sharon went after it.

"I got it! I got it!" The ball bounced thirty feet when it hit Bay Shore Drive, and Sharon chased it into the yacht basin. She came up with the ball, but the seawall was too high for her to climb out. Half the bullpen came to the rescue.

Sharon was sopping wet, looking hot, and two Yankees made crude remarks. She winked and gave them teasing looks over her shoulder as she walked toward the parking lot. One Yankee followed her to her car, and Serge followed the Yankee.

The murders of the Canadians made ripples in the press, but not as much as the robbery of the Yankees player. Serge had always wanted a World Series ring. For her part, Sharon hadn't exhibited the first hint of violence since that weekend. But under her vibe Serge and Coleman had become increasingly brutal in subsequent robberies.

There were the two Brits, who said something ill-advised like "Now look here. This just isn't civilized," and carried their teeth home in their pockets.

There was the Japanese businessman, who reacted by blinking four hundred times a minute and making high-pitched peeping sounds like a baby chick. So Serge and Coleman beat him into an express coma.

And after each robbery, Serge and Sharon resumed

combat and copulation in the backseat while Coleman chauffeured them around, wondering, Is this what they meant when they said I'd regret dropping out of school?

Coleman was deliriously content, but Serge had bigger dreams.

"Tell me 'bout the office in back of the club again," Serge asked Sharon.

"I told you already! Bunch of rich freaks. If they got enough money, they get whatever they want. One girl told me she made three hundred dollars sneezing on a guy's cock."

The next night Tiffany was on back-room watch, making sure nobody walked in on the action. Sharon handed Tiff a twenty, pointed a thumb at the man standing next to her. "Foot weirdo."

Serge smiled, holding a shoe bag. Tiffany blew a stream of clove smoke in his face.

Once inside the office, Serge pulled a camcorder out of the shoe bag and scanned the room.

"What are you looking—"

"Shut up!" Serge stood on a couch and stuck the camcorder on a shelf between a fern and a row of books. He bunched a small towel around it, concealing everything but the lens, and turned it on.

"I don't get it," said Coleman, watching a video in the shotgun cottage with Serge and Sharon. On TV, musical instrument cases lay open on the floor of the back office at The Red Snapper. A beautiful naked woman was playing the tuba badly for twin brothers. The brothers started arguing; one wanted her to switch to the slide trombone.

Serge hit the fast-forward. A man stuck a child's doll, headfirst, halfway down his throat, and clapped like a seal. Serge hit fast-forward again. "Okay, this is the money part. I think he's someone important. Sharon, see if you recognize him."

On TV, a flabby, middle-aged man in a three-piece suit walked into the office carrying a bowling-ball bag. He unzipped the bag and pulled out a large goldfish bowl. He lay down on the floor on his back and put the goldfish bowl over his head. A naked woman stood over him with a foot on each side of the bowl. She squatted down and her face strained.

A squeal of glee echoed out of the goldfish bowl.

"I may be sick," said Sharon.

"Can you get me his name?" said Serge.

Seven

The billboards started in Tampa and ran along Interstate 75 to Naples. The rough-and-tumble Jack Savage, has-been star of stage and screen, smiled down from the signs and pointed at passing motorists. He wore an unstrapped Army helmet that was his trademark from his biggest movie, the marginal hit *Guts and Glory*. There was a talk bubble next to his head: "Let's hit the beach at Puerto Lago Boca Vista Isles!" Underneath, a row of mobile homes and more writing. "Luxury prefab retirement living, from $39,900."

Near Exit 46, between Tampa and Bradenton, a man stood in saw palmettos beneath one of the billboards. It was a hot June day, four months before the World Series, but the man was wearing a long-sleeve blue-plaid shirt, jeans and a cowboy hat. He looked an athletic sixty years old. He waved an arm up at the sign and yelled at a man in a business suit, "Paint over those goddamn trailers. Shit, they look like goddamn tool sheds."

"But that's a photograph of your mobile homes," said the man in the suit.

"That's exactly why I want 'em gone. I'm selling an impression here. A false impression. And I don't need any photographic evidence to mess it up," the cowboy said. He climbed into a black Ford pickup with Yosemite Sam mudflaps that said, "Back off!"

"They'll find out soon enough," he yelled out the window and took off.

Florida developer Fred McJagger drove his pickup south on I-75 to the next exit, site of Vista Isles, Phases I–IV, twelve hundred trailers around five perfectly rectangular lakes. A giant clubhouse for bingo and thirty lighted shuffleboard courts. Everyone drove a golf cart.

On the other side of the interstate, Phase V was ready to roll. The sewer lines were run and the square lakes dug. McJagger met his ace salesman and fixer, Max Minimum, out where they were pouring the foundation for the new auditorium. A road grader roared and burped behind them.

"There's never been anything like this," McJagger said with the slight drawl of a Florida cattleman. "It's gonna get me on the cover of *Forbes*."

Minimum remembered his boss said the same thing before every new phase of Vista Isles. The "Isles" were eight miles inland, the lakes were retention ponds, and the beaches were light-gray fill dirt they'd poured instead of sodding up to the ponds because it was cheaper.

McJagger had filled the first lakes with ducks and

swans, but they flew away because the water was unacceptable. So Minimum was directed in the middle of the night to a warehouse in Ellenton, where McJagger had stored a new shipment of ducks and swans. Minimum's job: break their wings.

As the phases progressed, McJagger found if you broke just one wing, the birds would try to take off and go round and round in the water. He refined the technique, breaking the right wings of half the birds and the left wings of the other half, resulting in an elaborate water ballet of alternating concentric circles that the retirees thought was pretty.

Minimum was valuable to McJagger, first, because he'd sold 42 percent of all the trailers in Vista Isles, getting an average of sixty thousand for the "$39,000" model through fine print and outright fraud.

Second, he'd shown McJagger how to see beyond development. These weren't just home buyers. Minimum said he had to view them as frail old people that he had by the throats.

First came the maintenance fee for lawn mowing and upkeep of the shuffleboard courts and such. Start 'em at ninety-nine dollars a month and jack it up a hundred every six months until they die. What are they gonna do? We put in a clause that says they can't move the trailer. And who will buy into a mobile home with such high fees?

The bottom line, Minimum said: They were really easy to scare.

More than once, Minimum had had his arm around the shoulder of a shrunken old man when closing the sale, saying they'd take good care of him.

Two years later he was yelling at the same man, telling him he better damn well pay the maintenance fee or his keester would be out on the street digging through Dumpsters. They'd take away his trailer and sue his bank account dry for breach of contract. And the old man, a widower—a good man, a veteran, who'd worked too hard in his day and sacrificed everything for his children—was left near the end of his life crying and shaking all alone in what was essentially a large toolshed.

The retiree was being cannibalized by the New American, an untested, ungrateful, wet-behind-the-ears, fast-buck shit-ass like Minimum, who didn't know what had gone into the country under his feet and wouldn't care if he found out. To Minimum, no sacrifice was too small to pass on to someone else.

McJagger particularly liked Minimum's air-conditioner scam. Free AC inspections for the entire development that would lead to a thousand bucks of repairs that had to be done or the mobile home would be red-tagged for code violations and they'd be out on the street.

If the residents didn't believe the imaginary problems, the repairmen were coached to go out to the unit and break something. If they still resisted, the staff became physically menacing.

The purpose of the guard shack wasn't to protect the residents but to keep out reputable repair companies. When the service vans arrived, the guards at first offered fifty bucks to take over the service call.

Sometimes the repairmen flipped them off and drove through, and the guards activated road spikes.

McJagger was singularly impressed that Minimum turned the name, phone number and address of each resident into at least two hundred dollars on the phone-scam circuit. Each retiree could expect no less than fifteen boiler-room phone calls a day. Sweepstakes, world cruises, blind children, hospital wings, ballroom romance, missionaries held captive by pagans.

Minimum had a reputation among the residents of Vista Isles like that of an evil prison guard. The old people on their three-wheel bikes, electric wheelchairs, and Cushman carts booed and spat at Minimum when he showed new prospects around the Isles. Sometimes, to amuse himself, he'd glare back and jerk his thumb toward the entrance of Vista Isles, which meant "out on the street."

"Screw the bank," said the porcine man leaning forward on the edge of his couch, upholstered in brown corduroy. His madras Bermuda shorts were unbuckled, and his tank-top T-shirt was too small and stained in earth tones.

Max Minimum found himself staring down at the man's bald spot, which had been spray-painted with gloss black Krylon exterior enamel. Lester Frangipani had spent the early hours of the morning watching infomercials and drinking Tropical Depression Malt Liquor, whose cans depicted a fifty-foot sailboat being bashed to popsicle sticks on a jetty. Market researchers said the logo had the double benefit of appealing to both alcoholism and class warfare.

About three A.M., Frangipani had seen an infomercial about a new baldness camouflage in which three men sat on a stage atop stools, like *The Dating Game.* A studio audience "oooo"ed and "awww"ed as a Manhattan hair stylist sprayed "Liquid Appeal" on their heads. Lester was about to jot down the 800 number when the price appeared on the screen.

"Twenty-nine ninety-five my ass!" Lester changed the channel with the remote control. Former Cincinnati Reds catcher Johnny Bench came on the screen, shaking a metal ball inside a can of Krylon no-drip exterior.

To Minimum, the freshly painted, rust-resistant bald spot represented easy money. Minimum had found Frangipani's name and address in the foreclosure rolls at the Hillsborough County Courthouse, and Lester was now reading Minimum's sales brochure. "Foreclosure? Screw the bank!" began the pamphlet. There was a drawing of a big screw going through an even bigger bank. It explained how Minimum would take over the property, set Lester up in a modest but clean one-bedroom apartment, paying first and last months' rent and security deposit, and give him a thousand dollars of mad money. At the bottom was a cartoon of a wheelbarrow full of cash. It was pushed by a smiling bald man with a bushy mustache who looked like the guy on the Community Chest cards in Monopoly. Minimum had already researched the Seminole Heights house and determined that he would receive twenty-five thousand dollars of Lester's equity for less than four thousand dollars out of pocket.

"A month from now the bank'll have your house anyway," said Minimum. He made a hitchhiking gesture with his thumb over his shoulder. "You'll be out on the streets."

Frangipani glowered up at Minimum and popped another can of Tropical Depression Malt.

"The bank'll just sell your house again," Minimum continued. "They're the ones making you homeless— you gonna take that? You gonna let them get away with it?"

Lester gulped the malt liquor, tripping his gag reflex.

"I say, screw the bank!" said Minimum.

"Screw the bank!" echoed Lester. Minimum chalked it up as a positive sign.

"The bank is licking its chops, thinking about all that money they're about to steal from you!" Minimum said. "And we'll march in there together. I'll tell the bank, 'Go suck on your mortgage, fellas.' I'll hand them my certified check for back payments and there will be nothing they can do."

"Fuck the bank!" said Lester.

Jesus, this is too easy, thought Minimum. "Okay, you stay right here. I'll go cut the check and get the forms."

But Frangipani didn't stay there. As soon as Minimum was gone, he put on a beer helmet, stuck two cold malt liquors in the holders and the tubes in his mouth.

Lester drew attention at every stoplight, but he stared straight ahead, sucking on the beer tubes. Both hands were at the top of the steering wheel, one holding a shiny gun.

At Florida National Bank, six tellers called security when Frangipani strolled through the lobby to' the elevators, slurping on the beer tubes and acting as though there was no gun in the hand swinging by his side.

The security team would arrive thirty seconds too late. Next to the elevators, Lester scanned the menu of names and floors but none matched the autograph on his foreclosure letter. Because no such person existed, precisely to counter this eventuality. Lester rode the elevator to the top and got off on the forty-second floor. He walked past the receptionist and into the corner suite of Charles Saffron, president and CEO of New England Life and Casualty, who had nothing to do with the bank.

Saffron faced out the window in his high-back burgundy office chair. A medevac helicopter flew below his floor on its way to Tampa General. Two red-and-gray tanker ships headed out the channel at the Port of Tampa. A light haze hung over the bay, but traffic was moving well on the bridges.

Saffron yelled in the phone, "No excuses! Officially, there was no malathion in the house! . . . No, listen to me! It's *not* a good idea to say she drank just a *little* malathion! What drugs are you on! . . . What do you mean there's gonna be a toxicology! Get her cremated! . . . I don't care. Steal the body, go in at night, do whatever it is you do! I got enough to worry about—I'm up to my tits in medflies!"

Frangipani, standing in the doorway, emptied all six shots from the .22 pistol into the back of Saffron's chair.

Saffron heard six gunshots and felt six bullets punch the back of his chair before the slugs flattened out against its interior steel frame.

Saffron, still looking out the window, said calmly into the phone, "I gotta go."

The security team filed off the elevator and tackled Frangipani, whose pockets were full of literature from Max Minimum. The resulting threats of prosecution as an accessory prompted Minimum to gladly agree to leave the foreclosure market for life. In seeking a new field, Minimum considered his strengths and locale. He percolated Florida's opportunities down to their stairstep elements: fear, intimidation and exploitation.

In an epiphany, Minimum saw the future in two words. Old people.

The next morning Minimum shaved, put on a dry-cleaned suit and walked into the office of Puerto Lago Boca Vista Isles.

Surveys found the number one feature sought by the senior citizens selecting a retirement home was safety from crime. Due to the Machiavellian wages

Vista Isles paid its landscaping crew, this became their number one problem.

First, Minimum recruited the surliest of the crew to torch a few service vans of uncooperative repair companies. Then he used them to launch a war of nerves with troublesome trailer owners. Bushy-haired teenagers in Metallica shirts ran lawn mowers over beds of marigolds and chrysanthemums.

Minimum trained them for the park's air-conditioning and water-heater inspections, because of their aptitude for vandalizing large appliances.

The riding lawn mower was the plumb assignment, and Minimum doled it out based on loyalty and repair revenue; next was the chain saw. The others were relegated to a gas-powered, over-the-shoulder line of edgers, trimmers, mulchers, leaf blowers and hedge clippers. Minimum became concerned that maybe the crew was getting beyond his control. As their reign of terror escalated, the landscaping staff began and ended the day by marching down the main street of Vista Isles in a flying-V formation, the riding mower in the middle, all the others trailing off to the sides, gunning two-stroke engines.

Flanked by the edger and leaf blower men, Minimum circled the pool, enforcing the rules: no food, drink or loud talking. Any spark of fun prompted Minimum to run everyone out of the pool for a surprise chlorine analysis. Other times, Minimum would shock the pool before dawn with too much chemical, and laugh in the clubhouse as a dozen seventy-year-olds in the "Early Bird Aqua-Aerobics Club" ran from the pool yelling and clawing at their eyes.

By the end of each pool visit by Minimum, the crowd was silent and cheerless. "That's better," Minimum said. "You need to be more serious, set a better example for the youth." He gestured toward the landscapers with him.

"Shoot, you've got *very* serious things to think about, like how little time you have left."

Eight

In August and September, George Veale III improved teeth in two hundred mouths, crashed three cars, made eleven phone sex calls from his home, made one phone sex call from a crashed car, and went to the Red Snapper twenty-two times.

Veale was always exceedingly loud at the club and never sober. But he tipped in proportion to his obnoxiousness and was considered harmless, except to himself.

One time he stood on a chair, demonstrating to one dancer how he skied in Aspen, but the chair went out and he came down like a sack of cement, clipping his chin on the edge of a table and biting his tongue. Bouncers with rubber gloves paper-toweled the blood. Veale tipped twenties all around.

It was now October, World Series month, and on this night Veale was up to a hundred dollars with Sharon, who thrust to "Closer" by Nine Inch Nails.

Red and yellow lights strobed and swirled over the room, catching a dozen naked lap dancers in freeze-frame. The music was deafening and sexually narcotic and the dancers' humping fell in synch with the metronomic beat.

Serge and Coleman walked into the room unescorted. "Hey, you guys aren't allowed back here!" Sharon said. "Take Charlie Brown here and get the fuck out!"

Coleman's head was too big for his body, and he hated it when Sharon called him Charlie Brown or blockhead or "that funny round-headed kid."

Serge pulled up a chair. He straddled it backward and stared at Veale. He had a videocassette in his hand. "It's okay," he said, "you can finish your dance."

When the song ended, Serge told Sharon to get lost—he had business to discuss with Veale—and she left in a huff. Veale slurred his words all over the road and bragged to Serge what a successful and important orthodontist he was. Serge revised upward the amount of blackmail he'd demand.

"I have the biggest freakin' dental clinic in the richest part of town, goddammit!"

"Is that so?" said Serge, his mental tote board flipping over more numbers. Serge couldn't stop picturing Veale with a fishbowl on his head.

Veale held his hands up in front of him like a surgeon who had just scrubbed. "These hands are insured for five million dollars."

Serge's tote board cleared back to zero, and he slid

the video back into his leather jacket, thinking in a new direction.

"Is that so?"

Mortimer and Stella Hoffsner were lifelong Cleveland Browns ticket-holders, end-zone seats. They had been at Vista Isles less than a year but already the joy had evaporated from life. Mortimer suggested they treat themselves with a day away from the park.

On a Tuesday, the Hoffsners drove down to Sarasota and crossed the north bridge to Siesta Key, as they had done every year since they had begun vacationing in Florida in 1963. They turned onto Garden Lane, parked across from a harbor of distressed fishing boats, and ate smoked salmon and crab cakes outdoors at the Siesta Fish Market. Cats begged. The menu said Eleanor Roosevelt and Ted Williams had eaten there.

After lunch they followed Ocean Drive south, past the Stickney Point drawbridge, and stopped at the Crescent Club. It was named after the island's sugar-sand Crescent Beach.

The Hoffsners had first come to the club in their early thirties. Now in their mid-sixties, they didn't sit down, but walked around the room, looking for memories on the walls. There was a 1967 calendar from a Mishawaka, Indiana, machine supply store.

It was early on a summer afternoon. The front door of the Crescent was propped open to the street. A blinding rectangle of light and heat. Inside was dim with excess air-conditioning tonnage.

The Hoffsners picked a table near the door and talked about the park. "I can't take this," said Stella. "I didn't work this hard all my life to be miserable every day. Let's just move back to Dayton."

A voice from the bar said, "Dayton? You guys from Ohio?"

Six months ago, the Hoffsners would have recoiled at what they saw, but after dealing with Minimum's army of grunge, they didn't blink.

"Yep, Dayton," Stella answered.

"I'm from Dayton too!" said Stinky. Ringworm and Cheese-Dick turned on their stools to face the Hoffsners.

"Home of the Ohio Players," Stella said.

"I *love* the Ohio Players," said Ringworm. "Remember that rumor about 'Love Roller Coaster'?"

"Yeah," said Stella. "You're supposed to be able to hear the scream of a girl getting stabbed to death."

For three hours, the five got along famously and kept the pitchers coming.

Stella Hoffsner answered the early-morning knock at her door wearing Day-Glo hair curlers and a *Charlie's Angels* nightshirt.

"AC inspection," a punk said in an annoyed tone of voice, not looking her in the eyes, staring down the street.

"The air-conditioning is working fine," she said.

"Sorry, it's mandatory. Park rules," said the punk, still not looking at her. His black T-shirt listed Marilyn Manson's concert schedule.

"But you're just going to break it!" said Stella. "We don't have the money!"

The punk took a step into the trailer without being invited. He stood against Mrs. Hoffsner so that he stared down two feet into her eyes. He was amphetamine-skinny, at least six feet tall with shoulder-length unshampooed hair and halitosis. "Look, we can do this one of two ways," he said firmly.

"Your mother must be awfully proud!" Stella said and turned in retreat. The punk followed her through the trailer until they got to the kitchen. In the center of the table was a pile of steaming flapjacks being lowered by three men the size of barrels.

"Sons," said Stella, "I'd like you to meet this fine young gentleman from the park who is here to inspect our air-conditioning."

In the emergency room, doctors tied restraints on the young patient in the Marilyn Manson shirt to keep him from tearing at his skin. The hedge clipper guy had seen him first, but didn't know what he was looking at. Four crippled ducks perched on a silver tube floating in the middle of Vista Isles's main lake.

The man was in shock, and Minimum identified him to police as one of the landscaping crew last seen making inspections. Paramedics had waded into the lake and retrieved him, covered in duck droppings and wrapped tightly up to his nose in thick fiberglass insulation commonly used in air-conditioning work.

News spread and soon the residents and staff

knew what had happened. The only people who didn't were the police. Both sides decided to keep it that way.

Minimum went on the offensive. He stepped up appliance inspections, sent out free resident lists to rabid phone solicitors, and closed the pool for "health reasons." He secretly installed a microwave oven in the auditorium for the amusement of pacemaker users.

Members of the lawn crew began turning up across the park looking like the victims of vicious fraternity hazing. Minimum called off the offensive when the leaf blower guy walked into the office with his thumb Super Glued up his butt.

The coming months were halcyon days for the residents of Vista Isles. The park came alive with festivity. The bingo nights were rowdy, and the pool parties looked like MTV beach specials. Stinky, Cheese-Dick and Ringworm kicked back by the pool on chaise longues. The residents never let the bikers' beer mugs or nacho plates get empty.

In the clubhouse, Minimum and the lawn crew sat around a folding Samsonite table and plotted. Through the tinted, hurricane-tempered window they saw Mrs. Hoffsner and Mrs. Fishbine in the shallow end of the pool, carried around on Stinky's and Ringworm's shoulders, laughing and clobbering each other with colorful foam bats.

Stinky, Cheese-Dick and Ringworm went on the dinner circuit. The residents signed up on a rotating schedule to treat the bikers to lovingly prepared home cooking. They also got the biker "colors" they'd always wanted. One resident had made three large patches for their jackets with flaming skulls. But the patches were done in macramé. The resident also was color-blind. The patches came out looking like Don King.

One day in August, a hundred and twenty residents of Vista Isles gathered and led the three men blindfolded into the clubhouse parking lot. When the blindfolds were removed, the men saw three shimmering new Harleys.

McJagger sat behind his desk watching the Florida Marlins on television in the first round of the playoffs. Minimum knocked and opened the door.

"You paged me?" asked Minimum.

"Sit down!" barked McJagger.

McJagger got up, walked to the window and opened the curtains. The lawns were overgrown and the trees unpruned.

A pack of sixty motorized scooters passed the window and circled the road around McJagger's office. Stinky, Cheese-Dick and Ringworm were in front on Harleys, leading the residents two abreast down the center line. Most of them wore leather jackets with macramé patches.

"What are they doing?" Minimum asked as they passed the window again.

"I think they're on a run!" said McJagger. "Jesus, this is ridiculous! I've got fifteen buses coming in from Ohio tomorrow for the opening of Phase V."

Minimum joined McJagger at the window as the group made another pass.

"And look at the weeds!" said McJagger.

"The yard crew is afraid to go outdoors," Minimum said.

"Goddammit! Isn't that part of the whole concept of *yard* work? That you have to go *out in the yard?!*"

"There have been accidents."

"You're getting your butt whipped!" said McJagger. "Enough of this foolishness. I'm putting an end to it." He sat back down at his desk and pulled out a file. "When those buses arrive, the last thing I need is some geriatric rumble."

The pack made another pass. "Go call those bikers in here," he told Minimum. Something out the window caught his attention and he studied the riders more closely. "Is that Don King?"

Nine

Veale awoke in the afternoon, shielding his eyes from the blaze of sunlight. He was fully clothed on top of a still-made bed in a guest room of his house. His hangover was so bad he lay down in the shower and closed his eyes. While he was toweling off, the phone in the bathroom rang.

"Who? I don't know any Serge!" said Veale.

"The Red Snapper? What deal?" Veale continued, "I don't know about any deal. I was drunk. Fuck yourself!" And he hung up.

He wrapped the towel around his waist and walked downstairs. The doorbell rang. "Now what!"

As he got to the foyer, the door was kicked open and Serge entered with a grin. He held up a stolen cell phone. "Surprise! I was calling from your front porch."

Coleman walked in behind him and pull-started a sixteen-inch chain saw.

Veale had always secretly wondered how he

would react under major stress and now he knew. He screamed and ran naked like a bastard through the house.

Serge tackled him in the living room and they both splayed out across the Mexican tile. Without discussion, Serge put both knees on Veale's chest. He gripped Veale's left wrist and held it down against the tile. Coleman was right behind and brought the chain saw down like an ax. Two fingers and a vertical spray of blood hit the wall. A third finger was half off, and Coleman killed the chain saw.

"Let me give you a hand with that," Serge said. He grabbed the third finger, gave it a twist and yanked it off.

Serge picked up the towel Veale had dropped and came back to find Veale sitting up and staring blankly.

"Hey, let's see a smile," Serge said and wrapped the mangled hand in the towel. He pulled a tourniquet from his pocket. Veale threw up on himself.

"Ooops, had a little accident there," said Serge. He took Veale by the good arm and lifted. "Come on, big boy, let's get you to a hospital."

Veale was limp.

"He's freaking out," said Coleman.

"You freaking out, George?" Serge said. Veale turned and looked at him and started crying.

"Come over here and let me show you something," Serge said. He walked Veale over to the full-length mirror in the foyer, Veale's chest and legs streaked with blood and vomit. Serge and Veale stood facing the mirror, and Serge put his arm around Veale's shoulder and smiled like they were army buddies.

"You should be excited!" Serge said. "This is your big day. Serge and Coleman are on the case now!"

Coleman went into the courtyard and started the chain saw again. He cut down the Canary Island date palm and it crashed through the living-room roof.

"Okay, we gotta get moving," said Serge, still in the mirror. He gave Veale's shoulder a big squeeze and smiled large again. "Welcome to your new life!"

He hustled Veale out of the house and drove for the emergency room at Tampa General.

"You hired us to cut down that tree . . ." said Serge, speeding south on Bayshore.

"Canary Island date palm," Veale said, sheet-white, holding the bad hand against his bare stomach.

"Yeah, that's right. *Phoenix canariensis*," said Serge. "We were cutting it down and you came running out of the shower because we were doing it wrong. . . ."

"Nobody cuts down a Canary Island date palm," Veale said like a robot. "They add to the property value."

"Right, we were cutting down the wrong tree. That's it. See, you're thinking now, George, improving the story. Good to see you on board. . . ."

Veale stared ahead and started to hiccup.

"So you ran out and tried to stop us, but we didn't hear you because of the noise of the chain saw. You grabbed my arm, and I spun around with the saw. It was swinging right for your head, and you put up your hand to block it, and fingers went flying and blood everywhere.. Oh, it's too horrible to talk about anymore."

Coleman from the backseat to Serge: "He's a doctor, right? Can he get me some drugs?"

"Shut up with the drugs," said Serge. He turned right onto the Platt Street Bridge.

"I got his fingers back here," Coleman said. "I mean two of 'em. Couldn't find the last one. Want a look?" He reached over the front seat and displayed a ring and middle finger in his palm, then pulled it back.

Veale hiccupped.

"Now remember, George, stick with the story or we all go to jail," said Serge. "At least you will. I mean, we'll try not to roll over on you if we get caught, but you're the big fish here. After all, this was your idea."

Veale turned his head slowly to Serge.

"Don't you remember? You were in the strip club talking about how your hands were insured for five million and how you were sick of all the snooty moms and their bratty little shits, and I said maybe we could stage a little accident for, say, fifty thousand dollars. And you said, 'Fuckin'-A, fuck the insurance company!' And I asked if you were sure, and you said, 'Fuck the insurance company.' So I asked if today was good, but you just kept saying, 'Fuck the insurance company!' I know you'd had a little to drink, George, but your word has to stand for something. This is a question of character."

Coleman pointed. "The emergency room!"

Serge jumped the curb and ran around to the passenger side. He helped Veale out of the car and gave him an encouraging slap on the butt: "Go get 'em, tiger!"

"Don't forget the drugs," said Coleman.

"You assholes are costing me a lot of money!" said McJagger. Emphasis added by the large gun he was waving from behind his desk at Stinky, Cheese-Dick and Ringworm.

It was an old flintlock pirate gun, but the bikers just knew it was big, so they shut up and paid attention. They sat in a row of three chairs on the other side of McJagger's desk, each holding a Dixie cup of water from the cooler out in the lobby.

"But I'm a fair man. I'll make you a deal," said McJagger. "You like boats?"

"We were shrimpers once," said Cheese-Dick, and Ringworm elbowed him.

"Good, good," said McJagger, lighting a cigar with the replica pistol and replacing it in its holder. The three let out a deep breath.

"I've got a beautiful sailboat, a sixty-foot sloop. I'd like you to take a trip on it. Boca Grande, Marco Island, the Keys, wherever. Enjoy yourselves."

"What's the catch?" asked Ringworm.

McJagger pulled a real military .45 from a spring-release frame under his desk. "Don't come back for a week or I'll shoot you."

"You're a fair man," said Stinky.

* * *

Nothing anymore could surprise the insurance adjuster from New England Life and Casualty. Not on Monday, when the scorned wife drove her husband's airboat to the grocery store down US 301 and wedged it in the bread aisle. Not on Tuesday, when the stoned college student in the convertible MG drove around Dunedin in old roadster goggles and a fifteen-foot scarf, like the Red Baron. The scarf fell in the road at the first red light. When the light turned green, the scarf caught under the rear wheel, broke his neck.

So when the adjuster read Veale's claim, he simply clicked his pen and asked, "You haven't seen a lawyer, have you?"

Serge had been with Veale each step of the way, filling out forms and signing George's signature because Veale was in and out of catatonia.

George, sitting next to Serge, made a squeak. He looked up at New England Life's logo on the wall, a horseback Paul Revere, winking.

"This signature," said the adjuster, "it doesn't match the one in our records."

"For heaven's sake, look at the man's hand!" said Serge. "I signed it. I have power of attorney." And he produced a power of attorney document from a folder and handed it to the adjuster. "Of course, I had to sign that too."

The adjuster gathered up the papers and shook them into alignment.

"Obviously an unusual case, but everything seems

to be in order," he said, actually thinking that nothing about any of this seemed to be in order. The client was making chattering noises like a woodchuck, and his high-strung interpreter sat there with a Cheshire grin and took his picture.

On the other hand, sitting across the desk from the adjuster was some of the most irrefutable evidence of grotesque mutilation he had ever seen. Sometimes people would try to defraud the insurance company by snipping off the end of a digit at the knuckle closest to the tip; nobody did *this*.

I don't get paid enough, thought the adjuster. He stamped "approved," shooed the two out of his office and left for a two-hour lunch.

Over the next few weeks, the paperwork wound its way through the corporate rat maze of New England Life and Casualty, and five million dollars was deposited into the account of George Veale III.

Serge and Coleman had been calling every day to see if the money was in, and Veale kept them at bay by prescribing synthetic heroin for Coleman's impacted wisdom teeth. Then one afternoon in late October—opening day of the 1997 World Series—Veale called Serge and said he had good news, and they set up a meeting in the revolving bar atop the Palm-Aire Hotel on St. Pete Beach.

Veale rode the glass elevator on the outside of the hotel, breathing in a paper bag, telling himself to get it together. The sun had set a few minutes earlier. As the elevator ascended, Veale first saw over the fences of the waterfront homes and into living rooms glowing blue with televisions. A couple of floors higher he could see Boca Ciega Bay and the running lights on sailboats, and higher still, across the peninsula, a cruise ship lit up on Tampa Bay like a birthday cake.

He got out of the elevator and took forced steps, carrying a black leather toiletry bag jammed with packs of hundred-dollar bills. Serge and Coleman's cocktail table had rotated clockwise so it faced south toward the pink Don Cesar Hotel. To the left, spotlights illuminated the yellow triangular supports of the Sunshine Skyway bridge. Down on Gulf Boulevard they could make out blue, red and green light from an Eckerd's, a Burger King and a Publix.

Veale arrived at the table the same time as the waitress and ordered a triple Jack Daniel's before sitting.

"Another Perrier," said Serge. The waitress gave a dirty look at Coleman, facedown on the table. "Nothing for him," Serge said.

Veale sat and didn't move for several minutes as their table rotated until it was facing west toward the Gulf of Mexico. Veale discreetly lowered the toiletry bag to the floor and slid it slowly over to Serge with his foot.

Serge stared at Veale and raised his hand, talking into a make-believe wrist radio: "Agent Iguana to Captain Cavity. The Eagle has landed."

He grabbed the bag off the floor, turned it over and dumped the money on the table. Veale looked like he would stroke. The waitress arrived with their drinks, saw the money and said "Shit" under her breath.

"Oh, I'm sorry," Serge said and pushed the money aside to make room for the drinks. He peeled off a hundred, gave it to her and looked back down in the bag. The waitress opened her mouth to say something but left quickly instead.

"Where's the rest of it?" he said to Veale.

"What?"

"The rest of the money. I mean, this is a real sweet gesture, George, but when do we get the main money?"

"What do you mean?" said Veale, gulping for oxygen. "It's all there, fifty thousand."

"You're right. This is fifty thousand. But our share is three point three five million. Where is it?"

"Wha—?"

"Five million three ways. Coleman and my shares come to three point three five. This"—nodding at the pile on the table—"this rounds the outstanding balance to three point three."

"But you said fifty thousand!"

"When?"

"On the way to the hospital."

"You must have been delirious," said Serge. "Why would I settle for one percent? Is this going to get contentious, George?"

Veale felt hot surges of panic in his chest and neck. Serge packed the money back in the bag. As their table rotated to the north, the waitress pointed them out to her coworkers lined up at the end of the bar gawking.

George saw them looking. He ducked down and whispered, "We've been spotted!"

Serge looked up and waved to them. He pointed at Veale and yelled, "George Veale the Third, everyone, let's give him a big hand." He clapped robustly.

George fainted.

Serge splashed Perrier on the two men facedown at his table. Coleman looked around, disoriented, then Veale.

"George. Twenty-four hours!" Serge said, and he and Coleman left with the toiletry bag.

Ten

The sky was orange marmalade over Tampa Bay as the sun fell below the St. Petersburg skyline. The underlight caught some cirrus clouds, glowing pink-red.

Happy hour was under way at the bar Hammer-Time on the Courtney Campbell causeway. A typical Friday after-work Tampa crowd. Lots of Trans Ams in the parking lot. The bar's name was bent in red lights over the door. Just below it was a stuffed hammerhead shark wearing sunglasses and painted with electric-lime tiger stripes.

Souvenir T-shirts covered the ceiling, and the tables were old surfboards. The owners had bought up dozens of taxidermied fish—wahoo, cobia, amberjack—painted them wild like the shark out front and stuck them on the walls. A standing clientele coagulated traffic around the bar, and waitresses circulated with racks of test tubes filled with shots.

David Klein had been at the window table for two

hours, before the crowds, because he liked the view. He had a Coke and was halfway through a paperback.

David saw two sailboarders and the news helicopter doing traffic reports, and his mind drifted the way it did before sleep.

He thought back to the case he'd finished prosecuting that afternoon, another ATM stickup, open-and-shut, jury out twenty minutes. Where were they all coming from? Wave after wave of assailants. Carjackers, rapists, muggers, child abusers and people who'd simply decided it was time to start shooting. He averaged three death threats a month.

He thought back to Tampa High. David was seventeen, driving a carload of football players out into the county after another win. Out to the bootlegger on the Hillsborough River.

The sheriff's deputy was aware of the bootlegger, and when he saw the football players at that hour on that county road, he knew the reason.

He summarily pulled them over, found the moonshine and arrested everyone. He also charged David with reckless driving.

David's teammates laughed, but only as much as was polite, when David said he'd be their lawyer. He spent hours alone in the courthouse library.

In court, the prosecutor and judge were irked that the teens pushed for a trial instead of paying the misdemeanor fines. David's four teammates sat at the defendant table, two in letter-man jackets. Fourteen other players and cheerleaders sat in the wooden pews.

David asked the judge to combine all the defendants, but to separate his reckless driving charge into a separate trial.

The judge looked at the prosecutor, who shrugged. No objection.

The prosecutor put the deputy on the stand, and he described David driving over the center line, which everyone knew was a pretext for a search, but one that held up every time.

"Your witness," the prosecutor said, patronizing David.

"Was I speeding?" asked David.

"No."

"Were any other cars present?"

"No."

"Did you stop me for any other reason?"

The deputy lied about the moonshine suspicions. "Nope, just driving over the center line."

"No further questions," said David.

"The state rests," the prosecutor said with a smugness that made it clear this was beneath him, a game of legal putt-putt golf.

"The defense requests a directed verdict of acquittal based on the 1948 precedent of *Penrod v. Florida* in this circuit..." David handed copies made in the courthouse library to the judge and prosecutor. "... in which the judge ruled that driving down the center of a county road is a generally accepted safety measure in rural Florida, and without any other evidence is not in and of itself sufficient to support a charge of reckless driving."

The judge finished reading the court opinion and looked up at the prosecutor. "The state have anything?"

"But he was weaving too!" said the prosecutor.

"Too late," said the judge. "You had your chance on direct, and you rested. . . . Case dismissed."

"Okay," said the prosecutor, "now on the moonshine charges . . ."

"Your honor," interrupted David, "defense moves the alcohol charge be dismissed as it is the fruit of a search without probable cause, based upon the deficient traffic citation."

"The fruit?!" exclaimed the prosecutor. "Really, Your Honor, do we have to—"

The judge stopped him by holding up his hand. "He's right. Dismissed."

The judge looked at David and let a smile slip on his lips. "It'll be interesting to see which way you're gonna turn out."

A voice popped the daydream. "What are you reading?"

David looked back from the bay and saw Sean, who pulled out the empty chair across from him at Hammer-Time. David looked down at the book he'd forgotten he was holding. He turned it over to show Sean the cover. A drawing of a giant bug with a coke spoon hanging from his neck and submachine guns in its six arms under the title *The Cockroach Bay Story*.

"I remember that case," said Sean. "It was like the

typical eighties Florida crime story. Every cliché you ever heard about the Wild West cocaine frontier."

"That's it."

"Book any good?"

"I guess," said David. "Most of the facts are right. It's got the parts about the accidental coke drop and that big free-for-all when all those people found it."

"Isn't it amazing that's the same place we go fishing?"

"I know. I'm now at the part where everyone starts dying like grassy-knoll witnesses."

"It looked like you weren't at any part, looked more like staring out the window to me."

"Trying to forget work. These animals. They're like a different species."

David knew what Sean was going to say next. The state was rapidly dividing into two types of people. Those who made parents worry for their children, and those who didn't. David ascribed it to the fact that Sean had little kids. He also knew he was right.

"Now back to business," David said.

"Right," said Sean. "The annual fishing trip."

"The same one we have not been having for years. The tradition continues." Every year the same thing. Big talk. The big fishing trip. And then the big canceled fishing trip. Always something. Wedding, car accident, births.

"But this year . . ."

"Absolutely," said Sean.

"All the way to the Keys," said David. "I know a skiff rental place."

"I know these out-of-the-way cabins."

"It'll be a roadtrip."

"Easy Rider."

"Route 66."

"Lewis and Clark."

"Jack Kerouac."

"Thelma and Louise."

David stopped and looked at him.

"Can I be Thelma?" said Sean.

"Okay, here's the plan before we cancel it again this year."

"We're not gonna cancel it!" said Sean.

"It'll be the A-tour of Florida," said David. "We drive over to Cape Canaveral for a space shuttle launch. The next day we head south along the coast to Palm Beach, and hang there for a day. Then the same thing the next day in Miami Beach . . ."

Sean finished the thought: "And finally we drive all the way to Key West and break some fishing records . . ."

"Most Bait Wasted, Career," said David.

Laughter distracted them.

It was girls' night out at the next table. Five secretaries sipping stadium drinks, rum and Coke. They giggled and one took her bra off under her shirt to win a bet. One of the secretaries, the one with medium-length wavy black hair, saw David looking and held up her drink toward him and smiled. David smiled back and turned away to gaze at the pelicans skimming the bay. Two men on the make walked up to the secretaries. The women gave them good-natured patience, let 'em make their pitch. David heard the women groan at a punch line before the men were dispatched.

Another suitor approached the table. Green down vest and pointy cowboy boots. This one was getting a brisk rejection from the woman with the black wavy hair. He grabbed her wrist and she pulled it away. He took a step back and appeared to relax, ready to leave it alone.

But instead he grabbed her arm again, twisting it behind her back and pushing her head down to the table.

"I've had it with you, bitch!" the man yelled. Everyone froze. The only sound was the man's voice and U2 on the sound system, "Where the Streets Have No Name."

"You're fuckin' him! I oughtta break your fuckin' neck!"

In times of duress, when others might be non-plussed, David went to a different place. He stopped thinking verbally and began thinking in numbers. Not literally numerals. But distances, time, odds, spatial relationships, computer-modeling, assigning weights to outcomes, coefficients of opportunity. Extremely fast. It was what had made him such a successful quarterback. His effectiveness, however, depended on factoring out emotion. That was a challenge this time because the woman with her face pressed to the table was his sister, Sarah.

"You slut!" the man yelled, twisting her arm.

"Let me guess," said David, standing. "You were never very bright, even as a child."

Everyone looked at David like he had lost his mind. This guy was Paul Bunyan.

"What did you say?" the man growled.

"Oh, nothing," said David. "Just that it must be difficult going through life always the least intelligent person in any group."

"What?"

"But there's always hope," said David. "They have specially trained chimpanzees that can help you with daily tasks. I hear they're really smart."

The man let go of Sarah's arm and walked toward David. "I'll kill you!"

The man stepped right up to David, chest to chest, to scare the hell out of David before flattening him. The man pulled back a fist, but as he did, David gave a quick lean forward and head-butted him in the mouth. Bip! David got a little cut in the forehead, but it smashed the man's teeth up good. Hurt like the devil.

The man was ready to kill for real now. But instead of punching with his pulled-back arm, he reflexively went first to his injured mouth. That gave David time to pull his own fist back, and he piston-punched the man in the kidney. The man was off balance, his central nervous system telling him that things were going very badly on two fronts.

While the man was busy sorting it out, David didn't even have to be imaginative about the end. He picked up a chair and swung it sideways. In the movies, the chair splinters. In real life, bones splinter. The man put up an arm to shield himself, and it broke in two places before it was deflected away. The chair went on through and fractured his skull and collarbone. David wasn't done. He was down on top of the man, punching away. Would have killed him too if Sarah and Sean hadn't pulled him off.

After seeing David's gold assistant state attorney badge, the cops treated him like royalty. They cuffed the unconscious lumberjack.

Sean was driving. He looked over at David in the passenger seat and back to the road, then looked at David again. "Sometimes you scare me."

David was nonchalant. "Animals. Where do they keep coming from?"

"Let's go fishing," said Sean.

Eleven

Veale was at the dining room table with his wife and daughter, going over plans for the daughter's wedding in two weeks. He looked over his wife's shoulder at the TV in the other room and pregame coverage of the World Series.

"George, are you paying attention?"

George nodded.

He started hearing the voice before they did, the one calling him.

Then they all heard it: "Calling Captain Cavity!"

As his wife got up to investigate, Veale felt an oncoming four-wheel-drive panic attack. He had missed the twenty-four-hour deadline.

"George, there's two scary-looking men in our yard," said his wife. "Get rid of them!"

George and his daughter got up and joined her at the window.

Through the iron gate, the three saw Coleman out on the sidewalk, wearing army boots, skimpy silk running shorts and no shirt. He stood with legs apart and arms akimbo like Superman, and fixed a threatening mug on his face. Behind him, Serge leaned against a rusted-out Barracuda parked in the street.

Most intimidating was the giant tattoo on Coleman's chest that they could read even from the house: "Crucifixion Junkies." It was the name of a local death metal band, but the Veales didn't know that. They thought he was another bay-area devil-worshiper.

"We want our money," yelled Serge.

"George, do you know these men?!" asked his wife.

Veale said, "Hide me," but his voice was so high only dogs could hear it.

"George! Do something!" his wife yelled.

"Yeah, George, do something!" Serge yelled from the street.

So George got down on the floor and made himself into a ball.

"I'm calling the police!" his wife announced.

Serge and Coleman told the police that they were George's friends and only wanted to see if George could come out and play. "Isn't that right?" Serge yelled to Veale, who was hiding behind the stump of the Canary Island date palm.

The officer told Veale's wife that he was sorry. But since George refused to cooperate, or even come out from behind the stump, all he could do was tell the men to leave. He tipped his hat.

Veale's wife and daughter took matters into their

own hands and went shopping in Hyde Park.

After the women left, Serge and Coleman circled back to the house and walked through the unlocked door. George, in the living room, took off running.

Serge tackled him again on the Mexican tiles.

"George, we're not going to cut off any more fingers. We just want to show you something."

Serge pushed a videocassette into the VCR, and George watched himself with a fishbowl on his head.

"Now let's go for a ride, George," said Serge.

But George made himself back into a ball. So Serge and Coleman put him in a large laundry basket and carried him out to the Barracuda.

As Serge drove, he talked to Veale in the passenger seat. "Why haven't you paid us? You know it's the right thing. I can't believe you were intentionally trying to avoid us.

"Tell you what I'm going to do, George. I'm a motivational kind of guy. I deeply believe in inspiring the people around me, giving them a clear reason to do things."

Serge pulled out several sheets of paper stapled together. "We took the liberty of going through your mail. As a free service, of course, no charge. This was from your caterer, your daughter's final wedding guest list. About a hundred and fifty names, addresses too."

Serge pulled out ten rectangular boxes wrapped in brown paper, the size of videocassettes.

"These are the fishbowl chronicles," said Serge. "I've addressed them to the first ten people on the

wedding list. Every day you don't pay, I address another ten tapes."

Serge pulled the Barracuda over to the curb,
stepped out and dropped the ten tapes into a mailbox. George screamed, jumped out of the car and
jammed his arm into the mailbox up to his neck,
scraping off wads of skin, and got stuck for a half
hour.

With the three bikers on the sailboat and out of the
way, the unveiling of Puerto Lago Boca Vista Isles,
Phase V, went off without a snag. McJagger thought
it wise to keep the Ohio visitors in their buses, pre-
venting contact with the park's residents. A phalanx
of yard workers cleared one intersection of a block-
ade of electric scooters.

The mood at the park returned to interminable
funk. Minimum closed the pool again and ordered
the breakage of forty water heaters.

On October 14, just after noon, Minimum stood in
the driveway of Trailer #864, the Aloha model, brow-
beating an eighty-year-old woman to tears over the
maintenance fee. A crowd gathered and heckled him.

In Trailer #865, a widower in a walker went to the
closet and put on his Eighth Air Force bomber's
jacket with a small flak tear under the arm. He
reached behind a pile of newspapers and military
yearbooks and grabbed a lever-action Winchester.

A few onlookers noticed the gun barrel through a
screen on Trailer #865. They whispered and the
crowd slunk out of the line of fire. Minimum, con-

centrating on his intimidation, was the only one without a clue.

The doctor said the shot couldn't have hit Minimum's kneecap more directly or done more damage, even though the veteran told police repeatedly that he was aiming for his heart.

After at least six months of rehabilitation, Minimum would be able to get around with just a leg brace. Until then he'd have to use . . .

"No, not that!" said Minimum.

The residents hooted at Minimum as he hobbled around the complex with a walker. At the clubhouse, some tried to hook the legs of his device with their canes.

As for the veteran, that was something McJagger wanted to talk to Minimum about. McJagger, at his desk, harrumphed with impatience as Minimum moved like an escargot with the walker. He struggled to get into a chair.

"You comfy?" asked McJagger.

Minimum nodded.

"Good." He threw several newspapers hard across the desk and Minimum put up both hands to stop them from hitting his face.

"Look at those goddamn headlines. 'Shooting trial opens: Aging vet's last mission.' 'Retirement parks— hell on earth?' 'Gray Panthers blast Vista Isles.' They're making this guy out to be a hero. CNN even named a new syndrome after him. It's a goddamn nightmare. I got a twenty-million-dollar new phase about to go in the tank because of you. You're fired!"

"But what about all I've done for you?" said Minimum, on the business end of fear for the first time in his life.

"What about how you've treated all those old people!"

"But you wanted me to. I made you rich!"

"Oh! Blame others! That's the high road, you groveling little shit. You're weak; you can't even walk right anymore. You're yesterday's news," said McJagger. "How do you put it? You're out on the streets!"

Minimum sobbed without regard.

"Jesus Christ," said McJagger. "Be a man!"

Minimum fell to the floor and crawled around the desk. He grabbed McJagger by the leg and wouldn't let go, weeping on his socks.

"For the love of God!" yelled McJagger, trying to shake free. "Okay, okay, you're not fired. But you've got to disappear for a while, at least until the trial's over. The best thing we can do is make sure this guy doesn't get convicted. Get this off the front page."

"But he tried to kill me!"

"Don't cry to me. I'm on *his* side. Did you see the man's war record? Purple Heart, Flying Cross, thirty-six bombing runs over Germany, shot down twice, prisoner of war, tortured. I read the paper—couldn't believe how much money you swindled him out of. You're a sick man!"

"I gave the money to you!"

"That man is a real American hero! Cripes, you're just a little worm. Your kind has no values."

"But he shot me!"

"I would have shot you. I *will* shoot you if you don't shut up," and McJagger pulled the .45 from under his desk.

"Maybe you can sign some kind of affidavit," McJagger thought out loud. "Say you shot yourself cleaning your gun. It was a lovers' quarrel. A gang-related drive-by. Jealous husband. You were trying to buy drugs. Claim you're mentally unbalanced, mildly retarded. A transvestite . . ."

McJagger opened his desk drawer again and pulled out a zippered bank bag and threw it at Minimum.

"That's five grand and the keys to my Hatteras in Cape Coral, sleeps six. Take it and get lost," said McJagger. "Jesus, I'm running out of boats here."

Minimum rubbed his forehead where the bank bag had hit him.

"And if you see those bikers, tell 'em I want my sailboat back!"

Sean Breen and David Klein drove north from Tampa on Interstate 75. It was a warm Sunday morning and they were in Sean's Chrysler. David bought the gas when they stopped at a Cracker Barrel for biscuits.

They had open country driving through the Withlacoochee State Forest, slightly rolling, which is a mountain chain in Florida. Lots of pastures and hardwoods connected by strings of billboards for topless truck stops a hundred miles away.

It was a vintage 1985 New Yorker with a maroon interior, factory stereo. Eight hundred dollars of recent work on the air-conditioning. Mileage: unknown. David gave Sean relentless grief about trading it in. To hear Sean tell it, the car was good for another two hundred thousand, as long as he changed the oil on time.

The car began making a ker-chunk noise and puffs of smoke shot out the edges of the hood, but Sean continued driving.

"Don't you think you should pull over?" asked David.

Sean reached forward and turned off the air conditioner and the problem stopped. He rolled down his window.

"Why do you keep this car?" asked David. "How many miles has it got?"

"I don't know," said Sean. "The odometer's broken."

"So it's got a million miles and you have to have the air conditioner fixed every year, and a few months ago it failed the emission test. What was that? Another five hundred dollars?"

"Nine."

"Nine hundred!" David said and whistled.

"I just can't bring myself to get rid of it," said Sean. "I feel comfortable in it. It's like an old baseball glove."

"The rearview mirror is out of alignment in your baseball glove," said David. He reached up and turned the mirror slightly and it popped off the windshield in his hand.

"Whoops."

David tossed the mirror over his shoulder into the backseat. He turned and grinned with guilt at Sean, who glared back.

"They make a special glue," said David. "Sticks right to the glass."

"And you'll be finding where they sell it."

They took Exit 63 at Bushnell in south Sumter County and hooked back under the overpass. Sean drove briefly through the rural countryside until he saw large American flags. Florida National Cemetery.

They drove through tight grids of tombstones that formed different patterns depending on your angle. They only gave way to more fields of tombstones.

"It's over there," David said, pointing.

They parked on the road and began walking. Only one other person was in sight. An elderly woman knelt at a grave in the adjacent field, holding a rosary. Sean and David were in the newest section. They could tell because the tombstones ended in a ragged, nongeometric edge, and the land beyond was being backhoed and prepared for the advancing wave of white tablets.

In military cemeteries, plots aren't purchased in advance and spread out willy-nilly. They are dug in strict chronological order.

David and Sean walked through time as they checked the inscribed dates of death. 1988. 1989. 1990.

The pair slowed when they got to 1991. Up until then, the dates of birth had been mostly in the early part of the century as World War II and Korean vets died off. But now they began seeing a growing frequency of birth dates in the early 1970s mixed with the 1920s. The Gulf War. "A lot more than I thought," said Sean.

Most of the tombstones had crosses carved at the top. A distant second were six-pointed stars. There were rare Eastern Orthodox symbols. Following a series of eleven consecutive crosses was a Star of David and the name Reuben Klein.

David stopped and looked down and was quiet. Sean was glad he'd come, but he was uncomfortable because David's nature had been to aggressively avoid talking about his parents.

David started talking. "When he had his stroke, it looked like he would make it. I went with the whole family. Spent as little time as I could. Then my sister called and said I should see him. What she meant was if we had anything to say, there wouldn't be another chance. She knew why we didn't get along. It was because of the way he treated her. He didn't *mis*treat her. He just didn't treat her right. He was the colonel, very military, he was always cold and hard and never any affection or emotion. I could take it, but he treated Sarah like she was a buck private too. We always fought over it and when I was sixteen I took a swing at him and he decked me. After I left for college, I never said more than two words together to him, and that was only when I visited

Mom. Seemed fine with him; he never called or wrote."

Sean had never heard David talk remotely like this. David stared down at the tombstone the whole time he was talking.

"Sarah begged me to go back to the hospital and fix things. What do you fix? There was never anything there. I went early one Monday, but he was sleeping, tubes in his nose and mouth and arms. Machines tracking everything. He was helpless as a baby, and he slept like one. I sat there. Before I knew it I had been there two hours, and I left.

"I went to an artist I knew through a friend and told him I needed something quick—I'd pay extra. That Friday I went back to his room and this time he was awake. But no expression except maybe wondering what the heck I had wrapped in the brown paper. I held it up at the foot of the bed and took the paper off."

It was a painting of a beautiful P-38 Lightning flying over the Pacific Ocean. Tendrils of clouds seemed to zip by the plane, below the right wing and under its trademark twin nacelles. The sea was deliberately fuzzed up because David had rushed the artist and told him to cut corners on the background—he had to have the painting by the weekend. But the out-of-focus sea actually created a nice depth-of-field effect. On the horizon were traces of an island chain. The archipelago was anonymous in the painting, but the plane was not. Its numbers and markings were those of Klein's plane, and the pilot, though tiny, had Reuben's black hair and determined face. It was a clear sunny morning just after his twentieth birthday, and Reuben Klein had life by the tail as he roared through the wide-open sky.

Reuben Klein would have recognized the plane without the markings. The image in the painting was the same as in a sepia-toned black-and-white photo taken in 1945. Exactly the same. Every brushstroke precisely captured the details branded in his mind. The photo had been taken by another pilot that morning, looking back and to the right at Reuben's plane. For some reason it was the only photo Reuben had of himself flying during the war. In fact it was the only picture of him during the war, period. The other guys took snapshots of themselves all the time, but Reuben thought they were being childish. Years later, he regretted it. He kept the photo at home in a special cherry-wood box on his desk. Reuben Klein was not a materialistic man, except for that box. It also contained his pilot's wings, a couple of medals and the colonel insignias he would receive toward the end of his career. But that picture was the most special to him. If there was any emotion in Reuben Klein, it was when he opened the box once or twice a week and stared at it. His young heart was a lion in that cockpit and the world awaited. He didn't know at the time that it was his peak, but now he did.

David always wanted to be like his father, and, like his father, he stared at the photo of the P-38 for hours, committing every minute detail to memory.

Then he'd put it back in the box and carefully set it on his father's desk and sneak out of the room before his dad came home and caught him. David got more than one spanking for messing around with that box.

One night Reuben Klein was reading the newspaper when six-year-old David came up to give him something. He told his father he'd made it himself. It was a paper plate. Around the edge of the paper plate was a circle of hearts drawn with a red crayon. Glued into the middle of the plate with library paste was an airplane. David had cut it out of the black-and-white photo with his safety scissors and stuck it on the plate. He colored it with purple and yellow crayons and he put more paste on top of it and sprinkled silver and gold glitter.

"How do you like it?" David had said, beaming.

He got the worst spanking of his little life.

David stopped as he recounted all this for Sean in the cemetery, and Sean couldn't believe the always composed, private person transforming before him. David gathered himself and continued.

"I stood there at the foot of my father's hospital bed with the painting for what seemed like the longest time, and I said, 'How do you like it?' My dad's left eye looked up at me. The stroke had paralyzed the right side of his face and it was like stone, like that half was already dead. But his left eye started crying and the tears rolled off the side of his face onto the pillow. He desperately wanted to say something, but he had these tubes in his mouth, and the left half of his mouth tried to work the tubes out. I rubbed his arm and told him it was all right, but he kept trying to spit out the tubes like he had to say the most important thing in the world. The nurses came in, and they made me leave. I set the painting upright in a chair facing him. Late that night, actually closer to dawn, he went. By Monday he was here."

David turned his back to Sean, and Sean could see he was dabbing his eyes with the heel of his right hand. Sean looked away and wiped his own face. A few minutes passed without anyone talking. "Thanks for coming with me," he said, and they walked back to the car.

George Veale bonded out of the Hillsborough County Jail on Orient Road the morning after shooting his dog's leg off. He had shared a cell with a man who wore an aluminum-foil skullcap to keep out the gamma rays. He had eaten a dinner of food squares with the taste and texture of particle board. Sharing his table was a man who was somehow missing his nose and kept asking Veale, "What are you looking at, motherfucker!"

The only outdoor area in Cell Pod D was a tiny basketball court with four sheer, eighteen-foot-high concrete walls and a chain-link grating across the top. A basketball sat idle under the basket and Veale picked it up and started dribbling spastically like he was eight years old.

Two sinewy men sat in the corner of the court, and the taller one yelled, "Hey, Grampa, did we say you could touch that basketball?" He looked up at them and immediately put the basketball down.

"Did we say to put the ball down?" They came over and picked up the basketball and made Veale play dodge ball with them, Veale permanently on defense.

All in all, a rough twenty-four hours for George. After freeing his arm from the mailbox, Veale had camped at his wet bar for two hours and driven to the strip club, where he blabbed everything to Sharon and began wailing so loudly that he was thrown out of the Red Snapper for the first time.

Back at the homestead, Veale went into a paranoid fandango as he walked Van Damme in the front yard. He held the drink and cigar in his right hand, the good one, and in his left, with only a thumb and forefinger, he simultaneously gripped the end of the leash and a nickel-plated .45 automatic, the sight of which prompted seven neighbors to call the police.

Coleman and Serge made a slow left turn in the Barracuda from Obispo onto San Clemente, Veale's street. From the corner they could see Veale five houses up on the right, unraveling, marching back and forth with the dog, waving the gun and yelling at the sky.

As they approached Veale's house, Coleman glanced in the rearview mirror and nudged Serge, who turned his eyes to the mirror without moving his head. A Tampa police cruiser had fallen in behind the Barracuda.

Serge maintained his fifteen miles per hour, and Coleman waved like the Queen of England at Veale as they passed his house and kept going.

At the sight of them, Veale let out a sound one would expect to hear if somebody jumped on a small animal with both feet. A startled Van Damme bolted to the end of the leash, yanking Veale's trigger finger and firing the gun, blowing off one of Van Damme's back legs. The police officer gave a single whoop of his siren and jumped out with gun drawn.

Serge and Coleman returned in the Barracuda the next morning, staking out Veale's house for his release from jail. A late-model Camaro screeched up to the curb in front of them, blocking the view.

As president and CEO of New England Life and Casualty, Charles Saffron's job was to captain the company through treacherous financial straits. As a self-styled man of adventure, he sent the company's assets headlong into the world of cocaine trafficking, extortion, tax fraud, arms dealing, the occasional murder of a material witness, and campaign contributions to the Republican and Democratic National Committees.

While Saffron paid acute attention to his criminal enterprises, the company's legitimate ventures headed for the reef. But legitimate losses were only money; illegitimate losses could cost his life.

Saffron's largest off-the-books endeavor was money-laundering for the cartels, and he spent many an afternoon bouncing large deposits back and forth between Tampa and Caribbean islands.

His relationship with the cartels had begun on a

steamy July night in the Florida Keys in 1989. Saffron was at a cockfight in a tin building on one of the isolated, quarried islands in the back country between Sugarloaf and Key West. By four A.M., the crowd had dwindled to a sweaty clutch of people in light cotton shirts, holding cigars and shot glasses. After the place closed up, Saffron stood behind the open trunk of his Cadillac getting at a bottle of brandy. The moon was in first quarter and Saffron could see the shadow of a slumping man being dragged out behind the building and into the parched mangroves. Saffron followed quietly to a clearing and hid behind a gumbo-limbo tree.

The slumping man had already been beaten, and now one of his four assailants stepped up. He pressed a gun into his stomach and fired, and the man groaned faintly. The man's belly had acted as a silencer. The assailants apparently didn't want him dead yet; they still wanted to talk trash, and they babbled at him rapidly and angrily in Spanish.

Saffron stepped out from behind the tree. "Can I play too?"

The surprised men swung their guns at Saffron.

In Tampa, Saffron was an imposing figure. He was in his late forties but still in shape. He was just over six feet and his hair was black. His face was attractive but hard and rocky. A small scar ran from the underside of his lower lip. It added to his ruggedness.

But Saffron wasn't in Tampa anymore. He was big and hard enough, but the men with the guns looked first at his hands, which were soft, with trimmed fingernails. He was holding a bottle of brandy.

One of the men smiled and made an insulting aside to his friends. Saffron heard the word "gringo."

Saffron walked up to the man and gestured toward the sidearm in the man's waistband and then toward the dying man. "May I?"

The man smiled broadly under a Pancho Villa mustache. He took out his gun, cocked the slide and handed it butt first to Saffron. The others kept the guns pointed at Saffron.

"Hold this," said Saffron, and he slapped the bottle of brandy hard into the gut of the man handing him the gun. He turned and shot the injured man five times, fast, in the face, not worrying about the noise. The 9mm rounds boomed across the flats.

"God*damn* that was fun! Got anyone else you're pissed at?" said Saffron.

But the rest of the gang were startled by the noise. "Jesus! María! *Vamos!*"

They ran for their Jeep Cherokee, but the first guy there took off and left the rest in the parking lot, so they caught a getaway ride with Saffron.

There was much tension as they drove to Key West, but on Boca Chica one started laughing and then they all did and the brandy made the rounds and thin cigars were lit.

The sun was coming up as they hit Roosevelt Boulevard on Key West, and Saffron saw the first charter boat captain walking down the dock with a mug of coffee. The captain was dubious about the group but not about their two thousand in cash, and he couldn't cast off fast enough.

On the trip, Saffron hammered out a business arrangement. After that deal and a few more went profitably for all concerned, word got around the cocaine world and different cartels came calling.

"A good reputation is the best advertisement. That's what I always say," Saffron always said.

Saffron had short, coarse black hair and finely chiseled features. Unfortunately they looked like they'd been chiseled by Picasso, and he intimidated many people. He wore expensive suits that weren't flashy but drove a Lamborghini Countach. He ate lunch every other day at the club atop his bank building. He hated his cell phone and carried it everywhere.

The first and only office of New England Life was in downtown Tampa. In late 1997, Saffron stared out his office window and thought about third-quarter losses posted in no small part to the five-million-dollar payout to George Veale III. As point man for the corporation's money-laundering liaison with a Costa Gordan cocaine cartel, Saffron was getting nervous.

Costa Gorda had been calling on the hour since a duffel bag of American currency had not arrived on a tourist flight from Miami. In the first call, Saffron had sounded light, talking about debt-to-earning ratios, unanticipated claims and sunken capital. The Costa Gordans talked about exploratory surgery with a pruning saw, making Saffron's testicles retract into his lungs. When the subsequent calls came in, his secretary alternately said Saffron was in the executive washroom and out of town, and then both.

Saffron declared the payout to Veale a complete blunder, and the claims adjuster was given three months' paid vacation in Costa Gorda, most of which he needed to recover from a fractured femur. Even if the claim was legit, they still couldn't afford to pay, Saffron screamed. Drag it out, go to court, appear on *Larry King*. They weren't even in the insurance business anymore. All the legal money was gone, a deterioration begun with claims from Hurricane Andrew and finished with Saffron's greedy, head-long speculation in the joint underwriters market.

No, this was cocaine money, and one thing you never, ever do with cocaine money is give it to some fucked-up dentist in Tampa who cuts off his fingers. If it gets to the point where you were about to pay claims with it, you simply dissolve the company and pay off creditors, and all the ones at the head of that line were from Costa Gorda.

Saffron wasn't screaming this new mission statement at his staff. He was yelling into a cellular phone while driving over the bridge from downtown Tampa to his postmodern waterfront house on Davis Islands.

The phone asked a question.

Saffron yelled back, "Who cares what really happened! What it means is we're screwed. You and me both. We've been had. This is a bogus claim!"

"So you want me to investigate for fraud? Check the guy out?" asked the man on the phone, private investigator and state senator Mo Grenadine.

"No, I want you to get the money back. Steal it. Whack the guy if you have to!" said Saffron.

"That's not my field," said Grenadine.

"Why the hell do we pay you a twenty-thousand-dollar private investigator retainer?"

"You pay me to push legislation that favors your company," said Grenadine.

"And what have we gotten for our money? Jack shit. Not one of your bills ever passes. Not one!"

"It's the homosexual agenda—"

"Save it for your shitkicker listeners," Saffron hollered. "You go get the money or you've had it."

"You mean you'll withdraw support for my family-values campaign?"

"It means you go to jail! We've been taping everything," Saffron said and hung up.

Grenadine lay spread-eagled on his bed and didn't move for ten minutes. After, he searched around in his closet for his cheating-husband homing device—a modified stolen-car directional finder that allowed him to skip countless stakeout hours and go straight to the love nest.

The next morning he drove to San Clemente Street several hours before Veale would be released from jail, walked up to a red Aston Martin in the driveway, and stuck the homing device under the bumper.

He climbed back in his car and waited at the end of the block. A Barracuda pulled up two houses in front of him and nobody got out. Minutes later, a

Camaro screeched up in front of the Barracuda, and a dangerous woman opened the door.

"Christ," Serge muttered in the Barracuda.

A furious Sharon in chartreuse hot pants slammed the door of the Camaro and stomped up the street toward Serge's driver-side window. A long mane fell over the shoulders of her tight football jersey that was cut off just below her breasts—no bra. The tattoo on her left ankle was a rose dripping blood from its thorns. Her eyes were covered with Terminator sunglasses, and a cigarette dangled from her lips hooker-style.

"If it isn't Martha Stewart," said Serge. "What's today's tip, Martha? How to turn that cozy guest room into a dingy garage?"

"Fuck a duck," said Sharon.

"Wordsmith," said Serge.

Serge saw a cab drop Veale off in his driveway. "Quick, get in before he sees you," said Serge, and Sharon crawled in the backseat.

"You buttholes were gonna stiff me! George told me all about the insurance scam yesterday at the club!"

Serge ignored her and lifted a pair of stolen Bavarian binoculars. Veale was in the house less than fifteen minutes. When he hit the street again, he had shaved off his beard. He wore a curly blond wig, his wife's, under a Devil Rays baseball cap. He had on a full-length trench coat. He threw two suitcases and a gym bag into the Aston Martin and took off.

Serge and company followed him down MacDill

Avenue to Kennedy Boulevard and east over the
drawbridge to downtown Tampa. Veale parked in a
loading zone at the Florida National Bank tower and
walked inside with a suitcase.

"What's he gonna do, rob the place?" asked
Sharon.

"Dressed like Harpo Marx?" said Serge. "My guess
is he's about to make a withdrawal."

Through the front window, they saw Veale approach a teller and throw the suitcase on the counter
like he was checking luggage. The teller appeared to
talk excitedly, shaking her head from side to side,
and a bank vice president appeared. After a curt discussion, the vice president motioned for Veale to follow him around the corner and out of view.

Minutes later, Veale reappeared on the street with
the suitcase, having come out a different door.

Serge had planned to jump Veale outside the bank,
but Veale surprised him. He was in his car and gone
thirty seconds after they spotted him, getting on Interstate 4 at Malfunction Junction.

Two blocks east of Tampa International Airport,
the death metal band Crucifixion Junkies blew an
electrical fuse. The bass player accidentally spilled a
beaker of chicken blood into his amp during a song
urging violence against pacifists.

Tampa was—maybe still is—death metal capital of
the country, and the Junkies were working their way
up the pile. An alternative newspaper, *The Gotham
City News*, praised the band's recent performance at

the Ritz Theatre in Ybor City for its "delightful ba-
nality." Their guitars were crucifixes.

The five men had identical stringy, sweat-soaked
hair. Because of low-paying gigs and unwise home
economics, the quintet could only afford to practice
in a U-Store-It shed in an industrial park next to
Tampa International.

The Junkies' shed was number 9 in a row of
garage-type units with roll-down doors, and they
had just locked themselves in for the third time.

With the door rolled down, the power outage left
them in darkness, and the five bumped into each
other and stubbed toes and cursed.

The lead singer flicked a Bic lighter.

"It's hot as hell in here," griped the bass player.
"Why can't we practice with the door open?"

"I told you, because of noise complaints from the
airport!" said the singer.

The singer had an inverted cross burned into his
forehead. He had done it himself by heating a stationery wax stamp from a religious store.

A cell phone rang and the lead singer picked it up
with the hand that wasn't holding the lighter. The
conversation was short and one-sided. The voice on
the other end, Charles Saffron's, gave him two names
passed along by Mo Grenadine. Told him to consider
it an offering to the devil. And an easy five grand.

After he hung up, the bass player started bitching
again. "This storage shed sucks! Why do we have to
get so sweaty? Why can't we have a decent place to
practice?"

"Because we are the servants of Satan!" yelled the singer. "We are the embodiment of pure, merciless evil! We are the fucking lords of hellfire!"

The Bic lighter started burning the singer's hand. "Ouch! Owww! Ouch!" He dropped it, and the fucking lords of hellfire were bumping around in the dark again.

Twelve

It wasn't called *The Cockroach Bay Story* until it became a paperback and the subsequently forgettable TV movie of the week starring Jan-Michael Vincent as the misunderstood-cop-fighting-the-system and Suzanne Somers as the feisty-but-vulnerable love interest who didn't exist in the real story.

It was 1984, early November.

The sky slipped from black to deep gray over the Florida Keys, but the sun was a good half hour under the horizon. A twin-engine Beechcraft flew north two hundred feet above Cudjoe Key and the radar blimp called *Fat Albert* that was reeled in and moored. The pilot looked down on a flock of ibis heading east and wisps of ground clouds moving over the shallows. All his transponders were turned off.

At that moment, an identical plane took off from Key West on a vector that would intersect with the first Beechcraft fifty miles off Chokoloskee. The air force was already trying to contact the first pilot and had scrambled a chase plane.

When the Beechcrafts were on top of each other, the Key West pilot switched off his transmitters and the first pilot flipped his on, using the same electronic signature. The Key West plane continued on into the western Everglades and landed at a suspicious make-shift runway in the Corkscrew Swamp. No contra-band, papers in order.

Except the chase plane didn't follow the decoy. The switch was imperfect; there was the slightest shift in signal that couldn't be explained by electronic anom-aly. The radar operators stayed with the first plane.

The pilot was heading for a dawn drop among the countless islands off Homosassa halfway up Florida's west coast, but now it was taking frantic evasive ac-tion trying to shake the air force prop-jet.

It flew recklessly under the center spans of the Sunshine Skyway bridge across Tampa Bay, causing rear-enders in the stunned rush-hour traffic. The chase plane radioed the Beechcraft without response. It dipped wings and pulled alongside. The Beechcraft went on autopilot.

Cockroach Bay drafts just a few feet deep and is generally accessible only to flats boats. Cool morn-ings on the changing tide are ideal. Great snook, maybe even tarpon in the passes in June.

Seven boats sat still in the water, damp with dew. A johnboat, skiffs, bass boats. Most had poling platforms. Everyone using electric motors or push poles and talking in whispers.

One angler spotted redfish near some mangrove roots. He baled the orange line three times into his right hand and shallowed his breath. His heart sped as he hesitated a last moment before presenting a black-and-red, one-eyed fly lure he had tied the night before.

He let out the line from his right hand as he increased the whipping action of the cast, back and forth over his head. He looked up and over his shoulder as he brought the line around for the last time.

The fisherman stopped and the line fell limp in the water, the lure bouncing off the roots and snagging. The fisherman continued staring back over his shoulder at the sky. Something was zooming down toward Cockroach Bay at the end of what appeared to be a large, colorful streamer. The fisherman grabbed his binoculars and could see that the object flapped two arms.

Before the pilot had jumped, he had tethered three duffel bags to his parachute harness with D-rings. He banked the plane in autopilot so the Beechcraft would be a hundred miles offshore when its fuel tanks went dry and it crashed into the Gulf of Mexico.

The bags added five hundred pounds of cocaine to the job of the parachute, and when it popped open, half the shroud lines tore out of their stitching. The canopy sucked inside out like an umbrella.

The pilot hit the water with such force that the marine patrol would later scoop much of him out with pool skimmers. Only one other fishing boat had noticed the pilot; everyone else too busy with their rods or reading the water. When the middle of Cockroach Bay exploded, they thought they were taking howitzer fire.

After a pause to gather bearings, they started outboard engines to investigate.

The duffel bags had ruptured, as well as most of the tightly wrapped wax bricks inside. It looked like a cocaine piñata. Eighty-six one-kilo blocks had stayed intact, and it was first-come-first-served.

All the fishermen knew each other, but nobody said a word or exchanged looks as they scooped in the white bricks with trout nets.

In less than five minutes, all the bricks had been retrieved, but the flats boats were a jumble of bumper cars in the center of Cockroach Bay, pointed every which way, anchor lines twisted up. A new boat appeared from Tampa Bay and raced into the narrow entrance channel to Cockroach Bay. Then another. Both blue, numerous radio and radar masts.

"Shit! DEA!" one fisherman yelled.

The fishing boats came to life in a cacophony of different rpm's and levels of engine maintenance. They shot out in all directions, some without pulling anchor. Two boats opened up and went off at forty-five degrees from each other. Their anchor lines caught and jerked them around to face each other.

No reaction time. The engines drove the boats into

each other head on, and the fiberglass hulls shattered in a thunderclap.

The other skiffs scattered, each boater having a second to run all the waterways through his mind and place his bet. The main part of Cockroach Bay is an open dogleg of water, but the shores and western section are labyrinthine with mangrove islands and oyster bars.

Two boats shot into the Hole in the Wall Pass, making a run for Tampa Bay at Buoy Pass. The one heading toward Dung Islet would try to pull his boat ashore in the mangroves and hide. The one that cut in below Big Cockroach Mound wagered on escaping through the pass at Snake Key.

The DEA boats were bigger, drafted deeper and had it all over the skiffs in horsepower. They could run them down in short order, but if the shallower, shorter skiffs made it to the mangroves, they'd maneuver around the DEA at will.

Two fishermen from Riverview raced toward a clearing wide enough to take boats of excessive beam. But stretching just under the water was a thin, granite-hard oyster bar. In this tide, the fishermen calculated, it was six inches below the surface. Enough for their hull, as long as it stayed up on a high-speed plane, but not enough for the propeller. The DEA boat was gaining. Too late to change course; they were meat.

Thirty yards apart. The DEA boat closing fast. One fisherman crouched in the back of the skiff, leaning over the engine. Two agents sat up on the bow, brac-ing themselves, less than five yards range and still closing, almost near enough to reach out and grab the fishermen.

The next step became obvious. The skiff was too close to the sanctuary of the mangroves for the DEA boat to head it off. The agents were going to ram it from behind and send it out of control into the mangroves. Or ride right over the top of them.

The fisherman up front worked the power-tilt and the engine began lifting up from the water at an angle. Then it stopped, something hung up. The fisherman in the back of the skiff reached all the way over the twenty-five-horsepower Evinrude with both arms and grabbed it under the head. He jerked it hard and the mechanism came free. It shot a rooster tail of spray and the propeller popped out of the water and spun at high frequency in the air just feet from the agents' faces.

The pilot of the DEA boat knew the second he saw the gray-white through the water.

The fisherman up front held the propeller in the air, thinking in split seconds. He had yanked it out of the water at the last possible moment. Pulling it up too soon would have dropped the skiff off its elevated plane, and the hull would crash onto the oyster bar. Wait too long and the engine's lower unit would have smashed into the bar.

The DEA pilot didn't have time to curse before he was thrown over the windshield. The agents on the bow were tossed in the water as the oyster bar peeled open the underside of the hull. The two-hundred-horsepower Mercury sputtered and sank thirty feet behind the boat, where it had snapped off, and water poured in the transom.

The fisherman dropped the engine on the mark, and, at the precise second the skiff threatened to sink down into the water and muck, it roared back to life atop the surface and disappeared into the mangroves.

A new player, a green airboat from the sheriff's department, skimmed into the entrance channel of Cockroach and took south.

The two fishermen who'd set off for Dung Islet had landed on another island southwest. There was no shore, only a mangrove-root barricade around a half-acre circle of sand. The anglers fought and high-stepped their way through the roots with arms full of white bricks. A DEA helicopter buzzed the islands, but the fishermen had pulled their boat into a cove of red mangroves and the whole small island sat under a cover of sabal palms and sea grapes and black mangroves. The dense canopy darkened the middle of the island, with countless flecks of light dancing through the branches onto the sand. When the wind blew the trees, it made a disco-ball effect.

The fishermen dropped the bricks in a pile and went back for another load. They heard the airboat and crouched. The airboat slowed as it approached the cove with the hidden skiff. The older fisherman absolutely despised cops, having done time twice. One time for killing his wife, back when you could do it and still get out of jail young. Despite the short sentence, and the fact he'd shot his wife four times in the head, he blamed all his life's problems on the cops who arrested him. He raised a .38 with a six-inch barrel through the mangroves.

They couldn't see the airboat yet, but the roar of the aircraft propeller told them where it was.

The deputy was sure he'd seen the boat come in here, and he scanned the mangroves as he idled across the water. His gun was drawn.

They saw each other at the same time. The deputy raised his pistol, but the fisherman already had his level.

He shot the deputy off the airboat. The deputy fell in a foot of water, losing his gun, and the airboat kept on going.

"I hate fucking cops," said the ex-con, climbing out of the groves. He stopped six feet in front of the deputy, pointing the gun.

The bullet had torn into the deputy's side, just below the ribs. It had missed everything vital and there wasn't excessive bleeding. The fisherman standing over him fired again. The deputy turned reflexively and the bullet clipped his spinal cord. He lost touch with his legs. He lay bleeding in the water and groaned and with great effort pushed himself up into a sitting position.

The fisherman was tall and narrow with a Marine recruit haircut, his scalp nicked in places. His was the skin of the unintelligent, ravaged by sun, alcohol, nicotine and infection. An oversized wallet stuck out of encrusted jeans with a long chain looping to his belt.

His T-shirt advertised intolerance. His corneas had a turbid fogginess and his teeth showed abject neglect. The tattoos had faded to the color of veins.

The other fisherman looked young, Hispanic and scared.

With the hand that wasn't holding the gun, the fisherman fit a filterless Camel in his lips and lit it with a Zippo, exhaling through his nose. He took another drag.

"Cops fucked up my life. And now looky what I got here. A helpless cop."

Another drag. "Got a wife?"

"Widower."

"That's too bad. Any kids?"

"A daughter," said the deputy.

"How old?"

"Ten."

"What's her name?"

"Susan."

"Little Suzie. My, my. Ten-year-olds are lip-smacking good. Think I'm gonna go look her up after I kill you. Get me some of that! Hoo-weee."

Another drag on the Camel, exhaling as he talked.

"I'm sure you got a wallet on you, should be an address in there. Head over to your house, meet little Miss Suzie. Does it bother you you'll never see her again? I'll bet you're thinking about that right now.

"Shoot, she won't have a momma or a poppa anymore. Well, orphans taste that much sweeter. And you won't be anywhere to protect your precious little daughter anymore."

His voice became serious. "Don't worry, 'cause I'm gonna kill the bitch right after! God, you'd love to have your gun right now, wouldn't you? Stupid fucking cop."

He aimed and cocked the revolver.

"No!"

The fisherman, caught by surprise, turned to the kid. The kid said, "You're a piece of shit!"

The fisherman laughed, then mocked him. "I'm no good. My fishing buddy doesn't love me!" He pointed the gun back at the deputy and cocked it again.

A handful of mud hit the side of the fisherman's head.

He yelled at the kid, "Goddamn you little fuckin' bastard!"

In a rage, he swung the gun at the kid and marched three deliberate steps, sloshing through the water. The kid backstepped and fell. The fisherman raised the gun fast, and a shot echoed through the mangroves. Then another. And another. Evenly spaced a second apart, the deputy firing like a machine. Long after the fisherman was dead, still firing the gun he had pulled from his ankle holster, emptying all fifteen shots from the automatic. Then pulling the trigger of the empty gun another dozen times.

The deputy dragged himself over to the body and started punching. "Motherfucker!" He found a rock and bashed the fisherman's face to pudding before the kid pulled him off.

The deputy dropped his head and shook. The kid

came out of the cove pulling the skiff with about half the cocaine still in it.

The deputy told him to stop and pointed the automatic.

"Gun's empty," the kid said as he cleared branches away from the engine.

"Stop!" the deputy yelled again.

The kid turned and saw the deputy had found his service revolver.

"You won't shoot me," the kid said. The kid used a radio in the skiff to report the injured deputy. Then he cranked the engine, took off and never looked back. The deputy had already lowered his gun.

The youth steered his coke boat on the most difficult escape route, up by Camp Key toward Little Cockroach Bay. He pulled the engine up and got in the water to walk the boat through the shallowest parts.

He knew the water because this was where he took his canoe when he wanted to be by himself. He'd bring heavy work gloves, a hammer and chisel, a jar of cocktail sauce and a box of Saltines. He'd lean over the side of the boat and chip his dinner off an oyster bar. This was when you could eat shellfish out of Tampa Bay and not wonder if it would kill you. He'd lie there, watching the sun go down over St. Pete, kept company by the roseates at the other end of the bar popping oysters loose with spoonbills.

The memories served him and he skirted every submerged bar on the plane. He ran along a seawall behind a remote strip of old waterfront homes and

turned into the mouth of the Little Manatee River at
Goat Island. Two miles upriver, he pulled the bilge
plug and sank the skiff in a deep snook hole under
a broken bridge. He waded along the shore of a
bayou, pulling a small Styrofoam cooler in the water
behind him with a rope. He climbed up the incline
where the bridge on the Tamiami Trail crossed the
river.

A thirty-six-year-old auto mechanic took seventeen
kilos home from Cockroach Bay, pried up the floor-
boards in his lawn mower shed, dug a hole five feet
down and dropped them in. They sat untouched for
three years. During that time the mechanic developed
a constellation of facial ticks, stayed home more than
the average house arrest, cultivated a malignant
strain of dandruff, and became therapeutically de-
pendent on quick-release anti-anxiety medication. In
the middle of one night in 1987, the third in a row
without sleep, the mechanic dug up the bricks and
talked to them until dawn. That's when he poured
gasoline on the bricks and himself. His neighbors
said the fire left nothing but a five-foot crater.

Twenty-four bricks went to a twenty-three-year-
old bachelor, a rising advertising executive in a flats
boat with power trim, jackplate and twice the
horsepower he would ever use. Unlike the mechanic,
the ad exec broke out his stash immediately, and the
party lasted until early December. The stuff ended
up on every level, nonporous surface in his apartment. At first it was only his close, trusted friends.

That lasted two days. Then it was open to secretaries, clerks at the mall, every neighbor in his complex and people off the street. The occupancy of his one-bedroom unit never dipped below fourteen. The incident was featured in an article in *Business World* magazine when it took down the entire ad agency, which experienced a rash of unplanned pregnancies, white-collar accidents requiring emergency-room treatment and absenteeism that eventually spiked at 92 percent. The executive moved back in with his parents in Ohio.

A refrigerator repairman from Wimauma named Zach had never even seen cocaine in his life. Now he was staring at two hundred grand of the stuff, piled on top of the VCR in his single-wide trailer on the edge of a cow pasture. After two days he thought, what the hell, a little dab'll do ya. He tore a hole in the middle of one brick and sniffed at the little spot of white at the end of his index finger. Then snorted harder. He found a straw in the utensil drawer and stuck it in the torn hole in the brick. The sheriff's department received predawn complaints of someone riding a cow down State Road 674.

Since the mid-seventies there have been numerous published studies all involving a box holding a bunch of mice, a wedge of cheese and a pile of cocaine. In all the studies, the mice eventually stayed up round the clock doing the coke until they were found starved to death next to the untouched cheese.

Zach was the human version. He left the trailer less and less, until he stopped leaving at all. He ordered out for pizza and Chinese, then ceased that. His entire daily routine consisted of snorting coke and peeking out windows. Coke-thinking told him it was a good time to clean all his guns.

Deputies approaching the trailer at night saw shafts of TV lights flickering out dozens of bullet holes in the front of the residence. Zach's wasted, perforated body lay on the couch. The deputies backed out as soon as they opened the front door and called in a haz mat team. Ripped-open bricks of coke were strewn through every room, and all the furniture was coated with a thick, white film as if someone had gone through the trailer shucking sacks of flour in the air.

Rumors swept across Florida's Gulf Coast about a fortune in buried coke out in Cockroach Bay, and soon the whole mangrove flats—desolate bastions of the nature lover—were overrun by a motley crew of every asshole in the bay area who could lay his hands on a motorboat, canoe, Jet Ski, sailboard, or raft. They camped on the islands, threw trash everywhere, did nothing useful, played repetitive, bad music on tape decks and otherwise turned the bay into a Grateful Dead jamboree gone to sea.

The digging went on for months. The Florida Marine Patrol posted guards at the offshore Indian mound at the mouth of Cockroach Bay. That was after a pickup full of Gators fans drove to Tallahassee for the annual showdown with the Florida State Seminoles with a dug-up skull on the hood.

Nobody found a gram, and the flats resumed normalcy.

Eleven months later, however, the curse continued. A team of senior archaeologists from Gainesville, reconstructing apocryphal pirate stories, searched the islands on the southwest side of Cockroach Bay with metal detectors.

After six hours, they found a buried crab trap and a penny from 1971. Then one of their headphones beeped and the display lit up red. Digging revealed the detector had pinged on the metal zipper of a scuba bag and the two lead dive weights inside, along with thirty pounds of white brick.

Later that night, back on land, police reported foiling a brazen heist at the Museum of Natural History, twelve naked elderly men in white beards carrying the complete skeleton of a *Tyrannosaurus rex* out the front door on their backs.

The last twelve kilos ever recovered had gone to a twenty-two-year-old named Serge A. Storms. He was caught immediately.

A marine patrol officer was standing by the guardrail where the Tamiami Trail bridge crossed the Little Manatee River. He'd seen Serge coming ashore with the cooler and was expecting to find undersized snook or maybe illegal stone crabs. When he saw the cocaine in the cooler, he was so flustered his hand couldn't find the snap on his holster on the first try.

Hillsborough Deputy Sheriff Samuel Tchoupitoulas testified for the defense during the young man's cocaine trial and again at sentencing. Based on his statements, Serge A. Storms only got a year and a day at Starke. The things they do to someone Serge's age up there would last him the rest of his days.

Thirteen

The subtleties of mast and boom escaped Stinky, Cheese-Dick and Ringworm, and the sails stayed furled. The fifty-horsepower Johnson outboard was different; it was a small internal combustion engine, and they thought of it as a stripped motorcycle hanging off the back of McJagger's sailboat.

Ringworm manned the helm, and the three motored down the coast of southwest Florida in tattooed cellulite majesty. The boat had everything. A generator, stocked freezer, full kitchen, air-conditioning.

First they went naked. Then they dined on filet mignon and racks of lamb with their hands, and kept their spill-proof nautical coffee mugs filled with Maker's Mark. They lay on the deck until they got too hot, and they dove into the Gulf until they were cool. Then back spread across the deck. Munch a chunk of leftover pheasant lying around, some more booze, and when it got too hot again, back in the water.

These were pirate days. Laughter filled their lives. Lots of "Yo-ho-ho" and "Shiver me timbers." Cheese-Dick made an eye patch from a piece of Naugahyde. Stinky sat on the bow with a brandy snifter filled to the brim like a bear with a hive of honey.

They hugged the coast, less than a mile offshore, and watched the New World go by. Stilt homes at Midnight Pass, the twenty-four-hour pier by Venice, the lighthouse outside Charlotte Harbor, and the shorebirds of Cayo Costa and Captiva.

At night, they sat under the stars and watched lights twinkle from Fort Myers Beach. There was a cool breeze and they were still naked, but sunburns kept them warm. And they were overcome by a strange, almost paranormal feeling they couldn't quite put their fingers on. They were clean.

Three silhouettes sagged in deck chairs in the moonlight. The engine was off, and the sailboat left an opalescent wake of microscopic sea critters as it rode the Gulf Stream quietly toward the Florida Keys. The name on the stern was *Serendipity*.

The next day everything went south. Stinky was the first to awake, before dawn. There was no land anymore, no more food, and they had run out of gas. He was sure they were in the Bermuda Triangle, and he panicked. He grabbed the metal box of emergency gear and emptied it on the deck. He dumped green dye in the water, flashed a mirror at the sky and blew a referee's whistle. He strapped on a bandolier of flares and threw a strobing distress beacon over-board. He set off smoke charges on the bow, stern and midships. Ringworm and Cheese-Dick awoke choking and confused in a cloud of smoke to the air horn Stinky was blowing.

McJagger's sailboat had every essential and useless piece of radar, sonar, laser, loran, radio, telephone, and satellite-tracking, course-charting, weather-forecasting, fish-finding doodad ever overpriced at a marine store. To the bikers, it was all ballast. And in a crisis, ballast went overboard. They ripped out the big floating black globe of a compass in front of the helm and over it went too.

Stinky was messing with a large flare gun, smacking the back of it with his palm when the breech refused to latch. Kept smacking it, and it kicked with a quiet whoosh, and a trail of smoke laced across the deck. Stinky followed the trail and saw Cheese-Dick, surprised, staring down at this thing the size of a soup can lodged in his chest. The white-hot phosphorus lit up the inside of his rib cage like a jack-o'-lantern. A small parachute popped out of him and he fell backward into the water.

"You killed Cheese-Dick!" shouted Ringworm.

"It wasn't me! It's the curse of The Triangle!" said Stinky. "We're all gonna die!"

Ringworm slapped him around. "We've got work to do."

By midday, Stinky was sure they were near Africa, but the rudder had them turning in an ever-tightening circle due west of Naples until they were spinning in exactly one spot like they were over a bathtub drain.

Stinky found a block of frozen squid at the bottom of the freezer and gnawed on it with his dog teeth.

Ringworm found a chart and tried to read it. Stinky, squid in his beard, passed the frozen bait.

Serge had visual contact with Veale's Aston Martin as they passed the Lakeland exits on Interstate 4. On the radio, a guy was hawking beef jerky and calling homosexuals "fudgepackers." As they pushed east, the signal faded a bit, and the stream of bigotry acquired the backbeat of an urban contemporary station out of Orlando. Serge thought it sounded like rap music of The Third Reich—Master Race MC Eichmann. He went to change stations, but the knob came off. He handed it to Coleman, who put it in his mouth.

After seventy miles, Veale took the ramp to the Bee Line Expressway, skirting under Orlando.

"I spy with my little eye . . ." said Coleman.

"No road games," said Serge.

"What about songs?"

"No songs."

"I'm bored," said Coleman.

"I gotta take a piss," said Sharon.

Veale continued his neurotic escape flight until he was stopped by the Atlantic Ocean. He decided to spend the night, and in the morning head to Port Canaveral and take his chances on a cruise ship to anywhere else. He pulled into the motel parking lot, grabbed a suitcase and gym bag and walked toward the office. Serge was right behind. The Barracuda bottomed out as it sailed into the lot, and Serge sprang from the car.

Veale saw him and sprinted into the motel office. Serge thought better of it and got back in the car, watching Veale at the counter through the office's front window. Sharon got out of the Barracuda and walked cross-legged to Launch Pad Food Mart, where they gave her a restroom key chained to a hockey stick.

"Sean?" said an unfamiliar voice.

Sean, signing a credit card receipt in the motel office, looked up. He tensed at first. But he remembered it was Halloween Week as he looked at Harpo Marx.

"It's Sean, right?"

Sean studied him but nothing came. "I'm sorry. I don't think I remember . . ."

"It's me! George Veale! You were at my Gasparilla party in Tampa!"

Another pause. Sean said, "You're the one who blew the parrot through the window with the cannon?"

"You remember!" said Veale. "You decide to join the krewe yet? We're a fun bunch!"

Sean found it hard to ditch people, and he tended to give boring, cloying, overbearing cretins far more time than appropriate, which only encouraged them to sink their hooks deeper into his life like jumbo ticks. By the time Sean ultimately had to cut them loose, his delivery was abrupt and socially messy. "I want you to go away."

Veale walked out of the motel office with Sean, continuing an excruciating conversation as if they were on speaking terms. Sean loaded luggage into his car as Veale went on and on.

Sean and David had arrived the day before, taking in the attractions at the Kennedy Space Center. Now they were checking out of the motel to drive to a viewing area for an evening launch of the space shuttle *Columbia*.

Veale offered to help load Sean's car, which Sean thought was a little much, but a nice gesture all the same. The twelve-year-old Chrysler, a land yacht, was backed to the room. With the trunk lid up, Veale was blocked from the Barracuda and Serge's field of vision.

"What's he doing?" asked Coleman.

"Stalling," said Serge.

Veale glanced around the edge of the trunk lid; Serge still there. Veale correctly figured all the money would be lost if Serge caught him with it. Veale studied the trunk while talking to Sean, looking for a place to stash the suitcase. At least that way, there was a chance he could catch up with Sean later and get it back.

When Sean returned to the room to get another load, Veale tried to fit his suitcase this way and that in the trunk, under the other bags. Nothing worked; too conspicuous. Veale stood up and scratched his stomach, and he noticed the false panel leading to the wheel well behind the backseat. It was attached with plastic snaps and came off easy. A few automotive tools back there, and the spare tire was smaller than he'd thought. Plenty of room.

When Sean got back to the car, Veale looked up from the trunk as innocently as someone hiding a body. Sean only thought: Please let this end.

"So, where are you going?" he asked Sean.

"To the launch."

"The launch?" asked Veale.

Sean looked around them on the edge of Highway A1A. There were a dozen signs for sandwich shops, hardware stores and a lingerie place that all had "space shuttle" in the names. Logos of the space shuttle were everywhere. One shuttle had a smile and was waving hello.

"The space shuttle launch," Sean said.

"Right, right," said Veale. "Then where?"

"Just down the coast."

"Where ya gonna stay?"

"Play it by ear."

And this cat-and-mouse went on in agony, Veale desperately trying to cling to some scrap of itinerary so he could link up with Sean and retrieve the suitcase. And Sean deliberately nebulous so there'd be no conceivable way Veale could bump into them. Sean wished David wasn't next door at the Moon Hut restaurant and could get him out of this.

Veale kept glancing across the parking lot.

"What are you looking at?"

"Nothing," said a jumpy Veale. "So you're going to Key West? You know any good hotels?"

"We're staying at the Purple Pelican," Sean said,

assuming Key West was way too far to have to worry about Veale—and hoping a direct answer might eclipse the interrogation.

"The Purple Pelican, eh?" said Veale. He repeated "Purple Pelican" in his head eight times and made himself picture one.

"I think I'll go to Key West too," said Veale. "Maybe stay at the Purple Pelican."

Sean put a Post-it note in his brain to cancel reservations at the Purple Pelican.

"So, what's there to do in Key West?" asked Veale.

"Please go away," said Sean.

Fourteen

George Veale looked out the window of the second-floor room at the Orbit Motel. He would have enjoyed the ocean view more if he hadn't been tied up in a chair and gagged with duct tape.

"We need ice," said Coleman, trying to figure out the TV remote.

"I need cigarettes," said Sharon.

Serge closed his eyes and tightened a second at the sound of their voices. He wrapped duct tape and braided cord to fasten the end of the twelve-gauge shotgun to Veale's throat. He looked up at Veale's face. "You need anything, George?"

George shook his head no.

Serge turned back to the others. "See, now George is a good travel companion. Low maintenance, a happy camper. You should try it."

Serge had booked the room in the name on the stolen Visa card with a hologram logo of the Orlando Magic. They'd carried Veale up the stairs. One second after Serge had produced the shotgun, Veale had spoken in tongues. He'd told them where the suitcase was and about Sean and the Purple Pelican and had made a river of other language sounds that never quite became words.

In the parking lot, Mo Grenadine got out of a Lincoln Town Car and walked over to George's Aston Martin. He reached under the bumper and removed the metal box held to the car with a magnet. He walked over to the Barracuda and slipped it under the bumper. He got back in the Lincoln and unwrapped a beef jerky.

Serge told Coleman he needed to go out for more equipment and to keep an eye on Veale. He returned in forty minutes with a bag from Radio Shanty and another from Space Shuttle Hardware and Paint. He sent Coleman down to the car to bring up more stuff.

Serge spread out the bags' contents on the avocado carpet: copper wire, twelve-volt electric motor, twine, more duct tape, folding sawhorse, batteries, solenoid switch, tin shears, souvenir space shuttle key fob and *Apollo 13* baseball cap. Total: $61.78.

Veale had lost the Harpo wig and hat in the initial struggle, taking refuge in the vending machine alcove and fending off Serge and Coleman with the plastic ice-machine scoop. Serge put the baseball cap on Veale's head and began assembling his purchases. Coleman made two trips to the car and brought up three brown grocery sacks, a giant bag of Doritos sticking out of one. Also, a Styrofoam cooler, a case of Busch and two large foam fish that clamped on a person's head to indicate support for the Florida Marlins professional baseball organization.

Coleman held up the teal fish and studied it with a single knitted brow.

"I completely forgot," Serge said, pulling one of the fish onto his head, "the World Series is on tonight. Marlins and Indians tied two games each. Boy, have we been out of the loop."

Coleman wiggled the foam fish onto his head, a tight fit. Serge turned to Sharon. "Sorry, I only got two."

"I'll live," she said.

She sat on the edge of the bed with her back to him, a crossed leg swinging. Smoking and staring at a lithograph on the wall of a clown and two fat ladies at the beach.

Coleman dumped the grocery bags out on the bed. Onion dip, kaiser rolls, roast beef, Dijon mustard, sesame sticks, beer nuts, rolling papers, pickled cauliflower, grapefruit juice that wasn't from concentrate, microwave Tupperware, spicy fried chicken, three newspapers, deli packs of German potato salad, coleslaw and Swedish meatballs, six postcards for a dollar, a four-pack of C batteries, and a half-size souvenir World Series baseball bat.

Serge tossed the batteries underhand to Sharon, and they bounced on the mattress next to her. "I got those for your little vibrating friend," he said. "Lock and load!"

He turned to Coleman: "I made sure the whole food pyramid was represented. You got your nacho food group, the beer group, the hoagie group and the buffalo wing group."

"Why'd you get Busch? You got fifty thousand in that shaving kit," said Coleman, arranging the beer cans in the cooler for maximum storage.

"Habit of the damned," said Serge. "Like a rat that gets electric shocks so long he forgets to leave the cage when the door's open."

Serge tossed one of the beers to Coleman. "Kill that," said Serge. "I need the can."

Coleman popped the top on the Busch and took a motel pen sitting on some stationery and slammed it down on the can, puncturing a second hole on the other side of the top. He raised the can and shotgunned it. He tossed the empty to Serge, who clipped it apart with the tin shears.

The television was on Florida Cable News. A gray-haired man behind the anchor desk reported near tragedy at a state motor vehicle office, where a man who had failed the eye exam pulled a gun and fired fifteen shots at the staff, hitting nobody.

With unflagging persistence, Coleman poked at the remote control, getting no results. He Cheech-and-Chonged on a joint and switched the TV back and forth from video mode, changed the clock, switched it from stereo to mono, turned the set off and on and ran the volume bar left and right across the screen. He found the channel button and mashed it through sixty channels, accompanied by his stoned narrative: ". . . William Shatner's personal tragedy, remove unwanted facial hair with electrical tape, the gallery of unsellable homes, fishing with Jimbo, Jazz with Junkies, phone sex for shut-ins . . ."

"Gimme that!" Serge smacked Coleman on top of the head with the remote. He switched the TV to the NASA channel. Seven astronauts in orange pressure suits waved as they walked to the launch gantry. "It stays on that channel!" Serge said, and he threw the remote in the toilet.

Coleman broke out the cocaine, jarring Sharon from her indolent stupor. She picked up the plastic space shuttle tray next to the sink and flung the cellophane-wrapped shuttle cups into the corner. Urgency got the better of precision, and they dumped a gram and ran two lumpy lines across the tray with Coleman's driver's license. Sharon leaned her face down and made one long, guttural pull.

"What's that? More crank?" said Serge.

"No," said Coleman, "blow," and leaned over to take his turn.

"Shit, every day it's something else," said Serge.

"If it's Thursday, this must be cocaine," Coleman replied.

"One day it's meth, another day psilocybin; you drop acid on Sunday and Percodan on Monday," said Serge. "Then it's Thai sticks. And what about the time you boiled those flowers that were supposed to be like Aborigines' curare darts? Can't you just pick a drug and stick with it?"

Coleman said, completely serious: "I don't want to get hooked."

Sharon interrupted in a silly, pouting voice, "My

other nostril's jealous." So they tore off two more mondo lines.

"Look, a microwave!" said Coleman. "Let's make some crack!"

Coleman ran downstairs to the Launch Pad Food Mart and came back with an orange brick of baking soda. He produced a sandwich bag with the rest of his cocaine, and mixed the batter in the Tupperware. He slid it in the microwave and he and Sharon watched it through the window with their faces two inches from the glass.

"Hey, Betty Crocker, you ever heard not to watch the food cook?" said Serge.

There was a pop and a bright flash, and flames flicked inside the microwave. "Fuck!" said Coleman. He popped open the microwave door and a bunch of smoke came out. The Tupperware was empty. Sharon craned her neck and sniffed at the cloud of smoke. She turned and punched Coleman in the chest. "You stupid dickwipe! You just burned up a whole fucking eight-ball! And it was good, too!"

"I got some meth left," Coleman said sheepishly.

"Give it to me!"

He handed it to her wrapped in BC Powder paper. She went to the bed and turned into the corner of the room, protective, a cavewoman just handed a barbecued pterodactyl wing.

Serge installed a tension rod in the top of the bathroom doorframe and stuck his feet in antigravity boots. He grabbed the rod and swung his feet like a gymnast to attach the boots with special hooks. He hung upside down, crossed his arms over his chest and did inverted sit-ups.

On TV, the astronauts were at the top of the gantry climbing into the shuttle. Coleman said he and Sharon were going out for ice and cigarettes.

"Get some Perrier," said Serge, looking like a bat.

When he got down, Serge resumed work on his contraption. He tied the space shuttle key chain to the end of the copper wire, where it hung like a plumb bob. His project complete, he said "Ta-da!" to Veale.

Coleman and Sharon returned, and Coleman sat on the bed near the window, dipping Doritos. All the other food was open and arranged around him in a semicircle, equidistant to his hands. He converted the motel-room garbage can into an auxiliary cooler, icing down four beers on the nightstand.

"Move over," Serge told Coleman. "And beer me."

Coleman butt-walked sideways a foot and a half, making room on the bed for Serge, and handed him a beer dripping ice water. Serge tasted how cold it was and told Coleman good work. He slipped it into a NASA can insulator, lay back against the headboard, and reached for the window.

The curtains were motel grade that blocked X-rays, and when they were drawn it was a moonless night. Serge yanked down on the pulley, and the afternoon sun squeezed their pupils.

Anyone walking along the second-floor balcony of the Orbit Motel would have seen two men with foam marlin on their heads sitting up against the backboard of one bed covered in wing sauce. On the other bed, a gorgeous coke floozy licking the inside of a burnt Tupperware container like a Saint Bernard. And toward the bathroom, a man tied up and gagged with a shotgun strapped to his neck and an intricate contraption in front of him that looked part train set, part time machine.

After a single beer, Serge was half drunk and thoroughly insane. He ranted about the importance of the space shuttle program and the national imagination. He got up in a squat on the bed like he was telling a spooky campfire tale about the Cold War and the space race. In a rapid series, he imitated a beeping *Sputnik*, the average terrified American and a laughing Nikita Khrushchev. He adopted the German accent of Werner von Braun. He made himself rigid and narrow like a Redstone rocket, and he flailed around the floor like Gus Grissom after his *Liberty Bell* capsule sank. He floated in slow motion for America's first space walk.

Even Sharon was listening now, lying on her stomach and leaning forward on elbows.

For linear tension, Serge downshifted to pianissimo as he told of the Christmas flight of *Apollo 8* and the astronauts seeing the first earthrise. He built furiously through the liftoff of *Apollo 11*. For climax, he reenacted a splashdown off the USS *Kitty Hawk*, jumping in the air, bonking his head on the ceiling and coming down in a cannonball on Coleman's bed. Food flew everywhere—nuts, chips, salads and cold cuts. A glop of slaw hit Veale in the ear. Sharon was standing, and two meatballs thwacked her on the shirt.

"Wow," Coleman said.

"Look at my fucking shirt!" screamed Sharon. They slapped the daylights out of each other. She punched him in the stomach and pulled him down on top of her on the bed. She pounded her hips into him fast. "Say more about rockets, hurry!"

Veale watched in terror as Serge finally called out: "Godspeed, John Glenn!"

"Yi-Yi-Yi-Yi-Yi-Yi-Yi-Yi-Yi!"

"Hey!" Coleman yelled at Veale. "Don't be looking at them! What are you, some kind of sicko? That's a very special and private thing."

Sharon stood in front of the bathroom mirror pulling out a world-class coke booger. But it still had a lot of coke on it, so she put it back. Coleman lit a spliff, held the toke and said, "What happened after the moon missions?"

"That brings us to the space shuttle," said Serge.

He walked over to Veale. "You're probably wondering what all this is," gesturing at the wires, motor and switches. "George, you ever see a shuttle launch? You ever *feel* a shuttle launch?"

Veale blinked and looked over at Sharon and Coleman. "George, you're not paying attention." Serge flicked his nose. "This is important."

Serge pointed at the space shuttle dangling on the wire next to Veale's chair. "That little shuttle is the vibration sensor. If it swings far enough side to side, the wire it's hanging from will make contact with the collar—that's the piece of the Busch can. That, in turn, sends the electric current to the solenoid, turning on the motor, which winds up the string attached to the trigger, and boom!"

Veale was pixilated.

"Trust me," said Serge.

He pointed at the television set, where a giant digital countdown clock at the Cape was under two hours and counting. Serge turned the TV set to face Veale.

"That okay? Loud enough?"

George was blank.

"Good," said Serge. "Now when the shuttle first takes off, you won't hear anything, because of the distance. Give it, say, a minute, and you'll start to hear a rumble. A few seconds later, the shock waves hit. That'll make the little shuttle swing. As the real shuttle gets louder, it'll set up a harmonic rhythm with the little shuttle, making it swing more and more until it contacts the collar and sets off the shotgun. Whattaya think? Pretty clever?"

Still nothing from Veale.

"Now, if you're brave, you can try to counteract the swinging motion by shaking the chair a little, but it's really hard and you'll probably set the gun off early.

"And if you try to escape, it'll set it off too."

Serge shook the side of the chair and the shuttle swung into the beer-can collar, making a spark. The motor clicked on and the string pulled the trigger, making a dry click.

Veale felt the dry fire of the trigger vibrate through the barrel pressed against his throat. He thrashed wildly and screamed under the tape.

"It's not loaded yet," Serge said.

But Veale kept jerking around anyway, trying to wriggle the tape off his mouth.

"George," said Serge, "are you trying to tell me to take off the tape? You want to say something?"

Veale nodded yes urgently, his chin hitting the barrel of the shotgun. Serge pulled back the tape.

"I swear, I've told you everything!" said Veale.

Serge smiled as he put the tape back on Veale's mouth. "I know you have."

Fifteen

In what should have been a lazy sunset, thousands of motorists headed up A1A, bumper to bumper, a necklace of headlights along the shore from Satellite Beach to the Cape. They came from all over, in sedans, vans, sports cars and station wagons, ready to tailgate.

Sean and David drove over the causeway bridge near Port Canaveral. Sean, behind the wheel, turned onto the Kennedy Parkway and headed north until the security checkpoint. David had gotten a visitor's pass through work, and the guard noted the red placard in the windshield and waved them through.

Sean pointed out the Vehicle Assembly Building to David. As they approached the causeway at the Banana River, the space shuttle appeared over the water, in a crossfire of spotlights.

He followed the other cars onto the grass and parked. People unloaded lawn chairs from trunks, and kids ran around in pajamas. Parents broke out pizzas and KFC boxes. A souvenir trailer did brisk business in NASA pennants, mugs, hats, shot glasses and freeze-dried astronaut ice cream.

Back at the guard station, an untuned Barracuda backfired and the radio played "Tear the Roof off the Sucker" through the open windows.

Serge, in the driver's seat, sipped a steaming cup of Addiction World coffee and obnoxiously flapped a visitor's pass at the guard. Back at the convenience store, Serge had traded a hundred-dollar bill for the pass with a stunned family from Ocala.

The guard bent down and saw Coleman in the passenger seat, wearing the Marlin hat and raising a Slurpee cup to him in toast; Sharon sat in back with arms crossed, almost biting through the cigarette in her mouth. The guard couldn't wait to wave them through.

They parked on the causeway and spread motel towels. "What do we do now?" asked Coleman. "I mean about the money?"

"Nothing. We'll have to wait until that guy checks in at the Purple Pelican. Until then we're on vacation," said Serge. "How'd you like to see the real Florida?"

Sharon sneaked back in the car and snorted crank off a floor mat. Coleman sat on the edge of the Banana River drinking seven beers. Serge said he should probably move back from the water. The river is normally full of alligators, he said. But before each launch, trappers come in and secretly remove them. They're bound to miss a few.

"I think I see one!" said a drunk Coleman, pointing at a piece of cheeseburger floating by.

"I think you're right," said Serge, and Coleman scooted back to where Serge was sitting.

Communications between launch control and the shuttle were broadcast from loudspeakers attached to poles and echoed by hundreds of car radios tuned to local coverage. There were brief waves of celebration and relief at the countdown milestones. One hour, thirty minutes, ten minutes . . .

Sean and David sat in lawn chairs with binoculars and Chee-tos. They heard a commotion and turned up the riverbank. An intoxicated man with a foam fish on his head was beating a piece of litter on the edge of the water with a tire iron.

The loudspeakers broadcast that the weather was acceptable, and a NASA voice told the astronauts to "have a nice ride." Following the loudspeakers' cue, Sean and David and the rest of the crowd shouted in unison: ". . . ten, nine, eight, seven, six, five . . ."

In the distance were quiet pops and clicks. A flushing sound as tons of water hit the pad, a flicker of light, and the space shuttle disappeared as white smoke obscured everything. A David Copperfield trick. The crowd leaned forward, holding its breath. And after a theatrical delay, the space shuttle *Columbia* slowly poked its nose out of the top of the cloud, climbing sluggishly and twisting as the thrusters gimbaled.

A deep, tunneling sound began to build, that giant

worm from *Dune* coming straight at them, and the shock wave hit. It hammered up from the ground like they were standing on a big stereo speaker. A gray mass of birds filled the air in confusion over the distant marsh, and Serge thought of the Bible and locusts.

Veale watched the shuttle rising on TV but didn't hear anything. One of Serge's half-finished Perriers rested on the dresser, and Veale saw the surface of the mineral water start to vibrate. He heard a faraway rumble and looked down at the little shuttle hanging from the wire, starting to swing gently.

Veale prayed the shuttle would hurry up, get itself high enough in the air so the sound would peak before it was strong enough to trigger the booby trap. The little shuttle swung a bit farther, but still a good margin to go. And the big shuttle on TV now a healthy way up in the sky. Looking good for Veale. The distance and the speed of sound were deceptive, however, and a violent, tearing roar blew through the room. When the little shuttle swung into the collar and sparked, Veale had a massive heart attack.

It felt like a wrecking ball was pressing down on his chest. He saw the electric motor click on and wind string. The shuttle was so loud that nobody back in Cocoa Beach heard anything when Veale's eyes slammed wide open for good.

Serge insisted they have a late dinner at Bernard's Surf, but Sharon complained that she couldn't see what the big deal was.

"The big deal, you communist, is that the heroes who risked their lives for your freedom ate dinner there!"

"Whatever," said Sharon, rubbing a fingertip of crystal meth around her gums.

On the way to their table, Serge pointed out photos on the walls of Deke Slayton eating dinner and astronauts in convertibles waving to crowds during a parade that had passed the restaurant in 1962.

Coleman went to the restroom. Two guys talking sports at the hand-blowing machines.

He came running back to the table. "We forgot about the World Series!"

"Damn!" said Serge. He threw down a hundred. "Let's roll!"

"Fuck the World Series," Sharon said a little too loudly, turning heads. "You're not going anywhere. I'm not moving."

Serge blew. "Then you'll be a fucking pedestrian, 'cause I'm taking the car. No woman is gonna tell me I can't watch the World Series! Come on, Coleman."

The dining room was mortified, but two retired guys at a nearby table gave Serge a thumbs-up. Sharon cursed under her breath and chased them out.

Serge pushed the Barracuda two miles up A1A to the Cocoa Beach Pier. They walked eight hundred feet to the end and grabbed stools under a thatched hut.

It was getting late, windy and cold. Around the bar was a wide walkway, where men in rain slickers threw cast nets and landed pompano and jack with

heavy rods. Under the hut's rafters, the bar had plywood shutters that swung down to jam the wind. The
north and east sides of the bar were shuttered.

It was the third inning, and the three sat at the
southwest corner of the bar, watching a snowy TV
set whose guts crackled in the salt air like bacon.
Serge considered it a plus.

"Rumrunners?" asked the bartender.

"Go for it," said Coleman. Serge got a Dr Pepper.

The bartender—"Call me Gary"—brought back
hurricane glasses filled red. Serge had already stuck
a hundred under an ashtray and Gary brightened.
With an awkward attempt at style, Gary took a bottle
of Bacardi 151 and filled Coleman's and Sharon's
straws with a funnel.

"Hit it all at once so the rumrunner chases it," he
said. Coleman and Sharon complied.

The Indians led four–two and the bar was a dirge.
Sharon was still in a snit, and it needled Serge more
as Florida continued losing.

In the sixth inning, with one swing of the bat,
Moises Alou's three-run homer put the Marlins in the
lead. The bar erupted.

Mid-celebration, the TV exploded, shooting Roman
candles of electronic gizzards into the sea. Everyone
ducked. A fuse blew, cutting power to the pier. The
bar was in darkness except for a fire burning inside
the TV that cast a flickering glow through its vent
slits.

"Somebody do something!" said one customer. A
second responded by grabbing a fire extinguisher.

"No!" said the first customer. "Someone get another TV!"

Serge jogged to the car, retrieved a stolen five-inch battery-powered set, and ran back up the boardwalk. The bar huddled intimately around the unit. When the Marlins held on to win, the bar celebrated again. Serge left the hundred.

Sixteen

Early the next afternoon, a private twin-engine jet from the Lesser Antilles touched down at Tampa International Airport. A three-step staircase hydraulically unfolded from the fuselage. Four men in linen suits jumped to the tarmac without touching any of the steps and ran to a waiting Mercedes limousine.

A chauffeur held the back door open, and they climbed in. The tallest got in the driver's seat and took off, leaving the chauffeur on the runway.

Serge dumped the rest of his medicine down the toilet and announced he would show Coleman and Sharon the sights.

"Our lucky day," said Sharon.

Serge ran the Barracuda up to eighty heading north into Titusville on US 1. At the edge of the Indian River, he turned the wheel, hit the brakes and did a power slide into a public park. He jumped out with his camera. Sharon and Coleman straggled.

"There it is, the monument to the original *Mercury* 7 astronauts. There's another one out on the air station." They looked up at a giant aluminum 7 in a circle with a cross and a squiggly line.

"It looks like the symbol for the artist formerly known as Prince," said Sharon.

Serge glared at her.

"Did I see a place back there where we can get some beer?" said Coleman.

"Forget the beer," said Serge. "Look! Their handprints are in bronze all around the base."

Coleman put his hands in the prints for comparison, and asked about beer again.

They went to the Kennedy Space Center and Serge showed them space capsules that looked safe as barrels that had gone over Niagara Falls. Coleman wanted to buy a space helmet. Sharon tried to score dope in the rocket garden.

The Barracuda raced south from the center. They poked their heads in the Shuttle Grill and Bagel World and Alma's Italian restaurant, for the space memorabilia on the walls.

Alma's had a large photo of an astronaut walking on the Sea of Storms during *Apollo 12*. Inscribed: "I was the first man in history to eat spaghetti on the moon, but believe me it didn't equal yours. Alan Bean."

A waitress walked up with menus cradled. "Will that be three for lunch?"

"No," said Serge. "Just looking at the artifacts. But I'll take one of those menus, for my archives." He took a picture of the picture and herded Coleman and Sharon out the door.

The front wheels of the Barracuda left the ground as he crested the drawbridge onto the Canaveral Peninsula. He passed the turning basin and the cruise ships and slowed so he wouldn't draw suspicion at the air force guard station. "Going to the museum," he said, and the guard stepped back and motioned them on.

Serge told them the rocket gantries over the trees to their right were used for *Delta* and *Titan* launches. "The *Titans* are really top-secret spy shit."

Sharon blew an irritated breath, but Coleman was into the six-pack he'd picked up at Blast Off! Mart.

They parked in an empty lot by an anonymous beige building. Serge got out and danced around with his arms in the air like Rocky. "The Air Force Space and Missile Museum!" He stopped abruptly and ran inside.

When Sharon and Coleman walked in, Serge and two old guys were sitting on a couch in the museum's office, talking fast in a language they didn't understand. MA-6, Agena, geosynchronous, apogee kick, perigee burn, fly-by-wire, ha-ha-ha-ha.

Serge finally came to the office door, wiping tears of laughter from his eyes. He gestured back to the men, in their seventies. "These guys used to run the show. They manned the launches. Now they volunteer at this museum. The tour buses stop for a few minutes, but other than that, nobody comes out. I don't get it."

He pointed to a tiny window with green glass that looked a foot thick. "This was the blockhouse. Right out there they launched *Explorer*, our nation's first satellite."

Sharon twirled a finger. Big woop.

"You're killing the moment for me!" Serge snapped. "Here, for heaven's sake!" He reached in his pocket and tossed her the twisted-up corner of a sandwich baggie with cocaine packed down in the tip. He'd found it along the baseboard while sanitizing the motel room and had squirreled it away for just such an emergency.

"We have a hike ahead of us." Serge led them out of the blockhouse and they walked down a row of old launch pads, hundreds of yards through weeds and stickers and broken concrete. At the other end of the field was another beige building, but this one boarded up and locked, no employees. The first blockhouse was quiet, this was dead. Not a soul or sound in any direction.

Sharon finished the coke, stuck her tongue down into the corner of the baggie, then tossed it over her shoulder.

Serge told them that one May morning in 1961, every television set in the country had been tuned to this exact spot. Alan Shepard walking out in his silver pressure suit and climbing into the Mercury-Redstone to become the first American in space.

"Now look at the place!" said Serge. "It's like an abandoned gas station!"

There was a replica of the rocket standing on the

pad. Sharon walked up to it, pulled a key chain out of her pocket, and gouged a line through the paint.

Serge screamed and grabbed her arm. "Our heritage!"

"Your heritage, space boy, not mine!"

He slapped her across the face. She slapped him back. He knocked her down. She tried to get away by scrambling under the rocket, but Serge crawled in after her.

Coleman looked around the horizon, but they were still alone. He walked over to the blockhouse and read a plaque, giving Serge and Sharon their privacy.

Surf shacks and honky-tonks dotted the seaside south of Cape Canaveral. RVs squatted roadside at untended lots until they were told to move on.

"We need to buy more guns," said Serge.

"We're convicted felons," said Coleman. "And what about background checks and the waiting period?"

"That's what gun shows are for," said Serge.

The Barracuda didn't slow as it hit the swale at the Melbourne Armory. The marquee read, "Treasure Coast Gun Show," and below, "Limited-edition David Duke action figures, $25."

A large sign greeted visitors at an expansive table inside the hall: "Private dealer. We don't ask, you don't tell!"

Gun advocates had preserved the "private dealer" clause, exempting a bevy of regulations. Ostensibly, it was meant to allow neighborly sales over the backyard fence. Shockingly, it was used by arms dealers to place untraceable guns in the hands of untraceable criminals. Police chiefs across Florida cried foul. The gun lobby simultaneously labeled them jackboot fascists and ACLU bung-fodder.

The smiling salesman looked like no private dealer Serge had ever seen. His table was ninety feet long and staffed by eight salespeople in uniforms. He had two computerized cash registers and three VISA machines. A stack of background registration forms sat on a bottom shelf, holding up dust. The dealer wore a camouflage vest with mesh pockets, straps, clips, rings and secret compartments. He had a button pinned to the right breast pocket that read "Holy Moly is Right!"

Serge and Coleman squinted down the sights of assault pistols, which they accidentally pointed around the convention floor at other shoppers, who absentmindedly pointed guns back. Five salesmen clustered around Sharon, fitting her with a new line of sexy feminine body armor that made her look like Barbarella. She strolled and spun, modeling.

"It's you," said Serge.

Serge slapped a fifty-pack of hundred-dollar bills on the glass display case. Without even showing his false driver's license, Serge walked out the door with TEC-9 and MAC-10 burp guns, two Peacemakers, three hunting rifles, scopes and Sharon's Kevlar ensemble. He picked up a muzzle suppressor and the dealer showed him how to make it an operational silencer—"It's your Constitutional right."

* * *

In the high-rise offices of New England Life and Casualty, financial miscreation had reduced the company to a skeleton staff of agents, secretaries, mistresses and owners' nephews. None had left the forty-second-floor office yet, even though it was eight at night. None dared move an inch.

The only activity in the office was four Costa Gordan men in linen suits pacing. They had machine guns, small Israeli models with straps over the shoulder like purses. The leader had a Colt Python .357 with a laser sight, and kept dialing a phone number without success and cursing. The yuppie staff were surprised they could see no chest hairs or gold chains.

Costa Gorda was a small island nation in the Lesser Antilles. It was so small, in fact, that it existed only on paper, and it rented a post office box and a conference room on the island of Grenada. The sole purpose of Costa Gorda was to create jurisdictional confusion for shell corporations, offshore bankers, dummy partnerships, shadow firms, tax shelters and eighty-year-old Nazis. During the holidays it sold cheese wheels by catalog.

One of Costa Gorda's biggest clients was the Mierda Cartel, the sixty-eighth-largest cocaine producer in the world. Which was last place.

The law-abiding residents of Grenada acted intimidated, out of pity for their local cartel, which received unrelenting derision from the rest of the established cocaine world. At ribbon-cuttings, never an introduction; at banquets, never a trophy. In the yearbook they were named "most likely to be extradited."

The rare modicum of respect came when they flew into Tampa International, where they were mistaken for the thirty-fourth-largest cartel in the world.

Now, forty-two floors up, they had the complete attention of the New England Life staff.

At unequal intervals, the four stuck tiny crystal injectors in their noses and hit small amounts of blow, filling the office with an irregular nasal syncopation. They had broken into the liquor cabinet an hour ago and each carried a personal fifth at his side. They cranked up the stereo in the cabinet, "Hot Stuff" by the Rolling Stones.

One of the men half-stood, half-sat on the edge of a secretary's desk, trying to make time. Two looked west out the floor-to-ceiling window, mesmerized by the lights on Bayshore Boulevard and at MacDill Air Force Base. The tallest sat behind the office's largest desk in a high-back leather chair, still trying to work the phone, still swearing. The epoxy used to patch the six bullet holes in the back of the chair didn't quite match the burgundy.

One Costa Gordan found an ottoman on•casters. He put one foot on it and pushed himself around the office skateboard style. Then he got up on it with both feet and hung ten, sailing across the marble floor. "Look at me, everyone. I'm surfing!"

A secretary with big red hair and a Brooklyn

twang finally told the leader, "You have to dial nine to get out."

"Fuck!" said the leader, then smiled at the secretary.

This time the call connected and he spun the chair around, disappeared behind its back facing out the window. It was a quick conversation with an unmistakable tone. He slammed the receiver. "Damn!"

The leader walked to a spot in the middle of the office and turned slowly around the room with the Magnum so the laser sight scanned everyone's face.

"We're going to have a little party," he said.

He dumped two ounces of coke out on an onyx credenza. In the background, from left to right, a Costa Gordan skated fast across the office floor on an ottoman, arms straight out, flapping for balance.

A Lamborghini Countach sped past the Desert Inn in Yeehaw Junction, heading east. Charles Saffron punched furiously at the cell phone's button, still unable to reach Mo Grenadine.

He threw the phone down and it rang instantly. He picked it back up. "Hello!"

"We want our fucking five million." The accent was Costa Gordan. Saffron backpedaled with excuses.

"What are you doing heading for the east coast?" said the Costa Gordan. "Trying to run like a dog?"

"No, I'm tracking the thieves—to get your money back," said Saffron. "I'm getting close. Any day now. . . . What's all that music? Is that my Stones CD?"

"Saffron, you goat-fucker. We're gonna cut your *cojones* off and stuff 'em . . ."

"Your signal's breaking up," said Saffron, holding the phone at arm's length and making static sounds with his mouth. "I'm losing you. I can't hear . . ." And he hung up.

Back in Tampa, Saffron's employees were lined up single-file and made to snort coke at gunpoint. They were then forced into a second line, where a smiling Costa Gordan was pouring shots.

The cartel cycled everyone through both lines three times and sent them to their desks. Some of the staff swayed and forgot the no-talking rule. The leader had to keep threatening with the gun for them to shut up, and they'd look surprised, put hands over their mouths and giggle.

One of the employees raised his hand.

"This isn't school!" the tallest Latin said incredulously. "We don't take questions!"

"Yeah, but I'm real curious," said the accountant, his head lolling from the shots. "How do you smuggle cocaine?"

"Yeah, what do you hide it in?" asked the secretary.

"That's a secret!" said the Costa Gordan.

"I saw in the newspapers where they call you the Keystone Cartel," said someone else.

"The lies of Yankee pigs!" said the Costa Gordan.

"Do you hide it in your underwear?"

"Do you swallow balloons on tiny strings that come up your throat and are tied to your back teeth?"

"Shut up! Everyone! Right now!" said the Costa Gordan, waving the pistol fast around the room.

"I think you should pipe it in a slurry in long tubes."

"You should get a running start and run right up to the border and throw it really hard."

"You should sew it inside chickens."

"EVERYBODY SHUT UP!"

There was a tremendous crash. They all ran to the west window, now a jagged opening. Wind gusted through the hole high above downtown Tampa, knocking loose sharp triangles of safety glass, and they followed the rest of the window to the pavement.

Forty-two floors below on Ashley Street, a Costa Gordan in a suit lay on the sidewalk in a bed of glass ground to diamonds. The roof of a parked Jaguar was caved in from an ottoman.

"Shit!" said the leader. He raised his arms to get the room's attention. "Okay, we gotta leave now. Nobody move . . . and count to ten thousand. What's that state you say to count slow?"

"Mississippi," said Brooklyn.

"Mississippi, that's it," the leader said. "Let me hear all of you!"

The staff: "One Mississippi, two Mississippi, three Mississippi . . ."

The Mierda Cartel sprinted for the elevators.

Seventeen

Sean and David stood in silent shock upon entering their magnificent four-hundred-dollar room at the Palm Beach Surfside. They just stared out the window at the Atlantic Ocean and the tops of the palm trees barely peeking up over the balcony. Then they shook hands vigorously and back-slapped and insulted each other.

The room came with three courtesy newspapers, and they were soon spread over the beds, all turned to the sports sections, World Series coverage.

"You thinking what I'm thinking?" asked Sean.

"Who would have thought that back when we planned the trip . . ."

"If Cleveland wins tonight, we'll be forced to go to game seven in Miami. . . ."

They lapsed into a silliness that they only exhibited around each other and that had marked every reunion since high school.

"There'll be no choice."

"We couldn't help ourselves."

"Decades of genetic memory."

"A tractor beam grabbed us."

Laughing until hurting, dopamine everywhere.

Sean pointed at one paper that predicted scalping at one to two hundred dollars a ticket.

David pulled two Michelobs from the half-size room refrigerator. "Remind me to go to the convenience store to replace these. Otherwise they're five bucks each."

Sean admired David's drive and achievement. David's varsity good looks and poise still made him the most popular man in any room. He was the proverbial man that the women wanted and the men wanted to be like. In social settings, David always recognized and included Sean, who otherwise would have been happy to sit on the rim of the action.

David knew that Sean would say he was crazy if David ever told Sean that he secretly looked up to him. He viewed Sean as a considerate, honest family man with effortless character that exceeded his own.

That didn't stop David from teasing Sean mercilessly about his job.

David had the exciting position at the state attorney's office, but it was Sean who got the press.

First was a small profile article in *Tampa Business Times*, then the cover of *Tampa Bay* magazine and front-page articles in both *The Tampa Tribune* and the *St. Petersburg Times*.

While still the most junior advertising executive at Turbo-Image Corp., Sean had been dubbed "the Wizard" and "the Magician" in the media, and "Houdini" around the office.

As custom at Turbo-Image, the newest executives got the undesirable accounts. Sean was dealt the legislative reelection campaign of Mo Grenadine, following his problems in the hot tub. In-house, the account was considered a dog with fleas.

Nobody expected success—just the motions of work so Turbo could bill the hours. Sean went at it with an appreciation for the absurd, and he employed the Big Tobacco Theorem: Tell reality-defying lies with a straight face. He didn't consider it dishonesty but low comedy.

Sean launched a media campaign that blamed Mo's arrest on unspeakable acts of the newest threat to America: Urban Homosexual Terrorists. He said scientists had linked gun control to child molestation.

Sean wrote Mo's speeches and platform as those of a smug, sanctimonious sonuvabitch. His scripted attacks on the unfortunate, unpopular and downtrodden were the stuff of burlesque.

When Mo was reelected in a landslide, Turbo-Image was reviled on the editorial pages and praised in the business sections. Political wags proclaimed Sean a genius for setting up voter registration booths outside monster truck shows.

The senior executives at Turbo considered it a fluke. But when a scandal-pocked minister from north Tampa arrived at the offices of Turbo-Image with flames licking at his career, he would settle for none other than Sean Breen.

This wasn't funny anymore. This time his goal wasn't satire but sabotage.

Sean highlighted all folly and foibles in capital letters. The minister's coterie of bottom-feeding sycophants asked why Sean's press releases and speeches kept repeating the words "embezzlement," "extortion," "mistresses" and "tax evasion" in big, bold letters. And besides, they said, Sean was black! But the minister silenced them, saying that on their brightest day they couldn't comprehend what Sean was doing.

What Sean was doing was trying to sink the preacher. Press releases said that piles of cash diverted from church accounts were in "safekeeping from Satan." Luxury cars, diamonds, furs and beach houses bought with church funds were used to shelter the donations from "agents of the devil." Paid-off bimbos became salaried financial advisers whose advice was so valuable that God had told him not to reveal it lest secular institutions find out. He told the faithful to show that they were appalled by the media's bias toward the Antichrist—and asked them to write large checks directly to the minister's personal checking account.

The minister's bank account ballooned to seven digits while he was in jail on a five-hundred-count indictment.

New accounts to Turbo-Image came quickly and furiously. The more Sean tried to blow the campaigns, the more successful he became.

The Rapid Response corporation sought a makeover for its flagging Florida chain of convenience

stores. Sean renamed it "Addiction World" with
signs showing a smiley face with Spirograph eyes.
He introduced the Addiction World combo box: a
six-pack of beer, a pack of cigarettes and a lottery
ticket. The men's pack also had a copy of *Hustler*; the
women's pack a coupon for a pint of Häagen-Dazs
from the freezer.

Managers were skeptical but followed Sean's di-
rective to create entrance bulwarks of wine, malt liquor, tropical coolers, rolling papers, cigars and diet
pills. Addiction World earnings went vertical, and
imitators soon followed: Stoked Stores, Buzz Mart
and Drink-n-Drive.

The only account that didn't work out wasn't
Sean's fault.

The Florida Department of Agriculture needed to
change public perception in Tampa Bay. It was getting excessive grief for fighting the medfly by essentially carpet-bombing the area with the insecticide
known as malathion.

Sean proposed a campaign featuring Malley the
Dancing Malathion Bear. Early focus groups showed
he was so right, residents would start putting malathion on their cereal. A low-cost character actor was
suited up as a tap-dancing panda and began rehears-
ing. Instead of a cane, he held a spray wand used for
ground application of the insecticide. He pulled the
sprayer's trigger at prearranged points in his dance
routine, and the footlights lit up a mist over Malley's
head reminiscent of *Singin' in the Rain*.

Except the stage crew made the mistake of using real malathion during rehearsal.

Television news crews assembled for Malley's debut at the Li'l Bucs preschool near Tampa Stadium. By the time Malley tapped his way out in front of the five-year-olds, he looked drunk. Malley careened off the teacher's desk and fell to all fours, projectile-vomiting out the mouth hole of the bear mask.

The actor gasped for air, but the catch on the bear's head was stuck. Paramedics finally cut off the bear's snout with a circular saw used in traffic extrications. Tots shrieked, and news cameras recorded Malley's exit on a stretcher.

As the *Serendipity* drifted farther from shore and the batteries went dead, Stinky and Ringworm decided the only rational option was to finish off the booze.

When they awoke the next day, they were on another boat.

It was a big boat, and the two were sitting down on the swim platform. Cement blocks sat next to them. There were chains around their necks and their hands and feet were tied.

The boater kneeled behind the transom. He stuck a Barbie in his mouth. The boater's pulse rate seemed to rise. Without warning, he reached over with a gaff and toppled a cement block off the swim platform. Stinky was jerked by the neck off the platform and beneath the waves.

Ringworm stared up into the eyes of a long-gone

fetish aficionado getting off. Ringworm visited a land of panic that few ever know; he flopped around the platform, a fish on a hot sidewalk. The boater's breathing became more labored. He reached over again with the gaff. This time he pushed the block up on its edge to a teetering point and held it.

Ringworm's eyes locked on the cement block as it balanced precariously. The boater pushed the gaff and the block slipped and splashed into the water.

Eighteen

Serge crossed the Royal Palm Bridge onto Palm Beach at one o'clock and by one-ten had abandoned the car on the side of Worth Avenue.

"We don't need to live like this," he said of the car and everything. "We got more than forty grand left."

They took three shoulder bags from the trunk and walked up the avenue.

"Say whatever you want about Palm Beach," said Serge, "but ya gotta admit they have some bitchin' shrubbery."

They window-shopped for a block and Serge waved them into a boutique. "We have a wardrobe situation to fix."

Coleman held an Armani up in the mirror and Sharon checked out an Anna Sui. The staff blanched. Near the entrance, Serge found a silver service. "Ooooooo. Com-ple-men-tary cof-fee."

The head salesman, on bum patrol, asked Serge pointedly, "Can I help you?"

Serge tried to guess the man's weight as he took an extra-slow sip of coffee, forcing up the salesman's blood pressure.

"I'd like to see something that screams Miami Beach!" said Serge with caffeine confidence.

"Sir," the salesman said with a sweep of his hand that dismissed Serge, "I don't think you—"

"You don't think what?" Serge yelled, and stuck ten thousand dollars in the man's face. "Look at this wad, fuck-wad!"

For the next hour, they enjoyed free champagne and cigars as they spent the whole ten large.

Serge modeled a white number with a pink Ralph Lauren T-shirt. "Am I Don Johnson yet?" he asked.

The clothes cost eight of the ten thousand. Then Serge whispered in the manager's ear. The manager nodded and Serge stuck the other two grand in one of the manager's inside coat pockets. The manager held a private conversation with the salesman who had tried to roust Serge. There was a disagreement and the manager shouted down the salesman, who walked up to Serge and said nothing.

Serge punched him in the face, waved to the manager and left.

On Worth Avenue, a man got out of a Lincoln and retrieved a metal box from the bumper of an abandoned Barracuda. He parked outside a clothing store and read the sports section.

Coleman had gone Parisian and Sharon chose a low-cut red affair from Milan. They caught a taxi to

Palm Beach Exotic Motors, where the outfits drew a first-class welcome.

Exotic motors rented dream cars for nightmare prices. They looked at a Bentley Mulsanne, a Diablo roadster, a Viper, a Pantera, a Hummer and a De-Lorean.

"We need a good stereo with a large-capacity CD changer for our soundtrack," said Serge. "Did I tell you I'm a location scout for the studios? I can't work without tunes."

The salesman showed Serge something in a white, low-cut Lotus Esprit convertible for a thousand a day. A custom four-seater with fifty CDs in the trunk changer.

Serge presented another stolen Visa, but he had no photo ID. It was back at the hotel, said Serge, and they had to get to a tea.

"Sorry," said the salesman.

Serge stuck five hundreds in the man's shirt pocket and patted it.

"Drive carefully," the salesman said.

They raced the Lotus over to the Breakers Hotel and Serge checked in as a location scout for Paramour Studios. He asked at the desk how to get to Au Bar, the place where William Kennedy Smith and his uncle Ted hung out.

"We'll go and pretend we're Kennedys," Serge told Coleman. He lifted a pair of blank "Hi, my name is . . ." tags from a table outside a conference room in the hotel. "We'll write fake Kennedy names, and then act like we forgot to take off the tags."

Coleman tapped his head with a pen, trying to think of what name to use. "Don't use the actual name Kennedy," Serge advised. "Use one of the in-law names. It's more plausible, and we'll get the brainy chicks."

The three strolled into Au Bar, and the waiter smiled and said, "You forgot to take off your name tags"—leaning a little closer to read them—"Mr. Shriver . . . and . . . Mr. Schwarzenegger."

"I'm gonna mingle—I wanna find a *real* Kennedy," said Sharon, and she disappeared in the crowd.

Sharon rushed back to the table. "Quick, give me a hundred."

"Sure thing," said Serge. "The same day that I give you a tongue bath."

"No, really," said Sharon. "I need a hundred fast. A waiter said he'll give me a personal introduction to some Kennedys, but I have to tip him big first."

Serge handed her the C-note, and Sharon ran off and paid the waiter, who walked Sharon over and introduced her to Serge and Coleman.

Serge punched up the Talking Heads version of "Take Me to the River" on the CD player, cruising the Lotus along Flagler Drive in West Palm Beach, toward the Flagler Bridge. It was early in the evening, and Sharon leaned over forward and flicked a lighter below wind level. The car rode smooth enough for her to heat the heroin she'd bought at the techno dance club they'd hit after Au Bar. Serge crossed the bridge, drove to the ocean side of the island and turned south.

He yelled over his shoulder, "I've already counted five Rolls-Royces coming the other way, in case we're keeping track of such things."

Sharon found Serge's round tin watercolor mixing tray. The pockets around the rim contained dried paint residue, and Sharon had tapped out the heroin into the pocket reserved for lemon yellow. As it melted, it took on the hue of the paint.

Sharon dipped the syringe in the depression and drew up the plunger. Her respiration increased, Pavlovian. She didn't want marks to show, so she spiked a vein in the rose tattoo on her ankle. A dark purple drop of real blood beaded up next to a tattooed drop on the end of a thorn. She drew back on the plunger and a few cc's of her own blood squirted into the cylinder. Mixing with the translucent yellow in the clear tube, the blood formed tangerine blobs that floated in slow motion like a lava lamp. She reversed the plunger's direction and pushed it all home. She read the warmth in her leg as the beginning of the rush, but it was just the temperature from melting the opium.

Before she could get the needle out, she fell back against her seat. Her face turned sideways, against the headrest, looking out to sea. Sailing, above the grime of life, and the waves rolling in from the Atlantic broke on the shore in a symphony. Coleman pulled the syringe out of her ankle, refilled it and stuck it in the inside of his elbow, sending in a warm broth of horse and HIV. Serge raced the Lotus past Donald Trump's Mar-A-Lago estate.

"Marla Maples took a leak on the beach right there," said Serge, pointing. "At least that's what the newspaper in the supermarket said."

He punched up "Dark Side of the Moon" on the CD changer. The heavy-reverb guitar and cash registers of "Money" shook the car as Coleman's head fell backward over the headrest and he saw a shooting star.

Mo Grenadine folded the *Palm Beach Post* over to NFL coverage. The Tampa Bay Buccaneers finally had a winning record, which was being vaunted as one of the great all-time underdog stories of the sports world, along with the 1969 New York Jets and the 1900 Boxer Rebellion. Mo reached under the seat without looking, into a complimentary box of jerky sticks, and peeled one open. He threw the wrapper in the pile of cellophane on the passenger seat.

He dropped Visine and looked over the top of the newspaper at a martini bar on Clematis Avenue called the Atomic Olive. Every five minutes a large iridescent olive over the door belched a mushroom of smoke. A white Lotus sat at the curb. The small magnetic box had been under its bumper since Au Bar.

An hour earlier, the occupants of the Lotus had come out of a bookstore/coffeehouse across the street, where Carl Hiaasen was autographing stacks of green books. Waiting in line, Serge wagged a latent tail.

Now, a commotion on the outdoor patio caught Grenadine's attention. A bouncer yelled at a man taking pictures. The bouncer grabbed for the man, who jumped back out of reach and snapped more pictures.

The bouncer began a slow march toward the photographer that reeked of homicide. The man walked backward, taking pictures of the bouncer.

A tall blond ran from inside the club and jumped on the bouncer's back, and both began to spin with great centrifugal force. A man with a fish hat ran onto the patio with olive spears in both hands and stabbed them deep into the bouncer's buttocks. The photographer opened the Lotus's trunk and threw in the camera. He pulled out a TEC-9 and emptied the thirty-two-shot magazine in the air in three seconds, throwing the crowd into fits of nostalgia. Everyone else froze, and the three hopped in the Lotus without opening the doors and sped off.

Twenty-seven cars from the West Palm Beach Police Department and the Palm Beach County Sheriff's Office responded to the report of automatic weapon fire at the Atomic Olive. It would have been child's play locating a white Lotus, even in Palm Beach, except martinis caused the patrons to identify it variously as a Maserati, a Ferrari and "a Trans Am with everything."

Serge was three blocks away at an all-night knick-knack plaza, buying more postcards, lapel pins and a live caiman—a small South American crocodile sold to Florida tourists as faux alligator. They drove back across the Royal Poinciana Bridge to their room at the Breakers. Serge handed Coleman the caiman in a small rectangular cardboard box with little holes punched in it and told him to put it away.

Coleman turned the AC on full and reclined on the bed. He worked the remote control diligently, unable to punch up the World Series. Looking at herself in the mirror, Sharon felt a touch of class and refinement for the first time in her life as she squirmed out of the thousand-dollar dress and spit a cigarette into the toilet. Serge opened the courtesy fridge and scanned the price list. "Twelve dollars for mixed nuts! What do they do, make your dick hard?"

The TV was going back and forth from C-Span to off.

"You idiot!" Serge confiscated the remote control. He turned on the baseball game with one punch of the remote, opened the door and threw it in the pool.

Sharon was on the phone with the Psychic Pals Network, asking if they'd end up with the five million dollars or get caught for killing the dentist. Serge grabbed his head with both hands. "I'm surrounded by morons!"

He ripped the receiver from Sharon's hands and told the Psychic Pal, "I predict you will be raided by the IRS in ten minutes," and hung up.

The Indians were on top three–zip in the third. Coleman scooped miniature liquor bottles out of the fridge and dumped them in a pouch he created by stretching out the front of his four-hundred-dollar shirt. He climbed back onto the bed with Serge. They put on their foam Marlins and settled in for the game.

Sharon walked over and stood in front of the TV set, naked. "I'm bored," she said in a sultry voice.

Serge picked up the TEC-9 from the nightstand and pointed it at her. "Move."

Mo Grenadine had a wire running down from his left ear into a palm-size crystal TV. In the darkness of the Breakers parking garage, the two-inch screen dimly lit the Lincoln's interior. Grenadine saw the Marlins and Indians each add a run in the fifth before hotel security ran him off.

Sean and David switched to Cokes in the Surfside's bar as they watched the Indians carry their lead through the sixth, seventh and eighth innings.

On a sixty-inch home theater screen in a Palm Beach penthouse, the Indians celebrated the final out of the sixth game, pushing the World Series to a seventh. The sliding glass door of the penthouse was open. On the oceanfront balcony, Charles Saffron wore a powder-blue bathrobe and paced with a portable phone, fielding a long-distance death threat.

Nineteen

Coleman, coming to, felt someone playing bongos on his bare stomach.

"Wake up! It's World Series Day!" said Serge. "We need to tank up on breakfast. It's the most important meal of the day."

Some people fall asleep smoking in bed. Coleman had fallen asleep eating potato chips. He'd rolled around in the night, and he awoke in a film of vegetable oil, covered with crumbled-up chips like a breaded drumstick.

Serge ordered eggs Benedict and orange juice from room service. Coleman ordered the same and added three Bloody Marys. Sharon had meth and Marlboros.

Serge went to the mini-fridge and opened the freezer section for ice cubes. He saw a cardboard box with little holes in it.

He pulled out the frozen caiman and waved it in front of his face like a gator-pop.

"What the fuck!" Serge said to Coleman. "Why'd you put this in the freezer?"

"I thought it was some kind of dessert or candy that needed to be kept cold, like taffy."

Serge smacked the caiman's tail against the dresser, and it shattered like an icicle. "Unbelievable," he said and tossed it underhand into a satchel of dirty laundry.

Room service arrived. Coleman poked at his eggs Benedict tentatively until Serge said it was Mc-Muffins with secret sauce; then Coleman scarfed it up.

Serge called a bellhop and Coleman drank the last Bloody Mary and said he'd be in the bar.

Serge was tipping the bellhop and valet when shouting and general disagreement came from the Jacaranda Room and the Palm Beach society wedding inside. An heir to a bacon-bit fortune was marrying an heir to a sequin fortune. There were live peacocks, a hundred-foot-long ice sculpture of the Republican National Convention, and a life-size oil portrait of the bride and groom propped on a gigantic easel near the guest book.

Coleman thought it was just a really formal bar. He signed the pub's guest book and went in for a drink. Someone said Coleman had to leave. There were words. Shoving. Coleman lost his equilibrium.

It wasn't a quick fall, the kind where the person is smart enough to go straight down with minimal consequence. It was one of those stumbling, windmilling affairs that never ends well. Struggling for purchase,

Coleman pulled down a waiter's sterling tray of champagne flutes and fell through the oil painting.

When Serge got there, the bride was crying and a gaggle of tuxedos had Coleman pinned against a column from the Ottoman Empire. Serge got chest to chest with the largest one, where only a few people could see his pistol as he handed over a roll of bills in the three thousand neighborhood. Before the tuxes could react, he and Coleman jumped in the Lotus waiting at the curb with Sharon.

Coleman lit a Churchill joint as they rolled down A1A toward Miami and the World Series. Serge punched up "Rocky Mountain Way" on the CD.

"... *Bases are loaded and Casey's at bat* ..."

Inexplicably, the song changed to "Convoy." A few seconds later, "Afternoon Delight," and a few seconds more, "Muskrat Love."

Serge transfixed on the stereo, thinking gremlins. Then he noticed Coleman, who had discovered a remote control for the stereo somewhere and was pressing buttons.

The remote landed in a roadside lagoon and Serge manually clicked back to Joe Walsh.

"Where are we?" asked Sharon.

The pot told Coleman to free-associate: "... We're on the road to ruin, the highway to hell, going to hell in a handbasket, on the wrong side of the tracks, the last train to Clarksville, a bridge over troubled water, off the beaten path, between a rock and a hard place, at the school of hard knocks. . . ." Coleman took another Bob Marley.

". . . in Palookaville, dire straits, under the gun, up shit creek, the last resort, the end of the line—"

"Gimme that!" The joint followed the remote control out the window. "Enough weed for you!"

Sharon piped up, "Why do we have to go to the stupid World Series anyway? And where can we get some coke?"

Coleman: "I have a joke. An ant climbs up an elephant at the Miami Zoo and starts fucking the elephant . . ."

Serge squeezed the steering wheel and by force of will did not grab a gun.

". . . but the elephant, you know, doesn't notice 'cause ants are really small. And a coconut falls out of a tree and hits the elephant on the head, and the elephant goes, 'Ouch!' And the ant says, 'Take it, bitch!' "

Boynton Beach, Delray Beach, Pompano Beach. Salt air, sun, ocean's edge. Their hair blew back like a rental car commercial. When they got into Fort Lauderdale, Serge drove up the strip to the Bahia Mar Marina and parked.

"Why are we stopping?" asked Sharon.

"To pay tribute," said Serge.

"To what?" asked Coleman.

"Travis McGee," said Serge. *"The Deep Blue Goodbye, The Busted Flush."*

"Randy Travis? Where?" said Sharon.

"No, Travis *McGee*, errant knight of the John D. MacDonald classics! This is a fucking shrine!"

"I didn't think there was anything worse than the World Series," said Sharon, "but you've found it."

She got out and slammed the door, announcing she had to use the facilities. As she walked away, she leaned her head back and shook her hair, which she had begun doing for prurient effect and which was now unconscious habit.

Serge grimaced and turned to Coleman. "We're gonna kill her right now. I can't take this."

He pulled out the .380 but the silencer wouldn't fit. He tried again with the 9mm, but the threads didn't match it either. He tossed the silencer over his head into the backseat and pointed to the floor by Coleman's feet. "Hand me that grapefruit."

Sharon rejoined them out on the pier. They were alone. Serge took photos, and Coleman read the plaque at slip F-18, moving his lips and following with a finger: ". . . fictional hero & salvage consultant . . . designated a literary landmark February 21, 1987."

Sharon sat on the edge of the slip. She was never discreet about boredom and had the air of a child twisting at her mother's arm.

Serge moved behind her, removing the pistol and grapefruit-silencer from his camera bag, positioning them an inch behind her head. He glanced around, still alone. Perfect. She'd fall forward into the water, into noisy chops lapping the seawall.

He began to squeeze the trigger.

From behind them, a lively "Hey there!"

Serge let off the trigger and concealed the gun. The wind and waves had drowned out the idling motor until it was right on top of them, on the other side of the walkway, in the Intracoastal Waterway. A cigarette boat, aqua and orange stripe, number 13, with a tanned young man happy as a puppy dog.

Serge studied his face. Not Dan Marino, he thought.

"Y'all partying?" the man asked, looking only at Sharon. "My name's Johnny!"

He tapped a nostril and raised his eyebrows in a question mark. Sharon was on her feet. She told Johnny to hold on and ran to the car to fetch her beach bag, which contained her beach drug paraphernalia. She sprinted back with the bag and jumped in Johnny's boat.

"You kids go have fun," Serge said. "We'll just wait here."

He pulled stolen Bavarian binoculars from the camera bag and watched them motor away.

The boat planed up, but suddenly stopped in the middle of the intracoastal behind a seven-million-dollar Italianate mansion. Sharon bent over in a storm of coke-snorting activity that surprised even Johnny.

He tapped more coke onto the top of a first-aid kit. "Go for it!"

From the pier, Serge saw Sharon give Johnny a shove and grab him by the hair, shaking his head back and forth. She punched him and then pulled him down on top of her as they disappeared below the gunwales.

At first Johnny thought not only am I *not* scoring, I'm getting my ass kicked. Then he realized, as Sharon unzipped his pants, that this is it! After all those other times, I finally get some, and a wild tiger no less!

Sharon cursed and clawed Johnny.

Johnny was lost.

Unnerved and inept, he tried to follow her lead at dirty talk. He fumbled with a breast and stuttered, "S-s-son of a bitch, bastard, crap . . ."

"Ow, shit! What the hell? Ouch! Fuck!" yelled Sharon.

"Uh, damn," said Johnny, "fuckin'-A, farts . . ."

"No! Shit!" she said. "This isn't part of the sex! Something's biting me! Damn! Ouch!"

Neither Sharon nor Coleman nor even Serge had realized that caimans are cold-blooded, and when frozen they go into suspended animation. Serge's caiman had thawed out in his luggage and scampered around the trunk, settling in Sharon's beach bag.

Sharon leaped off of Johnny and looked down to see the foot-long reptile with no tail and a death grip on her ankle, trickles of blood running onto her foot.

Back on the dock, Serge watched through the binoculars as Sharon ran around the cigarette boat, Johnny chasing her and shooting at her feet with a fire extinguisher. "That's a new one," said Serge.

She dove over the side and the caiman let go and swam away. Johnny drove the boat alongside

Sharon, pleading for her to get back in, but she ignored him and swam the entire way to the pier.

Back at slip F-18, Sharon demanded, "Gimme your coke!" Johnny submissively handed it over, and Sharon went back to the car, having nothing more to do with him. He stared down sadly at his swim booties, thinking his losing streak would never end.

Serge gave Johnny a one-armed hug around the shoulder. "Consider yourself lucky," he said. "That woman is bad news with a four-inch headline."

Johnny remained pitiful.

"This'll cheer you up," said Serge. "Coleman's got a joke for you. You like animal jokes?"

After an inland loop to get around Port Everglades, Serge drove down to Miami Beach and the stretch of new condo construction on Collins Avenue.

They turned onto Ocean Drive. Serge said, "Hey, there's the Carlyle. That was one of the opening scenes in the *Miami Vice* pilot. Don Johnson and Jimmy Smits stood right there!"

Sharon threw a cigarette out the window and into a gold Cadillac Eldorado parked with its top down. She thought, If I kill these guys, I can keep all the money. And if I do it soon, I won't have to go to the stupid World Series.

Serge was thinking that game seven was only a few hours away. He'd have to kill Sharon soon if they were going to enjoy baseball at all tonight.

Serge said the Metropolis Hotel on South Beach was an architectural treasure, but Coleman thought

it looked like tutti-frutti ice cream. Shell white
trimmed with raspberry, lemon and lime sherbet.
Five stories and curved windows on all corners. The
name on the hotel was backlit with blue neon and
bookended by bronze sailfish.

The hotel's patio was one in a series of trendy sidewalk cafés, where tedious weirdness passed for style.
Two men with pierced nipples connected by jumper
cables. That sort of thing.

"Al Pacino shot that guy in *Scarface* right there!"
said Serge.

"Look at all the wedgies," said Coleman.

Valets worked the curb like pit crews at Daytona.
Serge jumped out of the Lotus and tossed his keys in
a Kareem Abdul-Jabbar skyhook, but they sailed over
the valet's fingertips into a twenty-dollar salad.

"Sorry," said Serge, waving at Jumper-Cable Men.

Bellhops rolled up with a luggage cart. Sharon was
in her Kevlar body armor. She attracted two body
builders from Caracas who rushed up to perform
synchronized pectoral popping.

The lobby of the Metropolis was an art deco orgy.
Twin rows of bromeliads flanked a line of domino
tables with lacquer inlays. The terrazzo floor was a
coral-and-alabaster checkerboard. With the two bellhops and a femme fatale in tow, and another Man
Friday parking his Lotus, Serge strode through the
hotel like The Great Gatsby.

Coleman had detoured to the bar, hewn from co-
quina rock and lit by a bronze Charles Atlas holding
a glowing orb on his back. The mauve, stiltlike chairs

were aesthetically grand and orthopedically suspect. Coleman tried one out and decided he was a bean bag man. He ran to catch the others at the elevator.

The three squinted when the bellhop opened the room. The elevator had been ancient, slow and dark, and the hallway a catacomb. But the room faced Miami Beach and the large wall of glass that wrapped around the corner of the hotel poured in the light. Serge took a deep, satisfied breath; he placed the tackle box on one of the beds and disgorged the contents onto the spread. Coleman popped a Coors. Sharon, excited, pressed her hands against the window. Old coconut palms lined the concourse across Ocean Drive, and along the shore was a row of brightly colored lifeguard shacks shaped like flying saucers. The Atlantic was dark blue and choppy, but the sky clear and warm. It was a world over-represented by sex, twelve-step programs and unnecessary surgery. Sharon's world.

Serge shaved in the bathroom mirror and scripted Sharon's demise. He'd bait her into going out of the room, maybe say he was going out too, and double back to prepare the trap. Lay out the polyurethane tarpaulin to catch the blood and stuff.

"I think I'm gonna head to the beach and take some pictures," Serge said, sticking his head out of the bathroom. "Probably be gone at least two hours."

Perfect, they'll be separated, Sharon thought as she lit one cigarette with another. I'll double back and kill Coleman, then set the trap for Serge.

"What are *you* gonna do?" Serge asked Sharon.

"I think I'll do some shopping, maybe lay out on the beach," she said. "Probably be gone a couple hours."

Perfect, Serge thought.

They left at the same time, both overacting casualness. Sharon got in the elevator and Serge said, "I think I'll take the stairs for exercise."

"Good for you," said Sharon. "Well, see you later."

"Have fun."

Sharon hid on the mezzanine and Serge hid in the stairwell.

Serge returned to the room first and found Coleman clicking a remote control at an unplugged TV set.

He heard a key in the door. "Shit, she's back. Don't tell her I'm here," and Serge ran in the bathroom.

He heard quiet talk and then nothing for an extended period. Eventually there was a whimper and more quiet talk, and Serge peeked around the corner.

Coleman was on his stomach on the bed. Sharon sat on his back, straddling him and holding the .380 automatic with a straight-armed, two-handed grip. Pointed at the base of his head.

"I'm gonna blow your brains out and there's nothing you can do about it," she said in a husky voice, breathing heavy. "Gonna shoot you in the skull in less than thirty seconds, send your brains out your eyes and nose."

She barked through clenched teeth: "Can you feel it coming? Huh, can you? Think about what it'll be like. . . ."

She pushed the barrel against his skull, Coleman weeping now.

"Here we go. Time to die. Ten seconds left. . . ."

Serge was unprepared; he had no weapons and it was too far to get the jump on someone with a gun.

"Cry, fucker, cry!" Sharon tormented him. "Tick-tock, tick-tock, tick-tock. Time's up!"

Serge grabbed the only thing he saw on the bathroom counter and charged the bed. Sharon heard him and spun. It became a split-second race. Sharon raised the barrel and Serge planted his feet.

The only alternative had been a hairbrush, so Serge had grabbed the miniature World Series souvenir bat. He had it in both hands and swung for the fences. Sharon fired.

The bat broke in two across Sharon's forehead as she pulled the trigger. The shot flew by Serge's left ear, and Sharon fell backward off the bed unconscious.

Serge looked around and picked up his tackle box.

Sharon drifted back from the ethereal, and her brain hung in a shroud as she opened her eyes halfway. She could feel some kind of tube running down her throat. Serge was kneeling over her and there was a hissing sound, like an aerosol can.

When the hissing stopped, Serge pulled the tube out of her throat and held a can up to her face.

Sharon read the label, "Fix-a-Flat," as she felt the rubber cement sealing up the inside of her lungs.

She mouthed without a voice: "No fair."

Twenty

"Tonight's the night!" read the outbreak-of-war headline atop the *Miami Herald*. Sean turned to the sports section and threw the rest in the backseat, joining the Styrofoam cups, napkins, burger wrappers, coffee lids and an empty quart of oil. David took Southern Boulevard to the Palm Beach International Airport and turned south on Interstate 95.

Two virgin Thirst Mutilators perspired in the cup holders.

"I remember the first time I went to Miami," said David. "I was a little kid. We went to the Seaquarium and I got a white plastic dolphin from one of those injection-molding machines under a see-through dome. It was supposed to be Carolina Snowball, the famous albino."

"I remember the last time," Sean said. "A squad of squeegee guys held my car hostage after midnight on Biscayne Boulevard. Then I got lost in the Omni parking garage. Car burglar alarms were going off all over the place. The only open door led into the mall and it was empty and dark and this guy started shadowing me. I had to run around like *The Fugitive*."

David tried the radio. "Fight the Powers That Be" came on and the two began to chicken-neck as they passed the Lantana exit.

"I love Public Enemy," said Sean. "Remember that Florida State student who did mushrooms and barricaded himself in the capitol demanding to talk to Flavor Flav?"

"You know, you still snore," said David. "I mean bad."

"Why do we still live here?" asked Sean. "The crime is crazy. Kids who think they're vampires and serial killers from Ohio . . ."

A Buick passed in the left lane with C-4 explosives and two bodies in the trunk.

"A personal question?" asked Sean. "You gonna have kids? I mean it's just incredible. The way it changes you . . ."

"Is this trip gonna turn into a chick movie?"

"Sorry. I just can't get the theme from *Muppet Babies* out of my head."

Dave saw the black limousine coming up in the rearview and fly past in the far left lane doing a hundred.

"Seriously, why do we stay in this state?" Sean asked.

"Co-dependency," said David.

"Look around," said Sean. "A lot of people don't seem right. Like that guy." Sean pointed at the

Honda next to them. "That's one scary-lookin' dude. We don't have any idea what he's up to."

"You're coming unwrapped," said David.

Every ten seconds the guy in the Honda threw a chunk of concrete down the embankment, each piece containing ground-up bits of corpse.

"I mean, you ever think how many undetected murderers drive down this road, past this very point every day?"

The answer was seventy-three. While they were talking, they passed seven graves just inside the woods along the interstate. Only two would be discovered in their lifetimes.

A Lincoln raced by on the inside lane. Mo Grenadine looked down in his lap at the homing monitor and followed it south.

The three men in white linen suits disassembled and cleaned automatic pistols in their laps. With one hand, the driver worked on the Walther laid out on a towel across his legs. He got a searching look on his face and turned to the man in the passenger seat. "Call it!"

The passenger looked up from his gun parts, apologetic. "Air biscuit."

The head of the man in the backseat shot up in alarm, and all three rolled down their electric windows with military precision.

Fifteen seconds later, the driver yelled, "Clear!" They simultaneously rolled up the windows and faced back down at gun parts.

The driver finished reassembling his gun and tapped on the wheel along with a Spanish radio station. The announcer came on at the bottom of the hour. The driver heard something that caught his attention. "World Series!" he yelled. *"El Series Mundo!"*

"Series Mundo! Series Mundo!" the others shouted.

The driver had taken the antikidnapping driving course in Bogotá during Cartel Safety Week. He hit the brakes and twisted the wheel, putting the Mercedes in a spin. The gloss-black limousine slid sideways across three lanes of traffic and into the median. Other cars sideswiped and ran off the shoulder.

"Series Mundo! Series Mundo!"

When the Mercedes was halfway across the median, the driver pulled the wheel back and pressed the gas pedal to the floor. He crossed to the opposite side of the interstate and headed toward the turnpike, to the baseball stadium.

The radio's volume was beyond its capacity for fidelity, and the speakers rattled like castanets inside the Yugo. A wall of fast, untuned guitars and lyrics about religious desecrations and infanticide.

Dar-Dar, lead singer for the Crucifixion Junkies, switched to the outside lane. He jerked his head violently, and his sweaty hair swung and slapped on the dashboard. He punched the armrest over and over. "Die, motherfucker! Meet Satan in all his killing glory! Bow down for the slaughter!"

The DJ announced there would be plenty more

music-without-hope still coming up on World Series
Death Jam Weekend!

Dar-Dar stopped pounding. "World Series?"

He came upon a massive pileup on the interstate,
where police were taking statements about a black
limousine. Dar-Dar drove the Yugo slow down the
breakdown lane and took the exit, working his way
around Opa-Locka until he was pointed at the baseball stadium.

Traffic backed up to the turnpike. Lines at the stadium entrance gates were long and chaotic. A Latin
man in a white suit peeled hundreds off a roll and
said "Three" to a fast-talking scalper in one of those
big, floppy Dr. Seuss hats. The Latins walked off to
the gate and, next in line, a young man with an inverted cross on his forehead stepped up to the
scalper. He raised an index finger and smiled. "One,
please."

David and Sean didn't budget enough time for
traffic. It was nearing first pitch when they made the
exit at Northwest 202nd Street. David turned the
wrong way and ended up on the side of the stadium
where the parking lots were full and closed. Sean saw
the Dr. Seuss hat first. It was on top of the only person in sight, and he was waving them over with a
hand that held four tickets.

"Ask him how much," David said, pulling to the
curb.

Sean rolled down the passenger window. "How much?"

"Homes, a buck each. Box seats behind home plate."

A buck, thought Sean, wow. This guy must not be having any luck; he's totally disgusted with the whole process. But Sean could see himself doing it, practically giving away extra tickets he couldn't sell minutes before the game, saying, "Aw, just give me a dollar." Sean pulled two single George Washingtons from his wallet and held them out to the scalper.

The scalper looked at Sean like a foot had sprouted from his forehead.

Sean might as well have pissed on the scalper's shoes. Here, homeboy, two fucking dollars, bite me! The insult was so aggressive the scalper was taken by surprise. He didn't know whether to go for his piece or run. He studied Sean for a clue but the little guy was ice cold, like James Bond. Probably had a gauge below the window.

The scalper suddenly laughed. "No, man, a buck is a hundred dollars!"

David leaned over. "A buck for both."

The scalper cringed for effect and quickly made the exchange.

"Shrewd negotiating strategy," David told Sean as they drove off. "Knock him off balance. Let him think there's no reasoning with us . . ."

"Shut up," said Sean.

"I mean, why even try to act street-wise when you can go for the much more intimidating surreal farce."

"I said shut up."

They asked the first security guard they saw where to park.

"Just keep driving around the stadium until you see someplace where cars are still parking," said the guard.

"Thanks," said David. "For a second I was worried there was no procedure in place."

They left their car somewhere in Broward County and hiked back to the stadium. Their seats were seven rows from the top of the stands behind the right-field foul pole, Section 433, Row 24, Seats 1 and 2.

"Hey, these are nowhere near home plate," said Sean. "That guy wasn't telling the truth."

David gave Sean the same look he had gotten from the scalper.

"How are we gonna get her body out of the room?" Coleman asked. "We'll have to go through the lobby!"

"Relax," said Serge. "We're in Miami Beach. Everything's backward. To get away with this, we need to *try* to attract attention, and then we'll be ignored. . . . I gotta go to the store."

Serge ran a fast errand to a specialty shop on Washington Avenue. Back at the room, he dumped a sack out on the bed.

Sharon was still wearing her Barbarella body armor, and Serge left it on. He fastened a handcuff around one of her wrists. He put a zippered leather hood with a Spider-Man design over her head and covered her crotch with a strap-on fluorescent wiener.

"She's ready," announced Serge, and phoned for the valet. They hoisted her up and carried her slouched between them like a drunk buddy, one of her arms around each of their necks. They headed for the elevator.

Serge and Coleman carried Sharon through the middle of the sidewalk café, ignored except for one of the jumper-cable men, who said to the other, "I want to party with *those* guys."

The valet held the passenger door of the Lotus open and helped Serge sit Sharon upright in the middle of the backseat.

"We're going to the World Series," Serge explained and handed him a hundred.

"Go Marlins," said the valet.

Serge waved and accelerated the Lotus into traffic as a fire engine headed the other way toward a fully engulfed Cadillac.

Serge whipped the Lotus around two sharp rights and into an alley, and they threw Sharon in the trunk. He checked his Indiglo watch. "We're late," said Serge. "Excellent timing."

Serge's philosophy was to arrive at the absolute last second for any big event, when everyone else had already parked, the roads were clear, and scalped tickets cheap.

Sure enough, they drove from the causeway over Biscayne Bay all the way to Miramar in zero traffic.

"We gotta ditch this car," Serge said. "It's getting too hot."

At the stadium, almost everyone was already inside. The national anthem played over the loudspeakers and the night air glowed from floodlights. The only parking left was on the south side, but Coleman and Serge had gotten off on the darkened north side, where there wasn't a person in sight. Except for a scalper in a Dr. Seuss hat waving two last stubs.

"Look!" yelled Serge. "Our tickets!"

He accelerated the Lotus, jumped the curb, and hit the scalper thigh-high, breaking both legs. The scalper bounced across the hood and rolled up the windshield like a ramp jump. Serge and Coleman ducked as the scalper flew over their heads, landing dead in the backseat. In fright, the scalper had tightened all his muscles and he still clutched the tickets.

The Lotus continued up the sharp incline of a grassy hill, spinning and slinging sod until it slammed sideways into the stadium.

Serge plucked the tickets from the scalper's hand, grabbed his gym bag and abandoned the Lotus, and he and Coleman walked around the corner and through the gate. Three minutes before the first pitch, he and Coleman took their seats in the right-field stands, Section 433, Section 24, Seats 3 and 4.

"Sodas! Get your ice-cold sodas!"

A man in a white linen suit held up three fingers, and Sean, David, Serge and Coleman passed money down the row to the vendor and the three Cokes back up the row.

"Excuse me, excuse me," said Dar-Dar, a souvenir World Series baseball cap covering the scar tissue on his forehead. He squeezed past Sean's and David's knees, carrying a cardboard tray with a hot dog, a bag of peanuts and a beer. "Pardon me, excuse me"—passing Serge's and Coleman's knees. He wore a Marlins T-shirt over his black tunic. "Coming through, sorry, excuse me"—passing the Latins, who twisted sideways in their seats to guard their sodas.

The Cleveland Indians took a two–zero lead in the third inning, and the Marlins remained lifeless through the seventh-inning stretch. In the bottom of the inning, Bobby Bonilla crushed a home run into the center-field stands, and the night sky over Dade County filled with screams.

Charles Saffron, sitting in a luxury skybox, was yelling too. He was yelling into a cellular phone. He clapped it closed. The Costa Gordans were calling from the right-field stands, wanting their money.

Saffron flipped the phone open again and punched a number.

"Grenadine, where the hell are you! Where's the money!"

Grenadine was outside the stadium. He held the small magnetic homing device he had just removed from the crashed Lotus. A dozen police cars were up on the grass, and blue and red lights swept across Grenadine's face as he talked to Saffron. The back of the coroner's van was open, one body already inside.

A detective with latex gloves popped the trunk and motioned for the evidence techs.

"We're staying on South Beach, the Metropolis," Serge said, making friends with Sean in the next seat. "Incredible place. Preservation people did a great job."

Coleman had bought a World Series helium balloon and tied it to a box of popcorn, weighing it down.

"Where are you guys staying?" asked Serge.

"Don't know yet. Guess we could try South Beach," David said. "We drove straight in from Palm Beach."

"We just came from Palm Beach too!" said Serge. "Stayed at the Breakers." He looked intensely into Sean's face, tilting his head off-center like a basset hound. "Have we met? You look familiar."

"Don't think so," said Sean.

Coleman ate popcorn until the box and the balloon were in weightless balance. He pushed them forward and they floated out over the field at a constant altitude of forty feet. An umpire called time out as they floated over second base, and a sharpshooter ran on the field and knocked the balloon out of the sky with a BB rifle.

"Those are really cool hats," Sean told Serge.

As time continued running out on the Marlins, a depression settled over the crowd like morning fog. Serge had to pace. He went out on the concourse, searching for souvenirs, and spotted Miami humor columnist Dave Barry in the liquor line.

Serge ran up to him hyper and insane-looking, and Barry took a step back. Awfully jumpy, Serge thought, must have some kind of nervous condition. Serge asked to get his ticket autographed, and he carefully wrapped it in three hot dog napkins, put it in a special compartment in his wallet, and ran away.

In the bottom of the ninth, the Marlins, piece by piece, assembled a tiny rally. A pop fly scored the tying run, and the crowd came apart.

The seventh game of the World Series was going into extra innings.

In the bottom of the eleventh, the Marlins loaded the bases with two outs.

David and Sean were talking about what hotel they wanted to stay at, South Beach, Biscayne Boulevard, the Holiday Inn at the racetrack.

"That reminds me," said Sean, "I still have to cancel the reservation at the Purple Pelican in Key West, unless we want to run into that Veale guy I told you about."

Through the roar of the crowd, the words "Purple Pelican" and "Veale" came unexpectedly to Serge and he turned and studied Sean's profile. Serge's face suddenly lengthened with realization.

Just then, Marlin Edgar Renteria singled up the middle, driving home the winning run of the World Series, and the stadium exploded. Fans leaped on each other and onto the field. Fireworks shot from the scoreboard behind the outfield stands. Coleman hugged Serge and lifted him off the ground.

David and Sean bounded down the aisle steps two at a time toward the exit, trying to beat the traffic.

"Put me down! Put me down!" Serge yelled at Coleman. "They're getting away! It's those guys! They were here the whole time!" Serge pounded on the top of Coleman's head with his fists, but Coleman kept hugging him.

After Serge finally got through to Coleman, they charged into the aisle. A beer-wobbled Coleman missed the edge of a step and fell into the back of Serge's legs, taking him and three other people down.

The people wanted an apology but Serge pushed them back down on the steps instead. "Come on, Coleman!"

Dar-Dar jumped around, double high-fiving two of the Latins. Through the cheering, he heard Serge screaming for Coleman, and Coleman yelled back, calling Serge by name.

Coleman? Serge? The targets Saffron had telephoned him about? A fire erupted in his soul. Dar-Dar climbed over two rows, fighting and shoving his way toward the aisle. "Satan's vengeance is nigh!"

Some of the Marlins ran along the outfield wall, smiling and waving up at the crowd. A stage was erected in the infield for televised presentation of the championship trophy.

The tallest Latin said to the others, "Let's wait till the traffic clears." He sat down in his stadium seat and sipped his soda.

By the time everyone reached the concourse, rivers

of people snaked out of the gates in all directions, and nobody could find anybody else.

"Let's get back to South Beach," Serge told Coleman. "They said they might stay there. We'll comb the strip."

Grenadine knew his only hope was for Serge and Coleman to leave by the same gate he'd seen them enter. Mo thought he'd never spot them in the mob, but there was Coleman, yelling "Wooooooooooo!" and thrusting a finger in the air: "We're Number One! We're Number One!" Serge reached back and grabbed him by the shirt and pulled him along.

They chose a yellow '72 Corvette in the VIP lot. People streamed by both sides of the car as Serge shattered the steering column; some noticed what he was doing but ignored it—there was a traffic jam to beat. Grenadine crouched behind the bumper, placed the magnetic homer and walked away against the tide of people.

Serge beat most of the pack, but when they turned onto the MacArthur Causeway, he merged with a new crowd. Partyers who had watched the game on TV and were heading to South Beach for postgame celebration. Some carried bail money.

The traffic exceeded eighty across the causeway, honking horns and flashing lights, people hanging out windows waving Marlins and Cuban flags. Coleman saw this and began climbing out his own window, still yelling "Wooooooooooooo!" As Coleman started falling out of the car, Serge reached across the passenger seat and hooked his fingers into the elastic waistband of Coleman's underwear, jerking him back inside.

Soon, Serge himself was tripping on Miami. On the left, little bridges spurred from the causeway for Palm, Hibiscus and Star islands. "Al Capone lived on one of those islands when he had cooties," said Serge. On the right, the illuminated downtown skyline gave him goose flesh. Serge imagined he was in all those great movie and TV chases over the same bridge. He looked over at Coleman, who was pretending to pick the foam Marlin's nose, and it broke the spell.

"Look at that building lit up all green." Coleman pointed at the skyline. "How do they do that?"

"Green lightbulbs," said Serge.

On South Beach, young people danced and disrobed in the back of pickup trucks cruising Collins Avenue. Five guys ran around an intersection with a giant Cuban flag. Serge's mind was on the money. He walked from the Park Central Hotel to the Clevelander, crossing to the beach side of the street, and waited for Sean and David. He sat on a bench with an open view of sidewalk traffic in front of the hotels and cafés. The Colony, the Beacon, the Avalon, the Starlite, the neon colors so evenly varied Serge thought they must have had a meeting.

Coleman bounded into the street. He grabbed a corner of the Cuban flag and ran around the intersection, picking up the chant, *"Cuba Libre!"*

Mo Grenadine sipped decaf at an outdoor table at

the News Café, watching Serge and Coleman and reading an overseas paper. It was after midnight, but people were still lined up nearby for souvenir flash photos in front of the Versace estate.

Twenty-one

When the Lotus was found, police appealed to the press for publicity. Blaine Crease immediately went on Florida Cable News, hanging from a blimp over the stadium, describing the killers as the criminal geniuses of the nineties, masters of disguise and escape.

Only three cars were stolen outside the World Series, a BMW, a Mercury Marquis, and a yellow Corvette, and police were looking for all of them.

Susan Tchoupitoulas of the Key West Police Department opened a briefcase at the kitchen table on Olivia Street, and pulled out a sheaf of paperwork. In the bundle was a bulletin from Miami. Murders at the World Series, complete with vehicle descriptions and suspect profiles. It said they were last seen heading south.

Susan made a few notes on a legal pad.

Former Hillsborough County deputy sheriff Samuel Tchoupitoulas wheeled himself into the kitchen of his Olivia Street home in Key West. He'd heard his daughter, Susan, come home from work.

"Hey, Sergeant," he called out with a smile, wheeling through the doorway.

"Hi, Daddy," said Sergeant S. Tchoupitoulas, putting the paperwork back in the briefcase. She got up and walked over and gave him a hug.

He tried to decipher the look on her face.

"Any problem with the Bubbas today?"

"Nothing I couldn't handle," she said.

The Bubbas on the force persisted as a small but definable number of ill-tempered and unprofessional officers. Through seniority and the inbred, small-palace politics of Key West, they bullied residents and tourists alike with impunity.

It was the cross all the good cops in Key West bore. Sergeant S. Tchoupitoulas had an additional challenge. Although she could run a six-minute mile and do every last duty of a police officer better than most of the department, she was still a woman. Which meant she had to put up with a strain of sexual innuendo that Susan found more lame than crass. Offend me, she thought, but at least make me laugh.

Friends and relatives didn't understand why Susan couldn't complain or file a sexual harassment suit. Her father knew exactly why, and asked her to quit the force. But he told her he'd be proud whatever she wanted. She wanted to be a cop. Like her dad. And cops didn't sue cops.

So that afternoon, when a Bubba escalated from unclever remarks to a hand on her breast, she didn't complain. She bent his pinky until she heard the sound of a piece of chalk snapping.

She chose not to tell her father about the incident, and the officer with the pinky splint sure wasn't talking.

Susan gave her father a second hug. "I have to go back in the office."

It was an outside chance but one that her responsible nature wouldn't let her leave uncovered. The suspects were southbound, and the permutations were endless. There was Homestead, or they could head into the Everglades or the migrant camps in Immokalee. They could always double back.

Or they could come to the Keys.

Her starting point would be tracking the yellow Corvette, but she assumed it had already been ditched. Maybe they were working their way through a series of cars.

Back at the department, Susan logged into a network of law enforcement computers and ordered spreads of all vehicles stolen in the last twenty-four hours south of the turnpike junction at Florida City.

Several spit out. A Ford Tempo, a Chevy Cavalier, a Coupe DeVille, a panel truck from Glotski's Bakery, a LeMans and the Oscar Mayer Wienermobile, which was on a promotional tour in the Keys when it was taken for a joyride over the Seven Mile Bridge by four high school students in Marathon.

She requested fingerprint results, and she filed them and cross-filed and tapped into the FBI computer and found a match with a murder scene at the Orbit Motel in Cocoa Beach. Roaming police computer systems was like surfing a secret Internet, except it was much, much slower and utterly disjointed. Susan kept making keystrokes down blind alleys, but the morsels she did find encouraged her to keep going. Three hours of trial-and-error later, she had a positive print match with the panel truck found ditched on the edge of Florida Bay, the room at the Orbit Motel and two small-time goofballs from Tampa. She couldn't believe the connection hadn't already been made, but then again she could. In coming years, police agencies would be universally connected for instant identifications. For now, however, the cops were at the mercy of meager local budgets, low manpower to input the data, and incomplete networking. In 1997, it still took days and sometimes weeks to make fundamental connections.

Her computer was downloading. Two criminal jackets and mug shots came up on her screen.

The phone tips had started coming into the Key West Police Department minutes after artist's conceptions of Serge and Coleman first appeared on Florida Cable News that Monday morning. The callers placed them all over the island, at the time when Serge and Coleman were still in Miami. One tip had them giving tours at Hemingway's House, another overcharging for a transmission near Searstown, and still another said they were on the naval base, training dolphins to plant bombs on the hulls of ships.

By Monday night, however, the calls began to come in with the cadence of credibility. Two calls put the suspects in a Cuban lunch counter and two more around the corner on north Duval Street.

Susan alerted the shift commander to what she had found on the computer and made a hundred enlarged copies of the mug shots. She grabbed them and ran out the door.

Dar-Dar drove with his elbows south on US 1. In one hand was a Bic lighter, and in the other a crucifix stationery stamp that heated quickly in the flame. The light ahead had turned red and he slowed to a stop. He realigned the rearview mirror to see himself and, for purposes of scar maintenance, pressed the heated stamp into his forehead. The smell of singed flesh filled the car and he let out a yodeling scream. Drivers around him responded by leaning on their horns, agreeing that the light was too long.

Just past the intersection, Dar-Dar pulled into the Rapid Response convenience store. The body of a flabby redneck lay in a pond of blood on the floor and had two hot dog spits sticking out of his chest. Dar-Dar stepped over the body and grabbed a pack of candied peanuts. He walked down the chips aisle toward the rest rooms, carrying a small wire cage containing two pigeons.

Clinton Ellrod was on the phone to the police. He put his hand over the receiver and yelled to Dar-Dar, "Hey you! No biting off the heads of birds in the rest rooms!"

Dar-Dar turned and stood still for a moment. He put the peanuts back on the shelf and walked back out of the store with the pigeons.

Twenty-two

As a child, Coleman probably would have raised his feet up when he crossed the drawbridge at Jewfish Creek, putting him officially in the Florida Keys. Instead, he placed a tiny square of paper with a grinning fiddler crab under his tongue.

"What's that?" asked Serge.

"If it's Monday, this must be acid," said Coleman.

"Oh, you're gonna be a treat!"

Coleman saw a mural of triggerfish and fan coral on the side of a building. "Dive trips, $25."

"Can we go? Please, can we?"

The cattle boat cast off from Key Largo for the afternoon snorkeling trip at John Pennekamp Coral Reef State Park.

The boat ran without wake through cuts in the coral. No margin for error. A deep, narrow channel, and on both sides, bright expanses of rock a few inches under the tide.

Once in deeper water, it throttled up and ran twenty customers out to the dive site. They anchored at the underwater Christ of the Deep statue, whose face and arms reached upward from the ocean floor, toward shafts of light.

Eighteen snorkelers in the water. Serge and Coleman in the boat.

Serge paced and took pictures. Coleman sat on the swim step, feet in the water, drinking from a plastic milk jug containing a batch of screwdrivers. The dive operators, a young man and woman in their mid-twenties, thought Serge was a harmless eccentric. Tall and thin, he had short, prematurely gray hair and lancing blue eyes. For some reason he was wearing long pants. And he was driving them nuts with all his questions: local history, marine biology, nightlife, politics. He only stopped asking questions when he was jotting in a leather notebook or taking more pictures.

Coleman was another story. He was the fuckup in the operation, no doubt about it. He had a chubby head that was a little too big for his body, and sunken, small eyes. In his resting state, ignorantly content. He was studying his hands, slowly turning them over and back.

Yelling came from the water. "Get off the coral!"

Others looked. A man was standing up to his waist in the water, exposing a bleached upper body. He was oblivious, adjusting his mask and destroying the reef.

Four other divers joined the yelling, almost in unison. "Get off the coral!" And next, everyone, including the dive operators and Serge: "Get off the coral!"

He continued to stand there, all fat and happy, not paying attention.

"He's from France!" someone in the water yelled. "He doesn't understand English!"

"Really? I speak French," said Serge. "Get off the *fucking* coral!" He pulled the Smith & Wesson from the gym bag and shot the water around the diver.

The tourist looked up, saw he was taking the gunfire he'd been expecting ever since landing at Miami International, and dove in the water.

"Eurocentric bastard!" said Serge.

The dive operators were staggered with fright, but most of the people in the water began clapping.

Serge smiled and waved at them with the hand that still held the gun. He tossed the .38 into the gym bag.

Serge walked over to the dive operators and said quietly, "That was pretty dramatic, but there was really no harm. And when we get back to the dock, we're going to get in our car and drive out of your lives. Or you can try to call the authorities on that radio or maybe make a stink back at the pier. In which case I will make sure our lives are entwined forever."

The two sprinted out of the dive shop. Coleman was hallucinating carnivorous sea horses, and Serge pulled him by the arm to keep him on track. The shooting on the reef was justifiable, of course. That

Frenchman had been stepping all over the coral. But he knew the French were a powerful people, and they would try to make an example of him.

The Corvette was on the far side of the lot, so they ditched it and jumped in a running panel truck delivering rolls to the convenience store next door.

Coleman thought Key Largo was ten miles of hell and sobbed. But Serge was getting excited, picking up the cues of building anticipation for the hundred-mile drive out to sea. Poincianas lined the median, and there was that squarish concrete tower on the right, whatever it was.

Plantation Key was more of the same, but by Islamorada the views began to open up, and Coleman settled down. One drawbridge spanned varying depths laid out in gradations of indigo and turquoise. Coconut palms angled out over the waves and charter boats lined up at a dock. Scales by the highway hung a swordfish, sea bass and bull shark.

Serge pulled over at a coral sculpture of a blowing palm, a monument for the victims of the Labor Day Hurricane of 1935. Coleman had gone into himself, entranced. Serge showed him Cheeca Lodge and the tiny Pioneer Cemetery that sat in the middle of the beach. A small square plot of nineteenth-century headstones and a cherub with a broken wing, surrounded by sunbathers.

They ditched the bakery truck in the Cheeca parking lot and switched to a restored red LeMans. Coleman told him the upholstery in the LeMans was alive with fire-tipped flagella. Serge pushed him in anyway and sped off.

Serge downshifted to climb the steep and high Channel Five Bridge. Coleman darted his eyes around, paranoid, preparing to light a joint. As they hit the crest of the bridge, Coleman deemed it safe and lit up. The drag was deep and calming.

Coleman blew the joint out of his mouth and yelled and crawled down to the floor to hide. Two Black-hawk military helicopters flew by slowly at window level on each side of the car, ported machine gun barrels glistening in the sun.

"Oh," said Serge. "George Bush must be down here bonefishing. They're just sweeping the area for terrorists."

Coleman didn't blink for five minutes.

Serge named the islands as they drove over them: Long Key, the Conch Keys, Duck, Grassy, Fat Deer, Crawl. They started out with brief glimpses of sea between long islands, and then it reversed, and they were touching down on brief islands between long, high bridges.

They were halfway out to Key West, approaching the Seven Mile Bridge. Serge told Coleman it was the longest bridge in the world. Just before the span, Serge looked over at one of his favorite restaurants but didn't stop. He saw the fifties-style sign over the lunch counter that was open to the highway. The Seven Mile Grill, one of those pieces of roadside Americana that the rest of the country lost when they put in the interstates. It was so popular he didn't wonder about the black limousine in the parking lot. Three men in white suits sat on stools, backs to the highway, eating the fish platter. Fried grouper with hush puppies and french fries on wax paper in plastic mesh baskets, coleslaw in paper cups. They had napkins tucked in their collars, and three machine guns rested on the counter; nobody in the place was moving. They tipped well and got sodas to go in souvenir can coolers depicting Pigeon Key.

Coleman told Serge the sky was convex, like a big blue punch bowl. He said the clouds were making sounds like a Wurlitzer organ. It dawned on him that their car had many, many moving parts.

At the beginning of the Seven Mile Bridge, Coleman was trying to get in the glove compartment. By the end he was tearing up the inside of the car like a cat on the way to the vet.

"Let's get you off the highway," said Serge.

He turned off US 1 and drove up Big Pine Key until they were back in the woods, and he kept driving. They approached the bridge across Bogie Channel, and Serge pulled over on the left. There were two other cars and a building partially obstructed in the trees. Coleman couldn't see any signs as he got out of the car and followed Serge through a flimsy screen door.

"The hallucinations are back," said Coleman. "There's money everywhere. We're rich!"

He saw thousands of scribbled-on one-dollar bills that covered the walls and ceiling of the No Name Pub. As remote and hidden as it was, the bar remained in another decade. Back when Zane Grey visited fish camps and ferries carried Studebakers across gaps in the Overseas Highway. Serge grabbed Coleman's hands, which had torn down some of the money. The bills read, "Billy and Sally's honeymoon," "Green Bay Packers rule!" and "Support mental health or I'll kill you!"

Serge apologized to the bartender and handed her the bills. It was a tiny place, the size of a living room, wrapped in an L around the bar. Children had taken over the single pool table.

"Look at this menu," he told Coleman. "Beer food from around the world. Pizza, chili, tacos, Philly cheese steak, calzones, smoked fish, barbecue . . ."

Coleman was looking up at the large animal head over the bar. A sign said "Largest Key Deer on Record, Shot at No Name Pub."

"It's a joke," said Serge. "That's the head of a regular deer. Real key deer are these miniature things. They're endangered, only a few hundred left. On this island we're on, Big Pine, they're like sacred cows in India. There's nothing these people wouldn't do to protect them. A little ways up, death threats are spray-painted in the road for anyone who messes with 'em."

Serge told Coleman about the times he'd come out to the No Name Pub years ago, how there used to be an antique mechanical baseball game that used steel balls, and an old stuffed deer that stood over the bar wearing a bow tie. He'd watched a Super Bowl here, when everyone wore 3-D glasses to watch the Coke commercials. . . .

Coleman interrupted, still staring up at the head. He whispered that the deer was telling him "to do bad things."

Serge suggested they leave and paid the tab. They drove farther, over the Bogie Channel Bridge onto No Name Key. It was a dead end, unsettled island with no utilities and a few dirt roads leading to places that didn't want visitors. This was body-dumping country, plenty of elbow room to deal with Coleman.

They got out of the car, and Serge sat on the hood. Coleman became mollified by a series of objects. A rock, a twig, a land crab. Coleman said wavy lines were coming off the end of the road, and Serge said that was real. A miniature deer came out of the woods and stood in the road facing them. It had long since become tame through food handouts. It smelled a smorgasbord on Coleman and walked toward him.

Coleman screamed. Before Serge could do anything, Coleman had grabbed the .38 out of the car and shot the deer until the air was full of fur.

It was Serge's turn to scream. He thought of the townfolks' reaction and imagined Coleman and him as the "after" photo of the Mussolinis.

He pushed Coleman into the car and hit the gas.

Mo Grenadine thought it was the first time he'd seen a brick fireplace next to a bright window view of tropical plants. A sailfish hung over the mantel and a cat rubbed his leg. He threw the cat a piece of jerky, but it was rejected.

The homing device sat on the table; a bright dot slowly approached from the east.

Grenadine fiddled with the remains of the steamed shrimp and ordered another beer. The restaurant sat back in the banana trees and he hadn't noticed it on the side of US 1 until it was too late and he had to backtrack. The Jamaican paint scheme had caught his attention, vibrant green and yellow, and a funky sign on the roof: Mangrove Mama's.

The dot on the homer was accelerating. Grenadine chugged the beer as the dot passed through the middle of the screen—his position—and kept going west. He left a twenty on the table and ran to his car.

The dot became stationary and Grenadine shook the homing device. But there it stayed. He slowed as he crossed Sugarloaf Key. He recognized the lodge, to his right. That old dolphin Sugar, who had lived in the pool out back for years, had died and it had made every paper south of Orlando. Grenadine was getting close to the dot, and he slowed and turned in the dirt road next to the lodge.

He approached an isolated airstrip—where they had filmed part of a movie when they needed a place with smuggler atmosphere. Over the tops of nuisance pine trees he saw the bat tower. It was a louvered gothic structure from the 1930s. Another developer's folly, but a creative one, put up in a vain attempt to colonize bats that would dine on mosquitoes.

Grenadine pulled around a bend in the road. He

parked the car and walked quietly on the gravel with his binoculars. First he saw the parked red LeMans, and then the full bat tower came into view. At its base, a slightly plump man had his arms and legs wrapped around one of the pylons, hanging on for life only a foot above the ground, and a taller, thinner man was trying to pry him off.

"Is it just a matter of time?" asked Sean. "Are we safe in this state, or have we just been beating the odds?"

"You're paranoid," said David, at the wheel, crossing Tavernier Creek. "I saw an article in the newspaper. It said Floridians are overly fearful of crime. There was this study that found residents fear violent attack about fifteen times greater than the rest of the country, when the actual threat is only ten times greater."

"That's comforting," said Sean. "Last year Karen and I were coming out of a video store just after dark. She was eight months' pregnant. Looked like she was about to pop, she walked like a freakin' penguin. These two guys followed us out. I didn't think anything of it 'cause I can't fathom the mind that would prey on someone that obviously pregnant."

"What happened?"

"I put Karen in the mini-van and was about to walk around to my side when I realized the guys had disappeared. I looked around and I finally bent down and looked under the car. There were two pair of feet on the other side. They were crouched down waiting for me to walk around. I got Karen back out of the car and we went back in the store as fast as we could. I can't tell you how frightened I was until we were back inside. But you know, once we were there, I started to get this feeling like I've never had before. I was so angry I wanted to kill those guys with my bare hands."

"I woulda helped," said David. "You found the traveler's checks yet?"

"No!"

"Just asking."

"I told you I hid them and I can't remember where. It'll come to me."

"Okay, okay."

The conversation stopped in a truce, and a minute later David asked Sean if he'd get the guidebooks back out. It was the division of labor; whoever wasn't driving would read from history and travel books, looking up facts and legends about whatever place they were driving through. They were traversing the causeway between Upper and Lower Matecumbe Keys.

"Okay, up ahead on the left," Sean said, looking down at a map and then out the window. "That should be Indian Key. That used to be the seat of Dade County. Back in 1840, the guy who developed the place, Jacob Houseman, offered to kill Indians for the government for two hundred dollars each.

"For some reason the Indians got upset. They came out there and massacred a bunch of people."

"And you're worried about muggers at a video store," said David.

"Shut up," said Sean. "Here's the wild part. There was a famous botanist, a Dr. Henry Perrine. He was hiding with his family. The Indians killing people all over the island. And the Indians are moving toward his house. So Perrine lowers his wife and three kids into the basement through a trapdoor. They expect him to come with them, but he figures the Indians are sure to discover the trapdoor and kill his family. So he closes them in and piles bags of seeds and junk over the door to conceal it. Then he waits up in the house and the Indians come in and butcher him. They never found the trapdoor—his family survived."

"Man, read something lighter," said David.

As soon as they arrived in Key West, Sean and David settled in at the Expatriate Café on Duval Street and watched the news. The Conch Train, an open-air sightseeing tram, clanged its bell as it went by, and a tourist took a picture of Sean and David.

On the side street, in the doorway shadows of a closed bric-a-brac shop, a man watched David and Sean.

Did they really want to go to Sloppy Joe's, David asked. Sean was ambivalent too, but it was a week-night, he said, when Joe's was a functional bar instead of a souvenir mall.

David and Sean had been looking out at the traffic on Duval as they talked, not looking at the man approaching the table from David's blind side. In the last few yards the man lunged. David's Canon camera with zoom lens was in the middle of the table, next to the lamp. While still looking at Duval, David's left hand shot out and landed atop the camera, a split second before the man's hand landed on top of David's.

David looked up at him. He said calmly, "You have a decision to make."

The man snarled, "I want the camera. Now!"

"Wrong decision."

David curled his right arm just behind the man's calves and slammed his shoulder into both his knees. The man went over backward like a tree. David was on him, and gave one quick rabbit punch below and behind his ear, knocking him out.

"How'd you know?" asked Sean as they walked down Duval. "I didn't even see him coming, and he was almost behind you."

"It's Florida," David shrugged. "It's like you're a small fish on the reef. You have to stay aware of your surroundings."

Up ahead, at Sloppy Joe's, Sean and David stuck their heads in the door from the sidewalk. They decided not to go in.

The bar was packed more than usual for that early, and especially a weekday. There was something odd about the crowd. They were all older men on the paunchy side. Gray or white hair with beards. Rosy, full faces, some sunburned, others with lots of cap-

illaries near the surface. Most of them in white tur-
tleneck sweaters.

"I think they're all supposed to be Hemingway,"
said Sean.

Since the early sixties, looking like Hemingway
had been a growing cottage industry in Key West. So
much so that by the time the annual Hemingway festival was unexpectedly canceled, it spelled a crisis of
confidence for the swelling numbers of look-alikes
who vacationed or had permanently relocated on the
island.

The colony even had a name, The Look-Alikes. In
1997, Hemingway's heirs decided to cancel the festival. They said they didn't like the rowdy image of
Key West's yearly festival, which disgraced Ernest's
memory by not giving them a big enough cut of the
profits.

They moved the festival to Sanibel and announced
there would be no drunken revelry; Hemingway
would be honored with more appropriate activities,
like golf.

The look-alikes moped around Key West for
weeks, some became surly, a few ended up on the
public dole. They had started meeting lately, trying
to figure something out. They hadn't made any progress against the Hemingway heirs or the city of Sanibel, but interest and hope were building. Each
Monday they held a meeting at Sloppy Joe's, but before they could stratify a legal or economic approach,
the gatherings inevitably unraveled into loud mis-
adventure.

The forums grew each week. It started with the previous year's eighty-three entrants in the look-alike contest, and grew to one-fifty the next week, and two hundred the week after that. Soon the weekly meetings generated so much sympathy that they were pulling in the cross-over look-alikes—those of Burl Ives, Orson Welles and Dom DeLuise, who, in a pinch, could do Hemingway in a crowd, if they were in the back rows.

This Monday, the meeting had ballooned to a record three hundred and forty. TV crews from Japan, England and Spain were on hand. But the meeting was well on the way to making no sense. One of the Hemingways tumbled onto the sidewalk and spilled a draft on Sean's shoes.

Sean and David agreed that no good could come of going inside, and they proceeded to Captain Tony's.

The chubby, belly-landing amphibious plane dropped its wheels and rolled onto the short Key West runway. A young man and woman in Bermudas directed taxiing planes around with lazy gestures. The woman chewed gum.

The Key West International Airport doesn't allow jets, because of noise rules, and the old prop planes lend romance. Much of the modest terminal is taken up by the Conch Flyer Lounge, which, in a display of priorities, sticks out onto the runway.

The door flopped down into a staircase from the green-and-white plane, and Charles Saffron trotted out, yelling into a cell phone. He marched to the terminal with the purpose of a man moving toward someone he wants to punch.

"You dumb sonuvabitch! Where's my money!"

"I'm real close, Mr. Saffron. Got 'em on the run," said the phone. "Just a little more time."

Grenadine, who had had a hundred miles of sea and sky to crunch the numbers, was no longer on the New England Life team, but it was no time to tell Saffron.

"Grenadine! Where are you! I want to see you right now!"

"Your signal's breaking up, Mr. Saffron," said Mo, holding the phone at arm's length. "I'm losing you. I can't hear . . ." and he hung up.

"Shit, shit, shit!" Saffron yelled next to a luggage cart. He bit the cell phone, breaking off the 6, 8 and 9 buttons.

Saffron entered the airport through the bar and punched a hole in a wicker butterfly chair. He ran out to the curb and hailed a cab the color of Pepto-Bismol.

The driver of the school bus had been crying off and on since they'd left Miami southbound on US 1. He turned around and looked at the men sitting behind him. "I love you guys." And started blubbering again.

Sixty middle-aged, overly happy men hugged each other often and sang, "Put your hand in the hand of the man who stilled the water . . ." They passed around pictures of their families and hugged and wept some more.

"Sorry you changed your mind," the desk clerk at the Purple Pelican said in the phone, jotting down the cancellation.

Sean, at a pay phone outside Captain Tony's, said he was sorry, too. Maybe next time.

The clerk was short, fiftyish, effeminate and well tanned. He had a white tank top, short blond hair, and an engaging personality. When he was finished writing, he looked up and saw two men approach.

"Welcome to the Purple Pelican," he said.

Serge's arms held a brown sack full of papaya, guavas, passion fruits, kumquats, pomegranates, limes, dates and coco plums. An hour earlier he had announced to Coleman that from now on his life was all about fruit. He decreed that he would drink only beverages that contained a tincture of banana.

"Any vacancy?" Serge asked.

"Usually we're booked solid," said the clerk, "but you're in luck. We just had a cancellation."

The clerk asked if they wanted to know where his favorite restaurant was and was told no.

"Blue Heaven," he said anyway. "Used to be a brothel. Roosters run around your table while you eat."

Serge looked down at a souvenir pelican trivet and took a bite of papaya while the clerk wrote down the make and model of their car. Serge went in the gift store and came back with a stack of postcards and a pair of souvenir Hemingway beards.

"The room I have for you is European bath facilities. That okay?" the clerk asked.

"European?" said Serge. "Wow, you make less service actually sound classier. We have to pay extra for that?"

The clerk dropped the smile. He handed over the key and said tersely, "Room three, upstairs."

In the room, Coleman became erratic, his skin clammy. He jerked his head around, looking.

Coleman stuck his head under one of the beds, and Serge finally said, "What!"

"Where's the TV?"

"There isn't one. A lot of guesthouses in Key West don't have 'em."

"Yeah, but . . ."

"But what?"

"Where's the TV?"

The hotel tucked itself between a used bookstore and a moped rental on Fleming Street, just around the corner from Duval Street and a block from La Cubaria. The lobby was flush against the sidewalk. A tiny spotlight illuminated a sign with a purple pelican in a Hawaiian shirt.

"I'll be out in the lobby," said Coleman, "by the TV."

Serge looked down from the window into the courtyard with a pair of royal palms. Ceramic tiles at the bottom of the pool formed yet another pelican. Serge installed the tension rod in the bathroom doorway. He put on his antigravity boots and hung upside down, working his abs.

Coleman ran back into the room. "We're on TV!"

They ran to the lobby but only caught the last seconds, the "armed and dangerous" part. Serge wondered how long the two giant pictures of them had been on the screen, Serge looking dangerous in his mug shot, Coleman smiling like a loon in his.

Serge looked over at the desk, but the clerk wasn't paying attention, working with a pencil and calculator.

They returned to the room and bolted the door. They waited an hour, until Florida Cable News looped back to the segment on Serge and Coleman. They went back downstairs to the lobby.

When they got there, however, the lobby was full of Belgian students on a youth hostel tour. They had switched the TV to the Home Usher Movie Channel, watching *Wayne's World*. Serge couldn't believe what he saw, the entire room swaying back and forth and singing "Bohemian Rhapsody."

"No, no, no!" yelled Serge, standing in front of the TV set and waving both arms at them. "That song is illegal in this country. You must now go to your rooms and await instruction."

"Weirdo," said one of the Belgians as they walked out onto the sidewalk. "Dork," said another, but Serge had already changed channels.

He and Coleman were right up to the set, blocking the view from anyone else, and the volume was low.

They saw crime scene tape outside the Orbit Motel.

They saw the Lotus outside the World Series and a sheet in the road on No Name Key.

"What do they mean, 'serial killers'!" said Serge. "Veale, okay. But Sharon was self-defense and the scalper—I mean, that was the World Series! You can call me a murderer, fair is fair, but as soon as you put 'serial' in front of it, everyone automatically thinks you're crazy."

"I only killed a deer," said Coleman, "and a turtle."

"We have to lay low and try to figure something out," said Serge.

"Yeah, but . . ."

"But what?"

"I wanted to go out and party."

The men in the school bus sang, *"I am woman, hear me roar,"* as they crossed the Seven Mile Bridge, but the driver didn't know the words and asked that they switch back to *"Put your hand in the hand."*

He blew his nose and dabbed his eyes with Kleenex and broke down again. They crested the Niles Channel Bridge and headed onto Summerland Key.

Dar-Dar hunched over the wheel, radio blaring. The sun had been down for two hours when the Yugo sputtered across the Saddlebunch Keys. He couldn't believe his luck. To his right: a red LeMans parked at the shoulder of the road, two shadows on the bridge with fishing poles.

He made a U-turn and parked on the opposite side of US 1. Waiting for a break in the traffic.

"Way too late in the year for tarpon," Serge told Coleman. Both were in their Hemingway beards. "Bonefish are out of the question too with this bait. Maybe get lucky with a trout."

Coleman reeled in his line and found something had chewed the shrimp off the hook. He hoisted the bait bucket out of the water and with clumsy effort retrieved another shrimp. He held it and the hook out to Serge.

"Okay," said Serge, "one more time. You can hook him through the face or under the tail or sideways through the carapace, but make sure you don't hit that black round thing inside. That's an important organ. He'll die right away; you'll get no action out of that bait. You can also twist that little fan thing off the end of the tail. It'll improve the cast and put more scent in the water, but you'll be doing way too many big things wrong for those little advantages to count."

With a rebaited hook, Coleman thought hard and flipped the bail on his spinning rod. Serge nodded so-far-so-good. Coleman stiffly whipped the rod and the line back over his shoulder, ready to cast.

A voice behind them yelled, "Watch it! You could put someone's eye out!"

Serge and Coleman turned. Dar-Dar held a sharp-looking scimitar. Without the baseball T-shirt and cap, and the scar on his forehead now showing, Dar-

Dar didn't look like the fan from the World Series. He wore an all-black outfit and ankle-length black trench coat. Cloven hooves were painted on his sneakers.

Serge studied the get-up and the inverted cross. "Who the hell are you supposed to be, Beelze*boob?*"

"I am Dar-Dar!" he said.

"Tartar?" asked Coleman. "Like fish sauce?"

"No! Dar-Dar! Lord of ultimate evil, pain and hopelessness!"

"Oh," said Serge. "*That* Dar-Dar."

Dar-Dar placed the point of the sword into the road and genuflected to one knee. He closed his eyes and prayed softly. Serge looked at Coleman and spun a finger at the side of his head, indicating insanity.

Dar-Dar continued his contrition. "I am not worthy, oh dark one. But thank you, great Satan, for the chance to offer you this humble blood sacrifice in the name of all that is unholy and shitty. . . . "

With long black hair and black clothes, kneeling at night on an unlighted bridge, Dar-Dar was invisible. There was faint singing in the night, *"Put your hand in the hand of the man who calmed the sea . . ."*

It grew louder, but Dar-Dar continued talking to the devil.

". . . hand in the hand of the man from Galilee . . ."

Dar-Dar looked up over the high headlights and saw a man behind the wheel with eyes streaming tears of joy. A banner hung across the top of the windshield.

Dar-Dar read the banner and said, "Goddammit!" and was crushed to death by a Promise Keeper bus.

Twenty-three

With Dar-Dar all over the road and Promise Keepers running everywhere, Serge decided they should leave before the authorities arrived.

An hour later they were ambling down Duval Street. Coleman wore a newly purchased T-shirt that said, "Mean people suck. . . . Nice people swallow."

"Maybe later we can go to the cockfights," said Serge. "They have them around here somewhere. I just have to get hooked up. We'll ask a cabdriver. They know where all the action's at."

They ate conch fritters with Key limes, sitting on the sidewalk, leaning against the front of the Southern Cross Hotel. A debutante from Jupiter Island mistook the bearded pair for vagrants and said, "Homeless and hungry, blah, blah, blah."

Serge spotted one of the half-bike/half-rickshaws in the loading zone. The driver said his name was Aubrey, from New Zealand. Twenty-two and not a bit wiser. He looked at their Hemingway beards.

"Hey! ZZ Top!" he said.

"ZZ Top wants the big tour," said Serge, climbing in back with Coleman.

"You got it."

After directing Aubrey through a series of stops, Serge and Coleman had sacks of take-out Cuban food, beer and Jack Daniel's in back with them.

"Have a beer," Serge told Aubrey.

"Not while working. I'll get fired."

Serge had him stop at a drugstore and bought a bicyclist's water bottle. He filled it with two cans of Miller and handed it over Aubrey's shoulder.

"Hey! Thanks!"

Over the next three hours, Serge and Coleman would make Aubrey a legend in his field, setting the Key West rickshaw record with a two-hundred-dollar fare. They saw Truman's southern white house, and they stopped to take pictures of the ten-ton concrete thimble at the ersatz Southernmost Point. In between were constant stops for rest rooms and tropical trinkets.

They rode down Olivia to Whitehead Street. At the corner of the Hemingway House they were beset by three competing crack dealers on mopeds, who appeared from behind bushes like motorcycle cops at a speed trap. "Psst, hey, I got what you want!"

Serge stood in the back of the rickshaw and pulled up his shirt to display the pistol in his waistband. The mopeds scattered.

Aubrey pedaled north on Duval.

Susan Tchoupitoulas walked south on the sidewalk, carrying flyers, darting in and out of stores where Serge and Coleman had been spotted.

She showed faxed photos of them in a kite factory, a body shampoo parlor and an art importer. The importers remembered the two all right, high breakage risks. Serge had handled and photographed everything. Coleman had bumped his marlin hat into a giant copper wind chime depicting a school of Spanish mackerel, and the staff had to get ladders to untangle him.

Susan walked in Southernmost Bong and Hookah, where Coleman had bought a ceramic toucan water pipe. The clerk yelled to another clerk, "Yo, Five-O! Five-O!"

"Bennie! It's me, Susan," Tchoupitoulas yelled as Bennie ran out the back door. "We went to high school together!"

Serge kept a steady flow of beer going to Aubrey, who lost inhibition and started taking pulls straight from the Jack Daniel's bottle in traffic in front of the Bull.

"You guys are the greatest," Aubrey declared.

"It's all relative," said Serge. "Turn around and watch the road."

When they got to Turtle Kraals, Aubrey was having trouble keeping the rickshaw on all three wheels. Leading to the Land's End Marina, in the darkness, was a winding downhill road. Aubrey took his feet off the pedals and let the bike freewheel. The pedals spun like fans, and Aubrey turned to an ashen Serge and Coleman. "Extreme, man!"

Somehow they found themselves going about thirty out on the wooden pier, vibrating like they were going down railroad tracks. They sailed off the end into the black water of Key West Bight.

A crack team of barflies ran down the pier and fished them out.

The rubber bands holding their beards had slipped down around their necks, and someone yelled, "It's those guys from TV, the deer killers!" Serge and Coleman fled sopping wet and ran out in front of a pink taxi driving by on Front Street. The driver hit the brakes and the two hopped in.

The taxi had a thick plastic body-fluid liner over everything in the backseat, and the driver ignored their wetness.

"Where to?" he asked.

"To the cockfights!" said Coleman.

"Ignore him," said Serge. "Start driving and I'll tell you when to turn."

They went west on Greene Street. Serge looked out the back window and saw a small mob running down the street chasing the cab. The cabbie studied them in the rearview mirror.

"Hey! You're the guys from TV! The murderers!" The hack hit the brakes, and Serge and Coleman bailed out and sprinted up Greene Street. The vigilantes ran by the cab in pursuit.

The mob was closing, about fifty yards behind Serge and Coleman, as they came to the intersection with Duval.

There was a lot of activity ahead in the road. On

the left-hand corner was Sloppy Joe's, and out on the sidewalk, spilling onto Duval, were the look-alikes. A few hundred, massing in the intersection.

They were in a tight knot in the street, mostly staggering, moving slow, or completely stopped, not appearing to be going anywhere soon, like cows when they're chewing. Blocking Serge and Coleman's escape. The mob right on them.

Serge reached the Hemingways, stopped and spun. Looking for an exit. He saw the mob a few feet away, about to pin them against the look-alikes. "Put your beard back on!" he told Coleman, and they pulled the rubber bands up behind their heads. Then they both turned their backs to the mob and pried their way into the Hemingways like they were climbing into a dense jungle.

The mob stopped at the edge of the Hemingways. They stood on their tiptoes and stretched their necks, trying to pick out Serge and Coleman. The pair burrowed deeper into the look-alikes.

One of the pursuers pointed and yelled, "There they are!" Serge saw the vigilantes start climbing in after them, and he pulled a pistol. He fired a fusillade in the air. The mob pulled back, tentative, and they dispersed when Serge fired two more shots.

Meanwhile, the Hemingways started moving slowly in the opposite direction, down Duval. In their dulled state, there was a calm confusion and general sluggishness of response. But as a few started moving, so did others. Slow at first, but soon all were under way, and the movement took on its own life.

The undulating, protoplasmic mass of Hemingways broke into a trot, then a run. In the middle, Serge and Coleman kept pace. By the time it got to Fleming Street it was a full-scale stampede. A clomping, reeling, wobbling herd of flatulence engines thundering across the island. A woman shrieked and a stranger darted into the street and pulled a small child from the path of the Hemingways. A moped slid out from under someone, and a man wearing a sandwich board that said "Repent" was trampled, footprints up and down his signs.

People ran hollering in the opposite direction; others dove for doorways or climbed on top of cars. Spooked cats came out of nowhere, running for their lives, adding to the panic. A tabby jumped onto one of the Hemingways' back and dug in its claws. The Hemingway twirled, yelling and flapping his arms behind him, trying to swat the cat just out of reach, and he ran up on the sidewalk and crashed through the front window of Margaritaville. A group of college thrill-seekers waited behind a fritter wagon, timing the herd. When it was alongside, the young men ran out into the Hemingways and down the street with them, dodging the men and their beer steins, trying not to get gored. Serge and Coleman worked their way to the eastern edge of the stampede and dove into a sunset cruise ticket booth at Angela Street.

The leading Hemingways ended up falling in the sea at the foot of Duval and others turned onto South Street until the matter petered out under its own specific gravity. The Japanese, English and Spanish television crews took news of the melee global. The following week, the look-alikes would be approached by a consortium from London, who would sign them to a lucrative deal to participate next year in the first annual Running of the Hemingways.

Serge and Coleman made their way through tiny backyards and victory gardens until they came out behind the garbage cans in an alley next to the Purple Pelican. In the distance, back toward Duval, they heard sirens and saw several spires of black smoke. They nonchalantly walked around the corner and into the Pelican's lobby. Serge waved as they walked by, soaking wet, filthy and winded, but the desk clerk showed disgusted indifference and returned to his crossword.

When Serge flicked on the light, he and Mo Grenadine surprised each other equally and both yelled. Grenadine had a flashlight and burglary tools in a drawstring Crown Royal pouch.

"Who are you?!" Serge asked.

"Southernmost Termite. The owner called and asked . . ."

"No you're not," said Coleman. "I know you. From the radio. You're Holy Moly! I love your show!"

Grenadine smiled, but Serge clubbed him to the ground anyway.

"I can't believe I'm really talking to Holy Moly in person!" said a starstruck Coleman as he and Serge tied him up in a chair.

"What are you doing here?" Coleman asked.

"You dolt!" said Serge. "He's looking for the money!"

Serge tied Grenadine's ankles together and went through his pants pockets.

"Get your hands off my dick, you fudgepacker!" Grenadine shouted. "Help! Help! Faggot attack!"

"That's it," said Serge and sealed Mo's mouth with duct tape. He flipped open a pocketknife and cut the ropes except the ones tying Mo's hands together. "Coleman, give me a hand here. Let's get him on his feet."

Coleman was looking for something for Grenadine to autograph.

"Coleman!"

Mo writhed and they sat him on the end of the bed. Coleman held Mo fast around the chest while Serge got the antigravity boots from his gym bag and put them on Mo's feet.

"Help me get him upside down," said Serge. They hung him by the hooks on the boots to the tension rod in the bathroom doorway. Serge opened his tackle box.

He squatted down and peered into Mo's inverted face. "You sure like to call people fudgepacker."

Grenadine's answer was muffled under the tape. Serge to Coleman: "Pull his pants down, I mean up."

Serge felt around inside the bag and pulled out a small plastic funnel used to change oil, some still coating it.

"Do you know what you make life like for a lot of people who have far more character and compassion than you?" This time Serge pulled back the tape to let Grenadine answer.

"Butt-snorkeler!"

Serge replaced the tape. "I suggest a toast. A toast to Holy Moly!"

He jammed the funnel between Grenadine's legs. "It's a special drink I've invented with you in mind. I call it the fudge daiquiri."

Serge opened a bottle of rum and poured it carefully into the funnel. "Bottoms up!"

Half the bottle went into Mo, and Serge corked up Grenadine with a pelican-shaped bar of hotel soap.

Serge explained to Grenadine, still upside down: "DUI in Florida is point oh eight percent blood alcohol content. At point forty, you're on your way to a coma, and you're pretty much dead at point sixty. What I've just poured in you should top out around point ninety. By bypassing the liver and going straight into the bloodstream through the intestines, the liquor will hit you in the next few minutes like a rocket sled."

Serge checked his watch.

"Here's your only hope for survival. And I think you, in particular, will appreciate this. In the next fifteen minutes you need to persuade someone to give you an immediate and massive enema. Your life depends on it."

They took Grenadine down from the tension rod and walked him out of the hotel room to the top of the stairs.

"You've heard of The Duval Crawl?" Serge asked,

referring to the bar-hopping tradition of Duval Street. "You're about to become the first person in history to do The Duval Crawl of Death!"

He cut Mo's wrists free, took the tape off his mouth and pushed him down the stairs.

"Rock on with your bad self, Beavis!" Serge called after him, and he and Coleman went back in room 3 and slammed the door.

The clerk at the front desk heard the rolling crash and sprang back. At the foot of the stairs, Grenadine pulled himself up by the banister. He could see at least five or six clerks at the reservation desk, circling in a kaleidoscope.

Mo charted a course for the desk, but he ended up moving like a guy in an initiation game after spinning around a baseball bat with his forehead on the handle. He overshot the desk and crashed into a potted croton. The clerk ran around the counter to help him, and Mo grabbed him by the shirt and demanded an enema.

Mo hit the sidewalk in front of the Purple Pelican on his back.

"And stay out!" yelled the clerk.

Even in his stupor, Mo knew time was critical. He stumbled his way across traffic on Duval and into the Charter Boat.

The Charter Boat was testosterone-rich, pea-brained and about as homophobic a bar as Key West can muster. The bartenders mixed drinks up on a tuna tower welded into the middle of the tavern. Behind it was a teak fighting chair, where patrons strapped themselves in, put their heads back and had margaritas mixed in their mouths. They yanked around with the aftertaste like they were fighting an eight-hundred-pound mako shark.

Mo careened into two guys on stools, spilling their beers.

"Help me. For the love of God. They're trying to kill me. They poisoned me with alcohol . . ."

Except it came out in a new, indecipherable language consisting entirely of vowels and drooling. Unfortunately for Mo, his enunciation congealed at the moment he got to the part about the enema.

Mo was strapped into the fighting chair, a big-armed man pinching his nose and another pouring double margaritas down his throat. Mo kicked furiously against the foot plate. Over the bar he saw an autographed photo of himself, inscribed, "Death to the Fudgepackers! Affectionately, Holy Moly."

Soon he was back flat on the sidewalk again, fuming high-proof from both ends. He righted himself on a bike rack and slalomed down the sidewalk, knocking over mopeds and banging into people, who shoved him into walls and lampposts. Duval Street had become an evil fun house, rocking, bending and weird.

On the sidewalk, he reached into his pants and between his legs without shame, trying to get at the pelican soap, but it was too far gone. He fell through the swinging saloon doors of Sting Rays, a gay dance club. A rainbow of laser beams sprayed the dark interior. Thousand-watt horn tweeters split his eardrums, and the subwoofers shook his ribs. Mo realized he was out on the dance floor, doing Joe Cocker.

"Bust a move!" shouted the man next to him. His partner smiled and nodded.

"I need an enema!" he shouted.

"What? Can't hear you!"

"I said, I need an enema!"

Mo thought: Are those jumper cables?

The men waved Mo over to a quieter area away from the dance floor.

"I said, I need an enema!"

The men laughed. "Don't we all!" More laughter.

"No, my life depends on it. I've got to have an enema . . ." He grabbed the jumper cables.

"Ow, that hurts!"

Literally, to save his life, Mo couldn't help himself: "You, you fudgepackers!"

"Well if that's the way you're going to be—" one of them began, but he was interrupted by someone else at the bar.

"That phrase. That *voice*. I know him. That's that fucker from Tampa."

"Just one enema, please!"

Instead he was given the bum's rush and socked in the jaw three times quick, reeling backward out the saloon doors and falling ass over teakettle into the middle of Duval Street.

Clang-clang. Clang-clang. Clang-clang.

Getting louder. Clang-clang. Mo stood up to see about the noise.

Bam! He was struck and dragged around all the finest points of interest in Key West by the Conch Train.

Twenty-four

Serge awoke before dawn in room 3 of the Purple Pelican when he heard the pop of a beer top and saw Coleman sitting in front of the dresser and watching it like a TV.

"I want to go out," said Coleman.

Serge was already ahead of him and hopped from bed.

Reluctant to go last night, Serge was driven to explore this morning. Overnight, the island had begun to metabolize in his system.

Serge always thought he'd die inside a month if he ever lived in Key West. While the balminess and quirky island lifestyle slowed time and energy for others, it only kick-started Serge's manicness. His interest in history, architecture, nature and all things Key West made him buzz around the island like a moth on speed.

Others might burn out on the alcohol and drugs that accompany the Keys' slothfulness; Serge would fry to a crisp trying to wholly consume its personality. But that was Key West. It searched out and exploited the hairline crack in each person's stability and crowbarred it open.

Serge went on a shopping spree and brought the bags back to the room. He pulled out a large backpack and pulled a smaller backpack out of it. He filled it with his native-tourist gear: camera, lenses, extra film, leather-bound journal, gravity-defiant pens, water bottle, the 1939 WPA guide to Florida, coupons, maps, AM/FM radio with weather alarm, a travel-size .25 automatic pistol and other people's credit cards. He left one compartment empty to collect more matchbooks, pins, patches and postcards. Coleman added into the bag a few beers, a bottle of bourbon, mixing shaker, to-go cups and a row of joints in a silver cigarette case from Germany during the war.

The backpack was heavier than Serge expected, so he hoisted it onto Coleman and handed him his beard. The desk clerk was dozing when Serge asked if there was any sign of a short black guy named Sean. The clerk opened his eyes to slits and was going to say no but closed his eyes again. A coffeepot was going somewhere. They walked out the lobby and into the blackness just before five A.M.

Vagrants lay in alleys and under the poinciana in front of St. Paul's Episcopal Church; young and old, in scales of life decline, The Evolution of the Sterno Bum.

The only others up were garbage collectors and

fishermen; no sounds except a chilly ocean breeze and the metal doors of newspaper boxes slamming shut now and then. As they walked south on Duval, crossing Truman, the sky didn't start showing light, just not as pure a black. And Serge introduced Coleman to The Routine.

He bought a *Miami Herald* and *Key West Citizen* and selected sidewalk seats on the elevated patio at the Sapodilla Inn. Breakfast ninety-nine cents. Serge and Coleman each got two. Buttermilk biscuits, sunny-side-up eggs, grits, bacon. Serge spread the yolk on everything. Coleman spiked his orange juice with Absolut.

Serge read about the baffling World Series murders in the papers as the sun came up in heavy clouds. He mopped up the plates with the biscuits.

"Let's rock!"

"Right," said Coleman.

Serge stuffed the newspapers in Coleman's backpack and dropped a ten on the table.

They continued south and crossed over to the foot of Whitehead Street. Serge took pictures of the concrete red-black-and-yellow buoy that marked the southernmost point, which he had photographed the night before. What he lacked in photographic training and talent he compensated for with electricity. He lay on the ground, looking through the 28mm wide-angle. Inching around in the road for another perspective that was never good enough, getting himself all dirty. The lens exaggerated the concrete buoy and bent the sky; waves smacked the seawall and shot spray into the air behind the marker, and Serge pressed the button.

The dawn had come up a battleship gray, and it stoned Serge on a depressing déjà vu he got whenever Key West was cold, empty and overcast.

"They put up that concrete marker because tourists kept stealing the signs," Serge explained.

They moved on. "It's not even the real southernmost point. That's on navy property." He pointed toward a fenced-off area and a bunch of directional antennas aimed at Cuba.

"See that place?" Serge indicated the Queen Anne residence that's known as the southernmost house.

"It's supposed to have secret trapdoors leading to a hidden basement. The owner put 'em in back in the early eighteen hundreds in case Indians attacked, which they had a habit of doing simply because we attacked them. You think we have a crime problem *now*? Imagine: You're in the kitchen baking a pie and arrows start coming through the window . . ."

Coleman nodded in feigned attention, sitting at the curb mixing a drink out of his backpack. Serge had them cross over to Simonton Street. They stopped for conch chowder at the lunch counter in Dennis Pharmacy.

They went to the Salvation Army and the dollar T-shirt rack. Serge whipped through the shirts and grabbed two. "Put this on," he said, and they changed in the middle of the store and paid the two dollars.

"We need these shirts to pass for locals. They'll

never be able to tell the difference." They walked down the street wearing Key West Electric Company T-shirts and fake Hemingway beards.

They came to the cemetery on the wrong side and climbed the fence. Serge gave Coleman the history of the USS *Maine*. "It all ties in with that time we visited the old Tampa Bay Hotel." He took pictures of the verdigris sculpture of a sailor scanning the horizon, where a silver prop plane descended over a row of coconut palms. Serge hurried Coleman into the Key West Island Bookstore and pointed at the signed author photos along the top of the walls. "The Pantheon!" Serge said. "That's Tom McGuane. And there's James Hall." He bought more postcards and rare used hardcovers and stuffed them in Coleman's backpack.

They walked briskly down Southard Street to the Five Brothers grocery, for cheese toast and café con leche. They ran over to Faustos, for Cuban salads at the deli to go. They dashed in an art gallery so Serge could show Coleman prints of Winslow Homer's *Hurricane* and *Stowing Sail*. Then they dashed out.

Serge was practically in a jog now.

"Hey, slow down," said Coleman, spilling a drink and trying to light a joint.

"Sorry," said Serge. They were crisscrossing the residential interior of Old Town in a grid. The wooden houses inspired Serge, and he pointed and offered an architecture class: "Classical revival . . . Victorian gothic . . . Creole . . ." He indicated gingerbread trim and widow's walks and shipbuilders' influence. "See how the roof comes down over the windows upstairs? That's called an eyebrow house."

Coleman took another puff of marijuana.

"More pot, eh?" said Serge.

Coleman: "Pot, grass, weed, dope, hemp, rope, thing, shit, gage, spliff, doobie, joint, number, ganja, blunt, Mary Jane, smoke, blow, roach, bone, jay, toke, hit, Bogart . . ."

Serge took the joint away from Coleman and stomped it out on Eaton Street. "That stuff's turning your brain to swamp cabbage."

"We need to stop and rest," said Coleman. "Where's a bar?"

The Bait House, on Garrison Bight, used to be a bait house. Bottles of beer floated in ice water in the old cement shrimp well. The bait pump still worked, and the bottles swam in a circle around the tank.

Coleman got a draft and Serge a bottle of Zephyrhills. "Finally, a place that has native water," he said.

Coleman looked at Serge's bottle of water. "What happened to the tincture of banana rule?"

"That was yesterday. I was talkin' shit."

The bar was in front of the bait tank and perpendicular to the door, and it was made of dense, dark lignum vitae wood. It was noon outside and midnight in the bar, only red light. Serge and Coleman took stools in the middle. There was no one between them and the door. On the other side, three stools down, was the only other person in the bar. A Dodge salesman down from Hialeah for a few days. He moved to the stool next to Serge.

"What're you drivin'? Cuz I bet I can put you in something better, and for a price you can't beat!" He smiled and thrust a hand forward with blind, hapless confidence, "The name's Archie Wallace." He handed them each a business card. Archie had full, droopy Deputy Dawg jowls and a forty-weight Dixie accent. He dipped a wad of tobacco into his lower lip.

"Damn, the Hurricanes had a butt-ugly season this year. I'm partial to the Crimson Tide myself, but when in Rome, ha ha ha. What're you boys drinkin'?"

Serge pointed to his water. "I'm fine."

Coleman, a beer sitting in front of him, smelled a free drink. "Dewar's!"

"Get the man a Dewar's!" Archie hollered to the bartender. "Shit, man, I love the Keys. Hopin' to get me a little something on the side if ya know what I mean. The women are damn fine! Hear the fishin' 's not shabby either. You fish? I'm a regular bass expert myself. Say, what's the deal with all the fairies down here? Bartender, where's that drink for my buddy!"

The front door flung open with a bang and Serge and Coleman shielded their eyes from the sunlight. Three men in dark suits walked in. They wore marksmen sunglasses and each had a small wire running out of his collar to an earpiece. Standard FBI/Secret Service haircuts.

"Shit!" whispered Serge and turned his face away from the men, looking at his water. He reached down with the hand opposite the door to the gun at his waist. He stared ahead at the mirror behind the bar and raised the water to his mouth with the other hand.

Coleman was sweating and fidgeted. "I'm scared," he said to Serge.

"Keep it in your pants," Serge whispered back. "We're not caught yet. Maybe I can talk our way out."

The agents looked in all directions as they walked unhurriedly through the bar. In the mirror, Serge saw they were three stools down from him, and he clicked the safety off his pistol.

When the agents were directly behind them, Serge began to rotate on his stool, thinking he'd say something disarming, possibly "How's it goin' today, fellas?"

He was a quarter way around, about to open his mouth. Two of the agents jumped back into wide shooting stances, pulled guns from armpit holsters and screamed, "Freeze, motherfucker!"

The third agent grabbed the Dodge salesman by the hair and smashed his face on the bar sideways. In front of his face the agent slapped down a warrant from Paraguay in connection with eleven terrorist bombings. It had a picture of the Dodge salesman and the name Che Mendez, also known as "The Wolverine," also known as "The Dingo," also known as "The Yellow-Banded Carpet Weevil."

"It's the end of the road, Che," said the agent.

A thick Spanish accent came out of the Dodge salesman. "*¡Viva la revolución!*" And they dragged him out the door.

"Let's go to another bar," said Coleman.

*   *   *

The next-to-last island on the Overseas Highway used to be Key West's barnyard, raising cattle for the residents, and it was named Stock Island.

Serge turned the LeMans north from US 1 onto Cross Street and took Fifth Street until he came to Cow Key Channel.

He drove across the parking lot to the dock and turned the car off. Coleman could see something had Serge shook up as he looked out at the cement-block building.

"It's gone!" said Serge.

"What is?"

"Cow Key Marina!"

Coleman looked at the peach-colored building and the fraternity brothers milling around by the Jet Skis, holding credit cards. Serge got out of the car and walked around with Coleman.

"This is where they filmed the movie!" said Serge. "Peter Fonda blew up a boat right there. That was during his *Dirty Mary, Crazy Larry* period. And over there is where Warren Oates and Harry Dean Stanton talked about murder. The shutters were painted with sailfish. Now it's a fucking snack display."

Coleman nodded.

Serge walked to a place in the gravel, pointing down. "This is where the tiki hut used to be, where Margot Kidder and Elizabeth Ashley got in a fight. I was out here in the eighties and a guy drove up in a Torino and pawned it for a six-pack. Then he walked home."

"Far out," said Coleman.

"This is a really bad sign," Serge said.

He moped on his way back to the car, and didn't speak as they drove to the dive boat docked a few blocks away.

Twenty-five

Captain Bradley Xeno got to be a captain by simply buying a boat, which Serge thought was a hell of a loophole. Serge insisted on addressing him as "Ensign," and Xeno hated him the second they met.

This put Serge in the company of every other paying customer Xeno ever had. Xeno owned a thirty-foot Wellcraft and made the payments by shuttling tourists on abbreviated snorkeling trips out to crappy, polluted reefs with no fish.

Standard reef trips by other boats ran a pleasant three to four hours, but about an hour and fifteen minutes into his excursions Xeno couldn't stand the thought of strangers on his boat any longer. He'd run everyone out of the water, race back and dump them on the dock, bewildered and bitter.

Considering it took forty-five minutes just to get to the reef, passengers had barely learned how to blow the spit out of their snorkels before they were marshaled back into the boat. He didn't allow talking on board.

Sometimes he'd wait at a dive site too long, giving passengers time to notice and ask, "Hey, where are the fish?"

At which times Xeno would say, "You want fish? Go to Red Lobster!"

He always had a week of stubble, because it made him feel studly. His glasses were green mirrors with a caution-yellow frame. He wore the tight mid-thigh shorts of football players at training camp.

He sold tickets out of a Duval Street booth and moored the boat at Cow Key Channel.

Serge and Coleman showed up in their beards. Xeno took one look and said, "No drinking until after diving."

Coleman opened a sixteen-ounce Bud in front of Xeno and guzzled it empty in one pull. He smiled at Xeno. "I've just finished diving for the day." He pushed past the captain and jumped into the boat, landing with a loud, flat-footed thud.

Xeno cringed. "Be careful!"

"There a problem, Ensign?" asked Serge.

Xeno turned back around and saw Serge and made a mental note to cut the trip even shorter today.

During the ride out, Xeno sighed and made facial contortions, constantly registering annoyance with everyone.

When Xeno told a single mother to "watch your

damn kid," he began an inexorable slide toward Serge.

Six miles out, near the reef, the small boy spotted something on the southern horizon, toward the Gulf Stream.

Serge checked with his binoculars. Five miles away were a half-dozen skinny men in rags on what looked like a bunch of bathtub toys lashed together.

"Rafters," said Serge. "They don't look good."

"Fuck 'em," said Xeno. "They come here to steal our jobs and end up sucking unemployment out of my pocket."

Xeno turned around and saw the end of a .38 snub-nose between his eyes. "Go pick 'em up," said Serge.

Steam was practically coming out of Xeno's ears as the six Cuban refugees climbed into his beloved boat, laughing, saluting and chanting, "U-S-A! U-S-A!"

Serge asked the single mom to walk her little boy up to the bow, and she did.

"What was that for?" said Xeno, cranky.

"Take your clothes off."

"You can't be serious!" said Xeno, dressed in rags, standing out on the raft. "I could die."

"It's all for the better," said Serge. "Like you just said, these refugees are just gonna take your job. You'll end up a displaced worker, and then I'll have to pay *your* unemployment out of *my* pocket."

As Serge untied the rope to the raft, Captain Xeno pleaded. Serge responded by singing Tom Petty. "You Don't Have to Live Like a Refugee."

Serge cast off the rope that had connected the raft

to the Wellcraft, and Xeno slowly floated out into the Gulf Stream.

Serge yelled, "We don't like bigots in this country!"

"Yeah," yelled Coleman. "We don't like Cubans either!"

Serge turned and gave him the stink eye.

"Sorry," said Coleman.

Serge was now off the chart, medication-wise. Under the spirit and letter of U.S. law, he was no longer competent to stand trial.

Instead of cruising to the nearest port, he piloted the boat back to the reef.

He handed out masks, snorkels, fins and safety vests to the refugees, who listened carefully and nodded, believing this might be naturalization training. What began as a celebration soured to befuddlement for the Cubans, who found themselves back in the water, forced to learn how to snorkel at gunpoint.

Serge leaned over the side of the boat, talking to the refugees with the revolver in one hand and a waterproof fish guide in the other. He tapped the plastic fish card twice with the gun barrel.

"Can any of you identify a sergeant major?"

The insurance industry has raised invasion of privacy to a level that makes the FBI salivate. So when Charles Saffron wanted info, he didn't have to look beyond his own company. New England Life trampled individual liberty with such delight that it did so even when it was easier and cheaper not to.

Saffron dialed his Tampa office from the presidential suite in the Ocean King Resort at the bottom of Simonton Street. He tracked Grenadine down to a spate of phone calls billed to his home number and placed from Shrimpboat Willie's Motel and Grill in Key West.

It couldn't be this simple, Saffron thought, standing in Grenadine's second-floor room fifteen minutes later. He didn't even need to use a credit card; the warped door popped open with a firm tug. And now, staring at him from a yellow legal pad on top of the television:

"Serge/Coleman [underlined], Purple Pelican, Room 3, 10/27."

He scrambled out the window and lowered himself hand over hand on a hurricane tie-down cable when he heard the Costa Gordans breaking in.

In room 3 of the Purple Pelican, Coleman was giving his new ceramic toucan water pipe a test spin. He crossed his legs in the middle of the floor and put his mouth over the end of the toucan's bright orange beak. The bird made the unmistakable bubbling sound as it filled with hash smoke. Coleman raised up and took a deep breath and tried to hold it as best he could, but he began sneezing it out his nose and then lost the whole thing in a massive coughing fit.

He sat there dazed in the illegal cloud. "Lung capacity ain't what it used to be," he said to himself. "Wonder why that is."

There was a knock at the door.

"Who is it?" asked Coleman.

"Southernmost Blintz."

"Munchies!" said Coleman. "Come in!"

Three Latin men entered the room and whipped Israeli submachine guns with silencers from their jackets. The three swept the ends of their guns from side to side as they sprayed the center of the room.

The silencers gave the guns a deceptively gentle purring sound as the ceramic toucan shattered and the colorful glass splinters showered the room. When they were done, they dragged Coleman's body out of the way and propped it in a corner, and then began pulling the place apart.

The purple bar of hotel soap shaped like a pelican made a metallic ping when it hit the stainless-steel tray. Dr. Sheldon Killjoy had dropped it there with what Susan Tchoupitoulas thought looked like a pair of salad tongs.

"They *are* salad tongs," said Killjoy.

The Southernmost Morgue on Atlantic Boulevard shared space with a clothing-optional laundromat and the Unofficial Jimmy Buffett Museum, which was facing torrential litigation.

Susan asked Killjoy about the soap extracted from the off-color Mo Grenadine lying before them.

"Still looks accidental," said Killjoy. "That bar of soap is nothing. You wouldn't believe what I find. Once there was a string of Christmas lights, and another time four pounds of quick-dry underwater concrete . . ."

Susan dumped out a large brown envelope on the

vacant slab next to Mo's. It held the contents of Mo's pockets: five pennies, a ball of brown thread, a matchbook from a scuba shop, two loose antacid tablets and a room key for Shrimpboat Willie's.

A young woman in a one-piece swimsuit and beach hat pushed open a pair of shutters at the pass-through office window. She had a four-foot inflatable salt shaker under her arm and a pair of pop-top earrings in her hand. "Do I pay for these here?"

"No," said Killjoy. He pointed with a bloody latex hand holding a liver. "The gift shop register is at the end of the next aisle."

Susan refilled the brown envelope, except for the room key, and put it on Killjoy's desk. "Thanks, Doc."

A Mickey Mouse toothbrush stuck out the corner of Serge's closed mouth as he walked down the second-floor hallway of the Purple Pelican and hummed "Smuggler's Blues." He wore a gamboge bathrobe with a pelican over the right breast, and he wondered when those two guys with the five million were going to show up. He had been checking with the desk clerk far past the threshold of harassment.

Serge had bought eighty-nine-cent plastic flip-flops at Eckerd's, to prevent athlete's foot in the European shower, and they slapped wet on the varnished wood floor. A towel was wrapped around his wet hair like a turban, which he had learned how to do as a child watching Haji on *Johnny Quest*.

Serge opened the door and had the feeling of a

foreign object in his heart. Coleman sat in the corner, his face shot off. Three Latin men in white suits with submachine guns were tossing the place.

They saw him.

He ducked from the doorway and pressed himself against the wall next to the door.

Normally, unarmed people facing three men with machine guns will run for their lives, and the Costa Gordans didn't think otherwise as they charged out the door. Serge clotheslined the first one with an elbow to the Adam's apple.

He then slammed the door on the other two and jumped to the opposite side of the doorway, grabbing the fallen Costa Gordan's machine gun on the way. The door swung back open into the hall and the other Costa Gordans ran out, looking the wrong way.

Serge shot blind through the back side of the door. Wood splinters, purple chips of paint and sawdust fluttered to the balcony floor.

He dragged the two bodies into the room. The third, who wasn't dead, clawed at his injured throat, and Serge knocked him unconscious with a glass pelican ashtray.

Serge walked over to Coleman and sat down on the floor next to him. He put a foam Marlin on Coleman's head and one on his own, and he stared at the ceiling.

The door creaked open. Charles Saffron walked in pointing a gun.

"If that's how you're gonna be, I'm definitely not buying any magazines," said Serge.

"I want the money," said Saffron.

Saffron looked down and saw the machine guns. "Silencers," he said. "All the better."

He grabbed one of the machine guns and reached behind him to return the pistol to a concealed holster in the small of his back.

Serge, sitting cross-legged on the floor next to his buddy, didn't care anymore. He told Saffron about Veale hiding the briefcase and the two guys at the World Series and the Purple Pelican.

Still holding the machine gun on Serge, Saffron dialed his office again and fed in the stray data.

Saffron emitted a series of "uh-huhs" as he received dossiers on Sean and David, including phone calls that morning from the Angel Fish Inn.

"It all checks out," said Saffron, and in that moment, Serge knew he was dead.

He asked Saffron, "Can you take a last photo of us?" He scooted over, put an arm around Coleman's shoulder and smiled.

Saffron was repulsed by the sight. Coleman's corpse had begun to attract dog peter gnats. "No way!" said Saffron.

"Please," pleaded Serge. He picked up the camera and held it toward Saffron. "It should be focused already."

"I said no!"

Serge pressed the shutter button and the xenon bulb flashed in Saffron's face, blinding him. Serge dove and came up with a machine gun. Saffron yelled and fired without aim.

Events moved slower and slower until time stood still, hanging a moment in the air like a pole vaulter atop the bar. Saffron was between shots, wildly off target; Serge had just reached Saffron's chest with the sight of the machine gun.

No air was moving. It was one of those slightly chilly days where you need a light coat on the street. But inside, with the sun filling the window, there was a cozy greenhouse effect. The light came in at a slant, making a bright tube of dancing dust. The temperature reminded Serge of a day with his mother in the early sixties, eating a tuna sandwich in the backyard.

Serge unconsciously bit a little on his tongue as he concentrated in a millisecond, aiming, ready to fire, when he felt an absolutely dumb-luck shot thump his chest. Under Serge's adrenaline, it was but a light tap.

Serge quick-inhaled half a breath. For some reason he pictured the view from the Seven Mile Bridge and thought what a great trip it had been as he hit the floor face first.

Twenty-six

Susan Tchoupitoulas found the room at Shrimpboat Willie's trashed. Part of it was the ransacking by the Costa Gordans, the rest was Grenadine's lifestyle. The mattresses and pillow were gutted, and the top of the dresser was littered with empty beer cans, dirty underwear and crushed pretzels. The lampshades were smeared with jerky-treat grease. A yellow legal pad was torn to confetti. A shred of paper caught her eye. It read "Serge/ Colem——" and was ripped right below.

Under the bed Susan found an electronic gizmo that glowed green when she pressed the "on" switch. An arrow pointed north to a green dot on the four-inch screen.

Back in her police car, Susan's attention was split between driving and watching the screen of the homing device, which led her up Elizabeth Street to a LeMans parked next to the Purple Pelican.

The desk clerk looked at the photos of Serge and

Coleman that Susan was holding and said, "Those guys!" He pointed overhead to the balcony. "Room three."

Susan went to her car and called for backup. Her old partner Jeff showed up first, followed by the original Bubba, Lieutenant Turdly.

Tchoupitoulas suggested they set up a perimeter but Turdly said, "Step aside, little girl," and blustered up the stairs. Saffron had left the door half open.

"Sir, I think we should . . ."

This time he brushed past her with an elbow to her ribs that was quick, subtle and unwitnessed.

"What a mess," said Turdly, patting his stomach and marking the target for the surviving Costa Gordan, who had recovered from his throat injury and was raising a machine gun.

"Watch out!" Susan yelled and aimed her gun, but Turdly's considerable displacement blocked the doorway and prevented a clean shot.

Susan belly-flopped on the floor behind the lieutenant, knocking the wind out of her. She fired between his legs, hitting the Costa Gordan in the mouth.

Turdly didn't say a word at first, then: "You think you're hot shit!" and shoved her into the door frame as he left the room.

Serge didn't know if he was in heaven or what. He was there on the floor, hearing voices, a gunshot echoing through a canyon, and a deep voice, ". . . think-

think-think you're-you're-you're hot-hot-hot shit-shit-shit."

There wasn't any tunnel or bright light or disembodied flying around the room. Serge just stared up from the floor unable to move. He tried to yell for help, but it was like in a dream when nothing comes out, and he was truly scared. He got his fingertips moving a bit first and then his neck and mouth. His panic thawed enough so that he thought better of calling out. About the time he could lift his head off the floor, his chest hurt like he'd been punched by a gorilla.

His shirt was moist with a large red stain in the middle. Saffron's shot had been luckier than he'd first thought. It was a ricochet, and it had glanced off his breastbone, causing heart arrhythmia and knocking him out.

The others had just left, and Turdly had placed an underling Bubba on guard on the balcony outside the room.

Serge zipped up a windbreaker to cover the bloodstain and grabbed his camera. He peered out the door and saw the officer not paying attention, gazing over the balcony's railing down into the lobby.

Serge backed up to the doorway with the camera and started taking pictures into the room. The officer heard him and turned.

"Hey you! You're not supposed to be in there! Get outta here!" The officer pointed down the stairs.

"Sure thing."

Susan was behind the front desk, taking a statement from the hotel manager, when the manager pointed at Serge coming down the stairs. He said offhand, "That's him right there."

Serge saw the woman in the sheriff's uniform over at the hotel desk, spinning toward him, going for her gun. But Serge already had his gun in hand, hidden under the windbreaker, and he pulled it and had it sighted on her immediately.

"Freeze!" he shouted. Susan stopped, her hand on the pistol, still in the holster.

They stared at each other, respective heartbeats blocking out everything. Serge saw the name plate on Susan's uniform. S. Tchoupitoulas.

"You're Suzie. Samuel's girl."

She nodded, looking down the barrel.

"Say hi to your dad for me," Serge said. He lowered the barrel and tossed the gun underhand, and it landed at Susan's feet. He turned and casually walked toward the door of the Purple Pelican.

Susan drew her own gun and held it in a two-handed grip. "Freeze!"

He kept walking.

"I'll shoot!" Susan shouted with more verve and determination this time.

Serge turned to face her from the doorway. "No you won't."

He turned his back to her again and ran out of the hotel. Susan raced to the door, but the street was empty by the time she got to the sidewalk.

* * *

Saffron spent two pissed-off hours searching another subtropical hotel room and canvassing another parking lot for a car he couldn't find. Time for the honest, direct approach; the truth never hurt. He marched into the office of the Angel Fish Inn.

After Saffron's explanation, the clerk told him that his high school classmates Sean Breen and David Klein must have skipped their reunion, because they had just taken a seaplane on a sightseeing flight out to Fort Jefferson.

"Where's that?" asked Saffron.

"The Dry Tortugas."

"Where's that?"

"You go to the end of Key West, and you swim another seventy miles."

Saffron looked around the office at vibrant oil and acrylic paintings of queen, blue and French angelfish. The hands of the office clock had a rock beauty and a clown fish on the ends.

"Does everything in this town have a theme?"

"What do you mean?" asked the clerk.

Saffron had the windows rolled down as he followed the map around Stock Island to the seaplane office. He unconsciously tapped along with "Hot Fun in the Summertime" on the Alpine stereo.

The white gravel crunched under his wheels as he drove through the parking lot of an old marina. He could see the seaplanes tethered on the far end, but he still hadn't found the office.

A man in sandals and a Blue Parrot T-shirt walked

out of a plywood shack that Saffron had thought was a failing snack bar. The man lowered a corrugated PVC shutter over the front of the hut.

Saffron was halfway to the man when he saw the burnt-orange windsock under his arm.

"Sorry, we sent the last flight out twenty minutes ago," he said. "Had to cancel the others. Storm front moving in."

Saffron pulled a thousand from his pocket.

"I mean, we're now boarding."

Sean's sinuses said the barometer was appropriate when he and David skimmed over the Marquesas Atoll at a hundred feet. The sky empty and bright except for the string of popcorn clouds toward Cuba. Three dolphin swam in a pod near the northwest shore of the atoll. A flock of gulls took off from the mast of a half-submerged, rusty wreck.

Their pilot looked like Jack Nicklaus on a bender. His cobalt-blue golf shirt was untucked and his sunburn line ended a half inch below the white sun visor. He worked the plane's pedals with designer sandals made from old tires and was otherwise wistful, laconic and punctual.

He had a case of Budweiser under his pilot's seat. The pilot saw Sean looking worried at the beer. "That's in case we run into the shrimpers," he said, and said no more.

They all wore headphones; the pilot had big red ones with a microphone he didn't use, and Sean and David had smaller models, yellow and blue. Sean noticed all the primary colors were represented but kept it to himself.

They had been flying about a half hour, and there was no longer any evidence of man. The last few mangrove islands dribbled off when the loggerhead turtles appeared, dozens of them scattered across the dead zone of the Gulf of Mexico, wiggling tiny flippers as the Cessna's shadow ran over them.

David checked the horizon over the cowling of the seaplane and saw it first. It reminded him of that smooth black thing on the moon in *2001: A Space Odyssey*.

This far out in the Gulf, in a world without corners, a long rectangle the size of a shopping mall started to rise out of the sea in the middle of nowhere and halfway to nowhere else.

As they got closer, Fort Jefferson took form, a brick hexagon. Jack Nicklaus banked and began his landing approach by circling the fort, which revealed a grassy courtyard inside three stories of masonry. It had a moat, bridge, dock, pockets of coconut palms and a sandy beach against the moat wall on the south side.

A collection of sailboats and yachts was anchored in the harbor, and the pilot split them with his landing. He cut the throttle back, and the plane fell, giving Sean and David a down-elevator feeling in their stomachs. The pontoons hit the water hard, seemed to bounce, and settled in as the Cessna taxied to the beach.

The front of the pontoons wedged into the sand.

Jack Nicklaus jumped down into the ankle-deep water. Sean and David climbed out more slowly.

David stood on the left pontoon, handing gear to Sean in the water. "This isn't the kind of place people end up by accident."

Sean slipped and fell to one knee. "But sometimes by mistake."

Charles Saffron's pilot was a talking machine. Lanky and activated, with curly, uncombed hair and a handlebar mustache. He looked like he was in his mid-twenties and had overslept his entire life.

"It's the whole Indiana Jones, Banana Republic, *Romancing the Stone* thing!" he said, flying happy. "Your own slice of paradise."

Most passengers want to sit in the copilot's seat when its available, but Saffron took one look at the pilot and went directly for the back of the plane. The pilot was somehow mellow and wired at the same time, and was too distracted to take offense by the reaction from Saffron, who was reminded of Mark Fidrych, the Detroit Tigers pitcher who talked to baseballs.

"Man, this is the beginning and the end of Florida. It's our answer to the top of Mount Everest, the bottom of Death Valley and last call at Rick's."

Don't call me "man," the voice inside Saffron's head said, and he opened a camouflage dry box in his lap.

"Man, the craziest things happen out here! You should hear the stories!"

No I shouldn't.

"First it was a fort, to protect shipping in the gulf, like Gibraltar. Can you dig?"

Nope. Saffron took pistols out of the box and loaded them.

"But soldiers caught yellow fever and fell like bowling pins. They quarantined them on a sandbar. Too much!"

Saffron inspected calibration of the sights.

"Then it was a prison. Guess what? A bunch of the prisoners went crazy. I know I would. They tried to swim over a hundred miles to the Everglades. Never found."

Halfway out to the Tortugas, the pilot said, "My name's Tom Johnson. But they call me Crash Johnson."

Crash had a habit of turning completely around to face Saffron in the backseat when he spoke. He detected Saffron's apprehension.

"Aw, this thing flies itself."

Saffron thought if it did, I'd have already shot you.

"The USS *Maine* sailed from here for Havana. That's where it got blown up. It started the Spanish-American War. You like history?"

Nope.

"Like the guy who shot Lincoln, right? There was this other guy, a doctor who didn't know who he was, and he fixed his broken leg. They threw him in jail anyway, 'cause they were *that* mad. Guess where they sent him?"

I have no idea.

"Right! Fort Jefferson. You can go in his cell—it's on the tour. You know that *tortugas* means turtles in Spanish? Or is it Mexican?"

Crash scratched his chin.

"Anyway, you probably wonder why they call it the Dry Tortugas out in the middle of all this friggin' water...."

Not once.

"There ain't no *fresh* water! You can die of thirst out here!" said Crash. "You see the pattern? People who come to the Tortugas have the kind of bad luck usually only seen in Greek plays."

That's how it's beginning to feel, thought Saffron.

"See that island over there? Know what sailors used to do? They'd step on all the birds' eggs and the birds would lay fresh ones in a few hours. Instant breakfast! Hey, you know what I think? ..."

Saffron wanted to carve a design in his own forehead with a scuba knife, but they were preparing to land and it would be over soon. Crash circled the fort an extra time on the approach to the harbor, because he couldn't explain all the historic features the first time around.

They landed far more smoothly than Saffron expected and parked on the beach next to another seaplane.

Crash climbed down and opened Saffron's door with effervescence. "Welcome to the nineteenth century!"

* * *

The moat wall was about eight feet across, wide enough for two-way foot traffic. Sean and David threw their gear under a palm tree and went for a walk on the wall to get the lay of the fort.

They began clockwise from the southern beach. The moat wall acted as a breaker for the surf from the Gulf, and it created distinct ecosystems on each side. On the left was typical open-sea terrain. A giant manta ray flapped slowly by an anchor from a forgotten galleon. A territorial barracuda ran off smaller fish at one corner of the moat wall. They could see tarpon fins at another.

To the right, the wall protected colonies of sea horses, squirts, urchins and anemones. A pulsing jellyfish floated by, a small hot-air balloon. A tourist coming toward them was walking his fish, literally. He broke off pieces of bread and threw them into the moat as he strolled. A fish snagged each piece of bread, keeping perfect pace with the man's stride.

Saffron wanted to know whether Sean and David were on the other seaplane, and he tried to strike up a conversation with Jack Nicklaus. He determined he needed dynamite to get the time of day. On average, he thought, the pilots were pleasant.

After five exhausting minutes, Saffron got a rough description of Sean and David, and he left without punctuating an end to the chat.

Saffron grabbed a sandwich from his collapsible cooler and started around the moat wall counterclockwise. He remembered how much he hated pimiento and started breaking pieces off the sandwich and throwing it to the fish in the moat.

The two men ahead on the moat wall fit the description he was looking for, and Saffron used the novelty of the trained fish to engage Sean and David in superficial talk. It wasn't unusual for strangers to drop guard in the Tortugas. There was the automatic bond of extraordinary effort to get this far from anything else.

Sean and David discovered others in the Tortugas weren't the old poolside gang from the Hilton. This was a slightly hardier confluence of lifestyles. Millionaire adventurers in yachts, marine biology students from the University of Florida, net fishermen from trawlers and a band of park rangers who inhabited a corner of the fort like a sect of monks.

Most urgent to Saffron was whether Sean and David had found the money. If not, he'd hang back and let them lead him to their car. If they had found it, the money undoubtedly had been moved and Sean and David were a flight risk. In that case he'd have to accelerate plans and initiate confrontation with overwhelming force.

Saffron wanted to construct a discussion that wouldn't appear too curious but would spring loose clues that they suddenly felt incredibly wealthy. New home, travel plans, premature retirement, kept women.

Saffron decided their answers were ambiguous and ambivalent. Could go either way. David was moving and Sean planned to leave his job. But he detected no wild new rhythms often found in lottery winners, like a nascent heroin habit.

On the other hand, they might have found the money and be playing it cool.

"Hey, guys!"

Oh no, thought Saffron. Coming down the moat wall in flippers and knee-length beach jams was Crash Johnson. His nose white from zinc sunblock. The beach jams were bright cadmium orange, and Saffron noticed they were covered with smiling octopuses wearing sailor hats.

"Sixteen million bricks, that's how many. They started building in 1846. I like to hang out on the roof. I pretend I'm the king," Crash said, putting his hands on his hips like Yul Brynner. His voice was nasal because of the swim plugs in his nose that were connected by a thin strip of pink rubber looping from nostril to nostril.

"That other island with the lighthouse is Loggerhead Key," he said, looking west four miles. "It's the very end of the keys, of all Florida in fact."

As Crash spoke, the three couldn't take their eyes off the thin rubber strip under his nose, and Crash scrunched his neck and bent his knees to get lower and lower into their line of sight.

"You need to bring dishwashing liquid to take a bath. Did you know regular soap won't lather in salt water? It's like rubbing a smooth stone on your skin. Found that out camping here three days once."

They stared at the pink rubber and Crash stood back up.

"Well, gotta go snorkeling." He waved.

Saffron hated him. The stupid bastard obviously had no money but was content as all outdoors, and Saffron was furious at the lack of justice in the world.

"Where were we?" he said to Sean and David.

Another voice interrupted, from the beach: "Shrimpers!"

It was Jack Nicklaus, and he was running for the seaplane.

Others on the beach sprinted across the sand for a row of beached dinghies and pushed them off in what looked like an emergency escape.

Around the corner of the fort, across the water, came the mechanical sound of general calamity. It had the backbeat of Creedence Clearwater.

"What kind of a verb is *chooglin'* anyway?" asked David.

A small, tattered diesel boat appeared. The crew of wildcat shrimpers laughed and hooted.

Jack Nicklaus pulled the case of Budweiser from under his pilot's seat and ran for the dock. Most of the dinghies had turned around and were racing back to the shore from the yachts and sailboats in the harbor. Loaded down with bottles of Beefeater and Stolichnaya. They joined the pilot on the dock.

As the shrimp boat pulled to the pier, the yachtsmen ran alongside, handing bottles over the railing before the boat had stopped.

A large shrimper in blue waders came up on deck carrying two five-gallon buckets. The others filled hefty plastic sacks from the buckets containing shrimp.

The yachters held up the giant bags of shrimp like the heads of their enemies; the shrimpers already had most of the bottles open. The one in waders announced, "All the best liquor and no mixers. I'll give a whole bag of shrimp for a single Coke." A man wearing Top-Siders and a Rolex ran for a cooler like the shrimper's own butler.

Soon, the western breeze would carry the scent of shrimp grilling across the beach.

From the moat wall, Sean, David and Saffron saw Crash talking with some shrimpers, gesticulating at different parts of the fort in a one-man stage production of history. The shrimpers laughed hard, slapped Crash on the back and invited him onto the boat.

Twenty-seven

Fred McJagger's yacht was anchored on the south side of Tortugas harbor, and Max Minimum had zipped ashore in a dinghy when he saw the shrimp trading.

Minimum brushed butter on the shrimp snapping and popping on a grill at the south end of the beach. He ate them with the Channellock pliers he'd found in a toolbox on the dinghy, which was aground between the pier and the coal docks. Those shrimpers made a stupid trade, Minimum thought.

The barbecued shrimp was succulent, and Minimum threw his trash on the beach. He went inside the fort to get tourist information and maybe take the tour of sights and mock the toil of history.

Sean and David climbed down a circular staircase from the top of the fort and ducked as they entered the low-ceilinged visitor center. They sorted through pamphlets.

"You guys like to snorkel?"

Sean and David turned to see Minimum.

"I came down here on my boss's yacht," Minimum said. "He sent me away from the office because I was making too many damn sales. They said they needed to let all the paperwork catch up."

He stopped to chuckle. "But I'm all alone and I wanted to do some snorkeling. I need some dive buddies."

David said there were always people diving near the moat wall.

Minimum shook his head negative. "I mean the real stuff. Out at Loggerhead." He cocked his head west.

"There's a great reef on the far side called Little Africa because that's what it's shaped like. I hear it's amazing, probably the finest in the Keys 'cause it's so isolated. Wanna go?"

Sean and David hesitated.

"Come on! You'll love it. I can't go alone," he pleaded. "Safety rules."

Sean and David looked at each other and shrugged. Why not?

"Good, good!" said Minimum. "Meet me at the dock in ten minutes."

"Can I come too?" Charles Saffron asked from the doorway.

A week at sea, Minimum was finally appearing natural behind the helm as he piloted the yacht into the deep, narrow channel between the fort and Bush

Key. He took the small ship on a curling course first northwest and then west-southwest.

Minimum yelled against the wind: "I hear there's killer lobster at the reef, but they're off limits under federal law."

The yacht was so sturdy, the deck barely moved in the mild, open-Gulf chop on the way to Loggerhead. Minimum's sailing jacket was open and the tail fluttered behind him. He turned the wheel with facility, an illusion of ruggedness. Saffron sat on his hands, deceptively harmless.

Sean and Dave were running out of money. They wouldn't be if Sean hadn't outsmarted himself and hidden the five hundred dollars of traveler's checks where he couldn't remember.

"I told you I hid it!"

"Where?"

"If I knew . . ." And so on.

Saffron picked up on the friction, but the words sailed downwind and out of earshot. When the wind died for a moment, all he heard was the last line of the conversation.

"When we get the money from where you hid it, we'll be set," said David. "It's our ticket out of here."

Bingo. Saffron fast-tracked his plans.

Minimum anchored the yacht in soft sand and twelve feet of water and the reef was between them and Loggerhead. They were even with the lighthouse.

Loggerhead faced them broadside, but the map told them it was a long sliver of island that came to a point on the southwestern end where the Gulf Stream filed it down. Minimum was in the water first. Sean and David next, and Saffron, who kept his shirt on to swim. They drifted over purple sea fans and orbs of brain coral. Staghorn and elkhorn coral, tube sponges, grunts, damsels, yellowtail snapper, tangs, parrotfish and even a flying gurnard.

A tarpon big enough to win the tournament at Boca Grande drifted feet from Sean. The silver wall startled him, which drove off the fish. Two black rays with seven-foot wingspans swam in slow motion between them.

As the four paddled, the coral came closer to their stomachs. Sean raised his mask and saw the beach twenty yards ahead. They worked their way over to a fissure and swam to the beach.

Sean imagined he was a shipwrecked sailor from the 1800s finally reaching safety, and what he saw was exactly what such a mariner would have found. It was a few dozen yards across the narrow part of the island to the lighthouse. Inside was one ranger, high up and asleep.

Sean and David said they wanted to go to the southwest end; they wanted to be able to say they'd reached the *real* end of the state. Saffron wanted to tag along.

Minimum said he would rest on the beach near the lighthouse. He pointed out an approaching squall line in the distance, to the west, and told them they didn't have a lot of time. Then he lay down for a nap.

Sean and David walked the few hundred yards to the bottom of the island, studying the low beach brush. The wind whipped up at once, and they looked out at a low-slung gray front coming in fast over a bright blue sky.

"We're almost there," Sean said. They reached the end of the island in another minute and took turns standing on the tip of the state, their feet dipping into the water at the sharp, sandy point.

"Forget 'southernmost point' in Key West," Sean said as David took his picture with a disposable waterproof camera. "This is The Spot."

"You've run out of Florida, assholes."

Saffron was pointing a Glock 9mm.

"Where's the five million?" he said.

"What?"

"The five million dollars that Veale gave you."

"Who?" asked David.

Sean showed recognition. "You mean that crazy doctor?"

"Right."

A faint yell came from up the island. Minimum ran toward them shouting they had to get off the island and back to safe harbor at Fort Jefferson. The storm was rolling in too fast.

Saffron concealed the gun against his side and faced Minimum, thirty yards up the beach. With his back to Sean and David he raised his shirttail and slipped the Glock back in the holster. "Be right there."

He turned back to Sean and David. "No scene. Not

one word to him or I'll fuckin' shoot all three of you. What's stopping me?"

It was a tense and bizarre swim back out to the boat. Minimum wondered what was up, the other three repeatedly stopping, looking at each other. The sky was black on the ride back toward Garden Key. No rain yet, but twenty degrees cooler.

Once Minimum was under way, he felt more confident about the weather and took time to change into long sweatpants. He threw extra pairs of sweats to the others. He handed out cups of coffee in mugs with the logo of Vista Lago Estates.

Sean awoke as he usually did when he slept in the middle of the day, not knowing when or where he was. He looked around in alarm at David and Saffron, who had regained consciousness earlier from the barbiturate-spiked coffees. Minimum stood on the fantail and stared down at them with a Barbie in his mouth.

The three were spread out sitting down on the swim platform, handcuffed behind their backs. Their ankles manacled and eight feet of chain connecting their necks to cement blocks. David in the middle; Saffron on the right.

The top of the fort was barely visible above the horizon, and David figured they were anchored about five miles off the far side of Loggerhead. It was still an hour until sunset, but the low-pressure front made it appear later. The sun peeked out under the cloud ceiling.

Minimum was on his knees behind the stern and breathing harder.

From the edge of David's sight, he noticed Saffron focused on Minimum and slowly lifting up his shirt-tail with handcuffed hands, going for his gun.

Minimum gave a sickening grunt and without warning leaned over the transom with the gaff and toppled Saffron's cement block into the water. The terror generated voltage inside Saffron and the veins in his neck and face popped to the surface; small blood vessels in the whites of his eyes broke. He was yanked off the platform and disappeared beneath the water.

Minimum, breathing even harder, leaned over again, reaching toward David's cement block.

David's eyes bulged and his system flooded with endocrine and steaming surges, and he saw Minimum liked it.

Minimum leaned forward with the gaff, and stopped halfway, to prolong. He reached farther until the tip of the gaff touched the block.

David had worked his feet up under him, and when Minimum was at the farthest point of his lean, David thrust upward. He intended to head-butt Minimum, but didn't get his legs set right and missed.

David's forehead would have hit Minimum in the mouth except Barbie was there, and he hit her square in the feet.

Minimum stumbled backward and clutched his throat like Kennedy in the Zapruder film. David was standing up straight now and could see into the boat.

Barbie had fallen out of Minimum's mouth onto the deck.

Except she had no head. It was lodged in Minimum's trachea like a Titleist golf ball. He reeled and staggered and finally tried to give himself a Heimlich. He charged at the railing and in his panic hit it far too hard and low, and he flipped over into the water.

David and Sean watched astonished as Minimum fought and splashed on his back in the Gulf, unable to drown because he was choking to death. He drifted west, gradually moving less until only an occasional twitch, and then completely still, a log of flotsam in the sunset.

David looked around for leverage to break the handcuff links. He steadied himself for balance when the front tossed up a series of chops that pitched the boat. He looked over at Sean and saw him trying to stand. As the yacht rolled, Sean's cement block slid closer and closer to the edge of the swim platform until it fell in the water.

Sean was gone.

David was thinking in numbers now and it was simple math: Sean had two kids and a wife. He didn't.

David kicked his own cement block into the water.

Twenty-eight

Salt water flooded into Sean's nostrils as he was pulled by his neck to the bottom of the Gulf. When the cement block stopped, Sean hung upside down eight feet above the ocean floor. Alongside was a dead Saffron. Sean's body jolted with glands that seared his insides and made muscles spasm and contort.

He felt as if his heart had burst and his chest cavity were full of boiling blood. He had gotten only a quick breath on the way down and it was long gone. Thirty feet under, the pressure stabbed his eardrums, and his lungs crushed. His mind was in hell.

There was large movement next to him as David's block hit the ocean floor, landing between Sean and Saffron.

David twisted through the water until the hands behind his back found Saffron. He had overestimated his air supply and it was already depleted. His chest started to thrust.

Upside down and disoriented, David found it harder than he'd expected. Blindly, he turned Saffron around little by little, a few inches of his shirt at a time. David's fingertips felt around behind him frantically. He grabbed Saffron's belt and turned him some more. His lungs were about to blow; he didn't even look to see how Sean was doing. He felt a leather strap a little lower on Saffron and followed it to the middle of his back and the holster. There was no time left, but he couldn't rush and drop the gun or it was over.

He came up with the pistol, and kicked away from Saffron. He bumped into Sean, this time luckier, and he quickly felt the chain at Sean's neck. He groped in the dark water and pressed the gun to the chain and pulled the trigger. As advertised, the Glock fired underwater.

Sean shot to the surface. He sneezed and inhaled water through his nose as the chops washed over his head. David doubled over below the Gulf, grabbed his own chain and fired again. He popped back up next to Sean, and they struggled, trying to tread water. Sean thought they'd escaped from the ocean floor only to drown on the surface, but David managed over the next few minutes to shoot through both their handcuffs.

They ripped the tape off their mouths and swam to the anchored yacht, *Serendipity II*.

When the radio call from the Fort Jefferson ranger's station came in to Key West, Susan Tchoupitoulas asked if she could fly out on the Coast Guard rescue helicopter.

The duty officer said the core of the storm was still on the way, but it was her call.

The chopper made time despite the headwind. A petty officer turned the searchlight down into the harbor, where there was growing confusion. Three marine biology students chased a dome tent that had pulled up its stakes in the wind and blew across the beach, a three-hundred-dollar nylon tumbleweed. Half the anchors had pulled loose from the soft bottom, and the boats blew toward the others. Collision sirens and klaxons went off. Several fired their engines and backed around in the close quarters in a high-stakes game of asteroids.

"This looks awful," said Tchoupitoulas.

"Actually, this is pretty tame for the Tortugas," said the petty officer.

In contrast to the pandemonium in the harbor, two park rangers escorted Sean and David calmly across the moat bridge to a clearing between the palm trees. The chopper lowered a rescue sling.

It hovered and Sean and David squinted in the downblast. Sean came up first. David was in five minutes later. The helicopter banked and accelerated. It cleared Bush and Long keys and flew out of the leading edge of the squall into the clear, toward Key West.

Sean and David were fine, but Susan told them they couldn't expect the sleep they coveted. They were material witnesses and low-order suspects, although she expected that to disappear after questioning. Things had gotten wiggy in Key West with the discovery of the dead serial killer from Tampa and the escape of the other suspect. A state legislator was killed under suspicious circumstances, and then four more bodies, all members of a cocaine cartel whose trail mysteriously ended in a post office box in Grenada.

Now add a dead manufactured-housing salesman and a Tampa insurance executive. Susan said it all seemed to spin around room 3 at the Purple Pelican. Below the helicopter, a catamaran sailed in the opposite direction toward the Tortugas, Blaine Crease in a safety harness.

Sean and David wrapped themselves in blankets and sipped cocoa on the copter. They gave exhaustive statements until after midnight at the police office, where they reclined in Police Athletic League jogging suits and ate fried calamari from the Crab Shack.

At one point Dave nodded toward Susan's badge and said, "Some last name."

"The T's silent," she said, jabbing back.

As midnight approached, Sean and David begged to go to sleep or have a beer or both.

Susan promised if they could hang with it another hour, the department would take them to dinner the next day, expenses be damned.

"Good," said David, "because this guy lost our traveler's checks."

*   *   *

Sean and David slept in past checkout at the Angelfish Inn. So late that upon waking, it was time to plan sunset activities. The phone in the room rang.

Susan Tchoupitoulas looked more disarming in cutoffs and an oversized jersey. It said "Fighting Conchs," her high school's nickname. Her hair was out of the small ponytail and brushed down, not quite long enough to touch her shoulders. She didn't need makeup.

When Susan saw Sean and David, she stood up from her outdoor table atop the La Concha Inn, the only high-rise on the island.

"Mallory Square is such a zoo," she said. "This is a little better."

The top floor of the hotel had an indoor lounge in the middle and a wraparound deck outside. Susan was at her favorite table at the northeast corner. Except it wasn't a real table; it was one of those cocktail deals, and their knees mashed together underneath. Sean was worried if he leaned too hard on the ledge, he might break loose a barrel tile and kill someone eight floors down on Duval Street.

"Hope you have a good restaurant in mind," she said. "I get to eat on the department tonight too."

Susan fulfilled her second promise, to fill them in on everything. There was no real investigation to jeopardize, because just about everyone was dead.

Susan told them about the missing five million dollars and the string of murders all over the island by and among drug enforcers and Florida lowlifes.

"What about us?" asked Sean.

"Looks like mistaken identity," she said. "We checked the records and room three at the Purple Pelican was your room before you canceled. There are no other links. As far as we're concerned, you're in the clear."

She took a sip of her Coke. A crowd of visitors from the suburbs of America filed onto the deck. In another corner, a two-piece band backed by a tape-deck set up. The crowd, fresh from the theme parks of Orlando, began shouting for "Margaritaville."

"People think these criminals were geniuses, especially that idiot Blaine Crease," said Susan. "They left a slick of evidence a mile wide."

"What about that doctor I met?" asked Sean.

"It appears the guys named Serge and Coleman killed him in Cocoa Beach and took the five million," Susan said. "They dropped a bread-crumb trail of hundred-dollar bills all down the coast. The serial numbers matched the bank in Tampa."

"So where's the money?" asked Sean.

"We'll probably never know," she said. "Serge and Coleman hid it somewhere. Doesn't really matter. It was all cocaine money, so nobody's making a stink. Everyone connected with the insurance company is running for cover."

A man who looked like Weird Al Yankovic sat on a stool holding a guitar. The tourists pressed closer and quieted.

Susan continued: "The district attorney's office says it's almost better if the money is never found. A Costa Gordan holding company has put in a claim for the cash. Everyone knows it's drug money, but the DA says the holding company has a better than even shot arguing that Saffron and New England Life stole it from them and it should be returned."

"What about those Latins?" asked Sean.

"You mean Uzbekistanians. Part of the new Russian mob in south Florida. They rented a postal drop in Grenada and tried to go native."

Susan looked at the singer in the corner and back at David. "I used to love Buffett."

Yankovic, in a bright shirt with parrots, began strumming. *"Nibblin' on sponge cake..."* The crowd went goofy.

"Let's go inside," Susan suggested.

They settled in at the bar with green frozen drinks. The TV was on Florida Cable News. Blaine Crease bobbed in his harness on the prow of the catamaran. In the background was Fort Jefferson, and next to him in a second safety harness was a young man in octopus beach jams.

Crease spoke dramatically at the camera. "Tonight we have an exclusive interview with Crash Johnson, The Hit Man's Pilot!"

Crash leaned into Crease's microphone. "Hi." He smiled and gave a quick wave.

"As the personal pilot to Charles Saffron..." began Crease.

"I wasn't actually his personal..."

"But as the pilot who spent a great deal of one-on-one time flying with the murderer..."

"He really didn't talk much."

"When did you first realize he was a time bomb, the infamous Keys Killer?"

"When you told me. Remember? Just before we put on these harnesses."

"Harnesses?" Crease laughed.

"Yeah, right under your suit there."

Crease cleared his throat.

"They used to have fresh water out here at Fort Jefferson, but you know what?" asked Crash. "All the cisterns cracked.... Guess what Tortugas means? . . ."

Crease broke in: "The murderous events of the last few days have taken their toll in the Florida Keys, including this brave young air force veteran who endured a life-or-death flight . . ."

"When was I in the air force?"

". . . and is clearly disoriented. That's our report this evening from the killing waters of the Dry Tortugas."

"Thanks, Blaine," said the spunky anchorwoman. "And now to the Krome Avenue immigration and detention center west of Miami. . . ."

The TV screen showed a diehard band of exiles waving Cuban and American flags. They had tables and chairs and beach umbrellas set up just outside the entrance gate. Buses from Immigration and Naturalization rolled through gates topped with barbed wire.

A young female correspondent in a red dress spoke to the camera: "Demonstrators have turned out to boost the spirits of the latest wave of Cuban freedom fighters to be brought to the detention center."

Two buses turned slowly into the compound, and the camera zoomed in on a third bus, where a bearded man was trying to climb out a window.

"I'm an American!" yelled Captain Xeno, dressed in an immigration jumpsuit.

The protesters erupted in cheers. Flags waved furiously. *"Libertad!"* someone yelled.

"No, I mean it! I really am an American!"

"Yes you are, my brother!" yelled someone in the back of the crowd, and the group exploded in cheers again. Captain Xeno disappeared into the compound.

David said to Susan, "Excuse us for a moment."

"Where are we going?" asked Sean.

David, standing, smacked Sean in the back where Susan couldn't see. "We'll be right back," said Sean, and they both went to the men's room.

When they came out, David sat back down, but Sean remained standing. He stretched and yawned. "Sorry to be a party-pooper, but I'm spent."

Sean left and Susan turned to David. "You always this obvious?"

David smiled. "I've got a restaurant in mind."

The Key West Police Department paid $127.42 for dinner at Louie's Backyard and drinks on the Afterdeck Bar and nothing for the stroll on the beach.

Twenty-nine

Late the next day. David didn't speak as he pumped gas at Dade Corners, a fueling/convenience megaplex outside Miami on the edge of the Everglades that carried shellacked alligator heads. Airboats filled the parking lot and newspaper racks showed photos of the Marlins victory parade.

David capped the tank and climbed behind the wheel. They started across the 'glades back toward Tampa.

"If you don't want to talk about it . . ." said Sean.

"I don't."

"Because if you did . . . I mean, I think she's perfect for you. You need some stability."

David turned on the stereo, Allman Brothers, and they began counting Indian concessions on the side of the Tamiami Trail.

The Allmans sang about being born in the backseat of a bus on Highway 41. David told Sean they were singing about this road, the Tamiami Trail, US Highway 41. Halfway across the swamp, they passed the last Gray Line tour of the day, pulled over on the south shoulder. Its sixty riders taking snapshots of a white wooden shack with a sign that read: "Ochopee, smallest post office in the United States of America."

"Did you notice about the trip?" Sean said.

"What?" asked David.

"No fish."

Out through the windshield, the sky was blood red over Naples, and in the rearview a deep violet above Miami as the Chrysler split the Everglades without another car in sight.

Back about forty miles, where the two-lane road started its western run across the swamp, a humble gopher tortoise had begun crossing the Tamiami Trail in the fading light. Its world suddenly became much brighter as the high beams of a black Mercedes limousine lit up the road.

The limo was on cruise control doing a hundred. In the driver's seat—actually sitting up in the driver's window outside the limo and driving with his right foot—a man was taking photographs of the magnificent sunset over Naples. The sun barely down, crimson shafts now sprayed up into a furnace of clouds. The limo's steering column was shattered and hotwired, and an impound ticket from the Key West Police Department lay crumpled on the floor.

At the last second, the driver noticed he was about to hit the turtle. In a reflexive evasive maneuver, he jerked the wheel with his foot. The car yanked hard left, missed the turtle and violently threw the driver back in the window, tossing him around the front seat at will—"Whooooooooaaaaaaaaa!"—as the car left the road and pounded through the sawgrass.

The driver grabbed the wheel and fought to hold it steady as he climbed up from the floor mats and back into the seat. The limousine crested the lip of a gator hole, but he managed to turn it back onto the pavement and into the proper lane.

"Geez, that turtle came out of nowhere," the man muttered to himself, loading a .357 Magnum. "I wouldn't have been able to live with myself if I'd hit it."

The limo raced west across the Everglades, closing distance, Serge looking out at the end of his high beams for a Chrysler.

What will become of the $5,000,000
in laundered drug money?
What will happen to our hapless heroes?
Will more cars be destroyed?
Will Johnny Vegas finally get laid?
Will Serge kill again?
And if so, how?

If you thought *Florida Roadkill* was a wild ride,
wait until you hear the rest of the story . . .

Hammerhead Ranch Motel

by Tim Dorsey
available wherever books are sold

Hammerhead Ranch Motel is a super-cheap, semi-dilapidated ex-tourist trap wedged between the ocean and a brand-new deluxe condominium development. The condo is full of paranoid cranks and hateful windbags. The Hammerhead Ranch is home to a motley assortment of dopers, dealers, swindlers, and other assorted misfits—the proverbial maggots in the underbelly of the Florida crime scene. Sounds like the perfect place for a kitsch-loving Floridaphile like Serge A. Storms to hole up . . .if only he can keep his eyes (and hands) on that elusive Haliburton full of cash. Here's a taste of Tim Dorsey's outrageous new novel.

Late the next morning, the first of the car thieves awoke in bright sunlight on the wooden floor of their Ybor City warehouse apartment, where they'd passed out just before daybreak.

He looked around, groggy. What happened? Snatches of memory filtered back. He remembered some guy back at the Wharf Rat helping them into a cab and paying the driver, then the ride back to the warehouse and the inebriated struggle up the steps, the three of them leaning against each other, an unstable tripod holding itself up. They must have made it into the apartment and lost consciousness on the floor because that's all he could remember. He couldn't remember anything at all about . . . the money! Where was the money? That bastard in the bar must have stolen it!

The car thief tried to spring up from the floor but couldn't move. He looked down and saw his entire body spooled tightly head to toe with hundred-pound-test fishing line, his arms pinned by his sides and his legs bound together. He looked over at his two comrades on the floor next to him wrapped in the nylon line.

"Hey, you guys! Wake up! There's trouble!"

The other two came around slowly at first, but then awoke all at once when they realized their situation. They thrashed around in panic.

"I wouldn't do that if I were you," said an unfamiliar voice. "That line will slice you to ribbons."

A stranger walked into the room from the kitchen and sat on the couch. He was wiry and casual, sitting there with a leg crossed, reading a *Tampa Tribune*. On the front of the newspaper the thieves saw a big headline, "Keys Killer Sought," and a large photo that matched the man holding the paper.

"Who are you?" said the first thief. Then he stopped and studied the stranger. Something familiar. "Hey—you're that guy we jumped last night coming out of the trailer."

Serge set the paper down. He leaned forward on the edge of the sofa cushion and spoke softly. "Where's my money?"

"What money?"

Serge reached around the side of the couch and slid a toolbox into view. He opened it and removed a pneumatic staple gun.

"Oh, *that* money. We don't have it anymore. Some guy took it."

Serge's voice was understated: "Where's my money?"

"I told you, we don't know where it is."

Serge didn't say a word. He got down on the floor and sat cross-legged next to the men.

"What are you going to do to us?"

Serge raised a single finger to his lips for them to be quiet. Slowly and with deliberate theatrics, he removed items from the toolbox and set them on the floor. The men lifted their heads the best they could to get a better look. A roll of metal wire, tubes of commercial solvents and epoxies, arsenical soap, gauze, highly elastic putty, steel wool and quick-dissolve surgical suture. The three faces went white. One of the thieves fainted, and his head hit the wooden floor with the clack of a billiard break.

Serge went into the kitchen and came back with two buckets and a large plastic mat, which he unrolled on the floor. He turned on a small electric air compressor.

Serge went to work with diligence, industry and master craftsmanship. Before the hour had passed, Serge had been told every single detail the thieves could remember about the money, and a few more they made up. Serge knew they weren't holding back. But it was too late; nothing could stop him once he was into one of his hobbies.

"Ever been to Ocklawaha?" Serge asked as he turned off the compressor.

Wide stares in response.

"You haven't! You don't know what you're missing—gotta go sometime. It's just up the road a ways between Orlando and Ocala. Famous four-hour shootout. That's where Hoover's G-men finally tracked down the notorious Ma Barker Gang. They raided their empty hideout in Chicago and found a map of Florida with Lake Weir circled. On January 16, 1935, they surrounded the two-story antique wooden house with a magnificent cracker porch. It was a crime in itself that they put three thousand bullets in it. Afterward, they found Fred Barker and Machine Gun Kate dead, and the locals later sold postcards showing their bodies at the morgue."

The car thieves continued staring in blank terror as Serge put down a tube of epoxy and picked up the staple gun. "What?" said Serge. "None of this registers? And you call yourselves criminals?"

Serge sighed in disappointment as he made a deft

cross-stitch with the suture. "What about Giuseppe Zangara? Ring any bells?"

Still nothing.

Serge threw up his arms. "If we can't remember our own history, what kind of state will we have to live in?"

He began rubbing with the arsenical soap. "Okay, but I'm only going to go through this once, so listen up. It was 1933; the place: Miami. Zangara was an unemployed bricklayer who had a chronic stomach-ache that he blamed on capitalism. To me, it sounds like he had some other problems, if you get my drift. Anyway, on Monday, February 13, Giuseppe buys a pistol in a pawnshop. He's just about to leave for Washington to shoot Hoover when he hears FDR is planning to visit Florida, so he decides to save gas money. President-elect Roosevelt is giving a speech in Miami's Bayfront Park. Guiseppe is only five feet tall, and he gets a chair to stand on. Suddenly he yells, 'Too many people are starving to death,' and opens fire. But he picked a crappy chair to stand on, and it wobbled. He missed Roosevelt and hit five other people, mortally wounding Chicago Mayor Anton Cermak. . . ."

Serge made a final suture stitch and sat back to admire. "There!" he said, and smiled proudly at the three men, seeking approval.

Four hours later, the trio lay on the floor, quiet, still alive for a little while longer. Three disbelieving mouths frozen open.

One of the thieves had a late resurgence of survival instinct, and he began to twitch on the floor.

"See, now you're wiggling around! Ruining all my work!" Serge let out a frustrated sigh and picked up the staple gun again.

Comic tales of Florida murder and mayhem
by TIM DORSEY

CADILLAC BEACH
0-06-055694-3 • $7.50 US • $9.99 Can

Serge A. Storms has busted out of the state mental hospital. It's all good for Serge. Not so much for anyone else.

THE STINGRAY SHUFFLE
0-06-055693-5/$7.50 US/$9.99 Can

When serial-killing local Florida historian Serge A. Storms is off his meds, no one is safe—especially when $5 million in cash is involved.

TRIGGERFISH TWIST
0-06-103155-0/$6.99 US/$9.99 Can

Ensconced in a lovely tropical villa, Jim Davenport anticipates the good life to come—but the neighborhood is not quite what it seems.

ORANGE CRUSH
0-06-103154-2/$6.99 US/$9.99 Can

Unthreatening Florida governor-by-default Marlon Conrad is a shoo-in for re-election, until he undergoes a radical personality shift during military action in the Balkans.

HAMMERHEAD RANCH MOTEL
0-380-73234-3/$6.99 US/$9.99 Can

Visitors come well armed to the Hammerhead Ranch Motel, because there's a different schemer or slimeball lurking behind every door.

FLORIDA ROADKILL
0-380-73233-5/$6.99 US/$9.99 Can

A handful of people are about to cross paths with a suitcase filled with five million dollars in stolen insurance money, and all of them want it.

And coming soon in hardcover

TORPEDO JUICE
0-06-058560-9/$24.95 US/$34.95 Can

Available wherever books are sold or please call 1-800-331-3761 to order.

TD 1004